Chicken
DANCE

Chicken DANCE

Jacques Couvillon

BLOOMSBURY

First published in Great Britain in 2008 by Bloomsbury Publishing Plc,
36 Soho Square, London, W1D 3QY

First published in the United States of America in 2007 by
Bloomsbury Publishing Plc, New York

A CIP catalogue record of this book is
available from the British Library

ISBN 978 0 7475 8930 3

Printed and bound in Great Britain by Clays Ltd, St Ives Plc

1 3 5 7 9 10 8 6 4 2

All papers used by Bloomsbury Publishing are natural,
recyclable products made from wood grown in well-managed
forests. The manufacturing processes conform to the environmental
regulations of the country of origin.

www.bloomsbury.com

For my parents,
Andrew and Julia Couvillon,
who always believed I could fly
and never asked me to dance.

ONE

My sister's name was Dawn, and my mother said she was named that because when she was born it was like the sun had just risen. My name is Stanley. My parents told me that they named me after my father's uncle, who left the country because he owed a lot of money to some loan sharks because he gambled and drank a lot. I don't remember being called Stanley because my parents always called me Don. They didn't tell me why they changed my name, except that they didn't like the name Stanley anymore.

What my parents told me wasn't really the truth, but I didn't find this out until I was twelve years old. Until then, I thought my name was Don. Actually, they told me my name was Stanley when I was eleven, but only because I found my birth certificate, because I was cleaning out the big closet, because my mother was having the "Power Couples" over to our house for dinner, because she thought she could get stuff from them if she gave them some eggs. I guess that doesn't really make sense, so maybe I should start from a couple of years ago, on my eleventh birthday, when things started happening.

But you know what? Maybe before I tell you that, I should tell you who I am and where I live and why I live there and some other stuff that you might want to know about me.

My name is Stanley Schmidt and I live on a chicken farm in Horse Island. It isn't really an island and there aren't a lot of horses there, but there are a lot of chickens. Almost everyone has them, and people drive from miles away just to buy their eggs in Horse Island. The town has always been filled with chicken farms, but it wasn't until one of the people from there, Jonathan Jacobs, moved to Lafayette and became a weatherman that people started wanting eggs from Horse Island chickens. He talked about the town all the time during his weather report and would say stuff like, "Tomorrow is going to be a sunny day. I'm sure all the chickens back on my parents' farm in Horse Island are going to enjoy it and give some delicious eggs. Maybe even a double yolk."

Because he talked about Horse Island all the time, people from other towns like Cow Island, Forked Island, Pecan Island, Kaplan, and Abbeville drove to Horse Island to buy eggs.

I wasn't born in Horse Island, though. I was born in

Shreveport, but when I was a baby, my parents and I moved to the chicken farm in Horse Island.

My sister, Dawn, didn't move with us because my mother told me that Dawn had died from scarlet fever when she was fifteen and I was just a baby. Although I didn't remember her, I knew what she looked like because we had a bunch of pictures of her in dance costumes all over the house.

Dawn and I didn't look alike at all, even though she was my sister. She was thin with straight brown hair, and her skin looked like she'd been out in the sun a lot, and her eyes were kind of the color of the insides of a pecan. I had green eyes and wore glasses and was short and I had reddish hair that was kind of curly and my skin was white, except for a bunch of freckles.

Anyway, the reason my parents and I moved from Shreveport was because my father inherited the chicken farm from his uncle. Not Stanley, whom I was supposedly named after, but Sam. In Uncle Sam's will, he said that my parents could live in the house for ten years if they kept at least twenty-five chickens at all times. Uncle Sam's lawyer had someone come and count the chickens every month and my mother called this person the "rodent counter." My parents were allowed three warnings if they didn't have twenty-five chickens when they were counted. After the third warning, the house and land would be donated to the American Poultry Association. After ten years of keeping twenty-five chickens, my parents could do whatever they wanted with the farm.

My mother said Uncle Sam had gone insane because he'd spent so many years alone with a bunch of chickens. I'd never met my father's uncle Sam or anyone else in my family. I didn't have any aunts or uncles that I knew about, and I'd never met my grandparents because my mother said that her mother and father had been killed when a tornado tore through their house. And that sharks had attacked my father's parents during a fishing trip off the coast of Texas.

But even though I'd never met my father's uncle Sam, I liked him a lot because I loved the chicken farm he'd given us. My mother wouldn't let me go into the coop alone because she was scared they'd peck my eyes out and then she'd have to go in and get me. So I spent all of my free time sitting near the fence that separated our backyard from the chicken yard.

The chicken yard was just a big yard surrounded by a chain-link fence. When the chickens weren't in their nests laying eggs, I'd watch them dance in the yard or roll in the dirt. When one got close enough to the fence, I'd poke my fingers through one of the holes and try to pet it.

Sometimes I'd even talk to them about stuff at school and about this kid named Leon Leonard, who made fun of me because my mother said we kept our chickens for ambience.

The chickens would answer me back and say stuff

like, "That's okay, Don. One day Leon Leonard is going to poop in his pants and not have any friends."

The chickens didn't really speak back to me. I only imagined that that's what they were saying. It was a lot more fun for me to make up what they were saying because that way they never said anything that I didn't like and so they became my best friends.

I really liked living on that farm, but my mother hated it. She never told that to people when they'd ask her why she and my father lived there. She would tell them that since she and my father were in their late thirties, they thought it was time to leave the city. Then she would add that we didn't keep the chickens to farm them because that would make us chicken farmers, and we were anything but that. She'd tell people that we kept chickens for ambience and because we loved fresh eggs.

I think this confused some people because a lot of them didn't know the meaning of the word *ambience*. And if they did, they didn't think scraping chicken poop off the bottoms of their shoes was ambience.

I guess I've told you all the stuff I need to for now, so I'm going to start telling you about the night of my eleventh birthday, when everything kind of started to change.

TWO

On the night of my eleventh birthday, my mother, father, and I were sitting in our living room eating TV dinners and watching television like we did every night. My father sat in a brown leather recliner and my mother on a dark pink velvet-covered love seat. It looked more like a chair to me, but my mother called it a love seat, and if my father or I called it a chair, she corrected us.

I sat on the dark pink velvet-covered sofa. If my father or I called it a couch, my mother corrected us and told us that she didn't know what we were talking about, because she didn't have a couch in her living room. She told us that she had a *sofa*, and that we should use the correct word.

She called it a sofa on my eleventh birthday when she shouted at me, "Don! Don't spill. Your sister loved that sofa. I'd hate to have a big stain on it because of your clumsiness."

My mother had broken the rule of no talking during regularly scheduled programs and my father, who had been taking a bite of his chicken cacciatore at the time, looked at her as if she had just given him a math problem that he didn't know the answer to.

Anyway, since it was my eleventh birthday, I decided I was going to ask my parents for a favor that I'd been wanting to ask for almost a year. It made me kind of nervous and so I started thinking about a KC and the Sunshine Band song to help me relax. I knew all of their songs because I'd won their greatest hits album at a chicken bingo at Horse Island Food and Furniture.

You see, Horse Island Food and Furniture had this contest where they put a chicken in a big cage, like about the size of a bed that two people can sleep in. On the floor of the cage was a white board with red numbers, like a big bingo card. Mr. Bufford, the owner of Horse Island Food and Furniture, put the chicken in the cage in the parking lot on Saturday mornings, right before the store opened, and everybody would watch what number the chicken used the bathroom on. Then they'd try to buy food and furniture that cost the same amount as that number. Mr. Bufford called it the "Magic Number" and one day it was 33, and my mother spent that exact amount by accident.

When it happened, the cashier smiled real big and told my mother, "Congratulations, you've reached the magic number. For one hundred dollars can you tell me 'the sentence that wins it'?"

My mother looked at the cashier and asked, "Excuse me?"

The cashier asked again, "For one hundred dollars, can you tell me 'the sentence that wins it'?"

I knew "the sentence that wins it," so I smiled and said, "Horse Island Food and Furniture does it the way I like it."

My mother looked at me and said, "Don, please. What did I tell you about not speaking unless you're spoken to?"

But then the cashier said, "He's right! Congratulations! You win one hundred dollars cash!"

My mother smiled and said, "Really? What a nice surprise!"

When the cashier gave the money to my mother, she put it all in her purse.

Then the cashier looked at me and said, "Since you helped your momma, young man, I'll give you the chance to win something as well. Can you tell me the name of the President of the United States?"

I smiled real big and said, "Jimmy Carter."

And the cashier said, "That's right. Congratulations! You have just won yourself a greatest hits album of KC and the Sunshine Band."

I had an old record player in my room and started to listen to the album every day and sometimes sang the songs in my head. Because I was trying so hard to think of the words, I'd forget what I was thinking about before I started singing. So sometimes if what I was thinking about made me nervous, I'd start singing a KC and the Sunshine Band song in my head. And it would help me forget what I was thinking about and then I wasn't so nervous.

So on the night of my eleventh birthday, I started singing "Boogie Shoes" to myself. But then I stopped because the opening song of "Happy Days" started playing on the television and my mother squealed like a pig.

Then she said, "That's 'Rock Around the Clock.' You know, that's the song Dawn danced to when she won her dance contest when she was thirteen years old."

She pointed with her chicken drumstick at Dawn's ballerina trophy that was at the top of this big bookcase in our living room.

"You know, she got her talent from me," she said. "I used to dance and could have been famous, but I decided to have a family instead."

Then my mother dropped her drumstick onto the aluminum platter and said, "I'm the one who taught her the routine."

My mother got up from her seat and started dancing to the television and pretending that she was spinning a baton. Then she kicked one leg a few times and spun around. She threw one hand in the air and said, "Dawn stole the competition by holding her right leg in the air with one hand and twirling a baton with the other. She could throw the baton in the air and then catch it with her mouth. It was really amazing and I think Dawn could have danced in Vegas if she wanted.

You'd think they would have given her more than that trophy."

Happy Days came on and so my mother sat back down and stopped talking and I looked up at Dawn's dance trophy. It was a shiny, gold-plated ballerina standing about a foot tall on one toe, on top of a green aluminum base. The top of her head was about six inches from the ceiling, and it was taller than anything else on the bookcase, including the television and my mother's music box.

If you opened the lid of the music box, a ballerina popped up from shiny, dark pink fabric that was the same color as our living room walls. The ballerina stood on one toe with her arms stretched out and spun around in circles to music. It almost looked like she wanted to fly, but since she couldn't, she stayed there and danced.

Sometimes my mother would take it down and wind it up and watch the ballerina dance. And sometimes she'd even dance with the ballerina and let me watch her. When I was a little kid, I saw that movie *Peter Pan* and I thought maybe the ballerina in the box was a fairy like Tinker Bell. I pretended that a witch had put a curse on her so that she had to live in that box. It made me sad that she had to live there and couldn't fly away and play with other fairies. So sometimes I'd pretend that if I wound the music box up all the way and whispered, "Fly," she would stop dancing and fly up in the air.

I had never tried it though, because my mother wouldn't let me touch the music box or even get close to it. I figured out, when I got older, that the ballerina was just a plastic doll and that she wouldn't fly away if I wound up the music box as tight as I could and whispered, "Fly." I still kind of wanted to do it, though. Just to make sure.

Anyway, during a commercial break from *Happy Days*, I took a deep breath and was about to ask my question, when my mother started crying. She said, "The Lord took Dawn because he needed another angel in the sky."

I imagined Dawn up in heaven with a chipped front tooth from a bad baton catch and wearing a white ballerina costume with wings on her back. She was standing on a tall white column and God was looking up at her while she held one leg in the air and twirled a baton with her other hand.

I was staring straight ahead thinking about this and it made me notice a picture of Dawn on her eleventh birthday. She had a blindfold on and was wearing a pink tutu and was trying to pin the tail on a picture of a donkey. I knew it was her eleventh birthday because she was wearing a T-shirt that said, "Kiss Me! I'm 11!"

It made me smile and I guess my mother saw me looking at the picture and smiling instead of looking at her.

She yelled at me, "Don! This is important. Listen to

us when we speak to you. Dick, tell him that this is important."

"This is important," my father said without looking at me, while scratching his underarm.

So I looked at my mother and saw her eyes were almost closed and her mouth was half open like she was going to cry. But then her favorite commercial came on and her eyes opened and her mouth closed.

It was a laundry detergent commercial about this Chinese couple who owned a laundry service, and when a customer asked how they got their clothes so clean, the Chinese man answered, "Ancient Chinese secret."

When the commercial was finished, my mother said, "I would love to go there because I heard that those Chinese ladies give a flawless pedicure for next to nothing. Anyway, so, Don, it's very disrespectful not to listen to me when I talk to you. Dawn would never disrespect me like that."

I looked at my mother and said, "Okay, ma'am."

When I was sure she wasn't going to talk to me anymore, I turned and looked at the television. A cake commercial came on and so I started smiling and watching my parents to see if they were thinking the same thing that I was. That there was a cake hidden somewhere in the kitchen for my birthday.

My mother looked at me and then back at the television and said, "I wish they had Chinese people in this town because we could really use a good restaurant like the one we used to eat at in Shreveport. You know, I want to move back to Shreveport and eat Chinese food."

I started thinking that maybe my mother had bought me a Chinese cake and that's why she was talking about Chinese food. I tried to imagine what Chinese cake looked like, but I couldn't, and then I started to think that maybe my parents had gotten me a Chinese clown.

But then I stopped thinking about that because my mother started talking again.

"Dick," she said, "can you stop off at an Oriental nail shop in Lafayette tomorrow and bring me back some red polish?"

My father looked at my mother and closed his eyes and then he opened them wide like he was surprised and said, "I'm not going to Lafayette tomorrow. I'm going to Baton Rouge for an aluminum siding convention and I'm going to have to spend a couple of days there."

"When were you going to tell me this?" my mother asked.

My father stared at my mother with a blank face until she yelled, "Answer me, Dick!"

Then *Happy Days* came back on. I wondered if my father was going to turn back and watch television, or break the rule of no talking during regularly scheduled programs and answer my mother. He looked back and forth between the television and my mother as if he were watching a tennis match.

After almost ten seconds he said, "I was going to tell you tonight. I just forgot about it."

"So I guess that means I'm going to have to take care of those rodents," my mother said real loud.

"Yes, dear," my father answered her. "You will have to feed the chickens."

For the next fifteen minutes my mother and father didn't speak. I knew that because my mother had to feed the chickens, my parents would have a fight. Because they always had a fight when my mother had to feed the chickens.

So after *Happy Days* was over, I got up from my seat, threw away my aluminum platter, folded up my tray, and excused myself to my room.

But before I got to my room, I heard my mother shout, "I hate it here!"

"Quiet," my father said. "He'll hear you."

Then my mother screamed louder, "I don't care if he does hear me! To think I gave up that dancing job in Las Vegas to marry you and end up on a chicken farm. I used to be Janice Remington, Dancer. I traded that in for Janice Schmidt, Chicken Farmer. I'd be famous right now if it weren't for you."

My father must not have liked that because then he yelled, "You weren't a dancer! You were a waitress at a drive-in where the manager let you dance for people's birthdays. I'm the one who was in college and had to drop out and do the honorable thing and marry you!"

I heard something that sounded like someone was

getting slapped, and right after, a dog food commercial and then the theme song to *Laverne and Shirley*.

I never understood what my father meant by "do the honorable thing and marry you." I knew what *honorable* was. It's like if someone drops their wallet and you find it. So I figured that my father had dropped his wallet and my mother found it and returned it to him and so since she had done the honorable thing, he did an honorable thing back and married her.

Anyway, right after the theme song to *Laverne and Shirley*, I heard my father say, "I'm sorry I yelled. But you know we can't go back to Shreveport."

"Why not?" my mother asked real loud. "Why can't you beg for your old job back?"

"Well," my father said, "for one, businesses don't usually hire back people they fire; for two, we're just starting to get out of debt and can't afford a move; and three, I couldn't stand to face any of our friends because I'm embarrassed about everything that happened."

"You know it's your fault!" my mother shouted back. "If you had taken family dance classes with us, this wouldn't have happened."

"Come on, Janice!" my father screamed. "It's my fault because I didn't run around in polka-dotted leotards and high heels, clopping like some wounded satyr?"

"A wounded satyr?" my mother yelled.

And my father shouted back, "I call them like I see them!"

Then I heard another slap and footsteps that sounded like they were going toward the kitchen. So I opened my door, stepped out into the hall, and tiptoed into the living room. I could hear pots hitting the floor and plates crashing into the sink. This happened in most of the fights even though we ate out of the TV trays and never used the pots or dishes.

After a few minutes, the pot and plate sounds stopped. That's when I walked out of the living room and into the foyer. I knelt behind a bookcase and right when I did, I heard my father say, "Listen, I'm sorry, Janice, but don't blame me for what happened. That's cruel, and I'm just as upset as you."

Then it sounded like a hundred forks and spoons fell on the floor and my mother let out this really loud scream. It kind of scared me and I wondered if I should run back to my room and lock the door.

But I didn't because then my father said, "I promise that next year when the house becomes ours, we'll sell it and move to another city. Until then, it's all we've got. We spent all of our savings on Mr. Munson. So if you'll be a little patient, this will pay off. And I can buy you that convertible you always wanted."

My mother started crying and my father said, "Everything is going to work out, Janice. I promise."

Nobody talked for a few minutes and then my father asked, "Would you like to go to New Orleans this weekend and get your hair done at one of those fancy salons?"

"Can we go to a dance club?" my mother asked.

"Yes," he told her. "We can go to a dance club."

"Oh, thank you, Dick," my mother said. "That would take off some of the pressures I have."

The arguments happened I guess every month from as far back as I can remember. The one on my eleventh birthday started because my mother had to feed the chickens, but sometimes they were because the weather was too hot or the townspeople were too stupid or because the hair salon didn't have banana-pineapple–scented shampoo. But during all of them, my mother always screamed, "I hate it here!"

When the arguments first started happening, I would sit in my room and listen to them like their voices were coming from the radio. When I first started learning to write, I copied some of the arguments in a notebook. I was about six and since I couldn't write out the whole argument, I'd write the words I knew like *the*, *hair*, *dance*, *job*. The words I didn't know the meaning or spelling of, I'd sound out and then look up in the dictionary. I found the words *leotard* and *honorable* easily. I could never find the word *satyr* in the dictionary, though, because when I'd sound it out, I imagined it to be spelled *sat tire*, or *satire*, but never *satyr*. I found out at school one day that a satyr is a thing that is half man and half goat. We also found out that a centaur is a thing that is half man and half horse. I think that would have been a better word for my father to call my mother, because a horse clops more than a goat.

Anyway, after each argument, I'd look at my notes from the one before and compare them with the new one. I couldn't always hear what my parents were saying. Some months I'd hear, "It's my fault because I didn't run around." Then other times I'd hear, "didn't run around in polka-dotted leotards and high heels, clopping like some wounded satyr?" After a while I could write the whole sentence out and then the whole argument and that's when I started to realize that maybe my parents were hiding something from me.

After I was sure that the argument on my eleventh birthday was over, I walked real fast to my room. I hadn't had a chance to ask my parents my question and they still hadn't given me a cake or birthday presents or a Chinese clown. I thought that at any moment they would call me to go and meet them in the kitchen where they would be waiting to wish me happy birthday. I didn't want to look like I was waiting for them so I changed into my pajamas and lay in my bed awake. After a few minutes I heard a knock at my door.

This is it, I thought. They were going to call me into the kitchen and give me a T-shirt that said, "Kiss Me! I'm 11!"

The door opened and my mother stepped into my room and I looked at her and smiled. She didn't smile back or say, "Come to the kitchen" or, "Happy birthday."

Instead she said, "Don! I'm turning off your light. It's past your bedtime."

I lay awake for the next hour thinking that she was

trying to fool me. She'd never surprised me before on my birthday, but I was sure that this was the year it was going to happen because the picture of Dawn made me think that eleventh birthdays were a really big deal.

An hour after my mother turned off my lights, I fell asleep and dreamed about a Chinese clown. It didn't look that different from a regular clown.

But anyway, when I walked into the kitchen the next morning, my parents were sitting at the table. My father stared straight ahead while he ate a banana and my mother bounced around in her chair while she ate a donut.

When my mother finished eating, she said, "Don, your father and I have an announcement to make. Don't we, Dick?"

My father nodded and scratched the bald spot on his head and then my mother said, "We're going to New Orleans this weekend, so you'll be staying with the babysitter."

My mother stood up and walked over to the radio and said, "I'm so excited. I need to practice dancing for New Orleans."

She turned on the radio and the song "Love Will Keep Us Together" by Captain and Tenille was playing.

I closed my eyes and tapped my fork against the table and moved from side to side with the music until my mother said, "Don! Stop tapping that fork. You're messing up my rhythm."

I opened my eyes and saw my mother spinning

around. She looked like she was in a good mood so I decided I would ask her the question I'd wanted to ask the night before. I took a deep breath and was about to ask if I could start taking care of the chickens. But something else fell out of my mouth and I said, "Yesterday was my birthday."

My father turned and looked at me. My mother, who was kicking her leg in the air, froze for a few seconds. Then it was like she melted, and she dropped her leg down and said, "Oh. Happy birthday. You know, I'm sorry, we forgot. I don't always have time to remember these things. I mean, I cook and clean all day, every day. You mustn't try to make me feel bad about this. Dick, tell him not to make me feel bad about this."

My father looked at me for a couple of seconds and then at my mother. He did something funny with his eyes that made him look like he was thinking. Then my mother crossed her arms in front of her and looked at him. My father closed his eyes and then said, "Don, don't make your mother feel bad about this."

THREE

My mother called the chickens "The Feathered Curse." The reason she didn't just call them "The Curse" was because she used that name to talk about her menstrual cycle. I overheard her tell my father several times that the chickens caused just as much pain and suffering as her menstrual cycle, but couldn't be controlled with sanitary napkins and pain relievers. I didn't know what my mother meant the first time I heard her use the words *menstrual cycle*. All I knew was that it was bad and that you probably couldn't ride it like a motorcycle.

Both curses put my mother in a bad mood. On days when she would wake up with puffy eyes and complained more than usual, I'd check the front foyer of our house to see if my father had packed a suitcase and was heading out of town. If there wasn't a suitcase, I knew my mother was acting the way she was because of "The Curse" and that I should stay in my room and away from her. If there was a suitcase, I knew it was "The Feathered Curse" and I'd get happy because I knew I'd get to watch her feed the chickens.

Even though feeding the chickens was like a menstrual cycle to my mother, I liked watching them being fed because they always seemed so excited. They each had their own way of getting over to the grain. Some of them would spin around in circles, roll around in the dirt, fly a few feet, and then flap their wings the rest of the way. Sometimes a group of them would line up like they were playing that game Red Rover, and then they'd run over together to the grain. Some of the smaller, lighter ones could fly the few feet over to where the grain had landed, but the heavier, older ones couldn't, so they danced over.

Sometimes my mother didn't feed the chickens because she decided it was too much of a bother for her. There were a few times when some of them died and lay in the middle of the pen until my father came back from his business trip and got rid of them. The next day, the dead chickens would be replaced with others, so we always had twenty-five of them, because of the will.

My mother eventually figured out that it was better to feed the chickens than to let them die and stink up the yard. But even though she stopped starving the chickens, the yard still stank because of the eggs.

You see, since my mother was so scared of the chickens, she never collected their eggs, but instead left them in the nest until my father got back from his business trips. After a while they started to rot and smell up the yard. My mother decided one day to replace the hens with roosters so they wouldn't lay any more eggs.

I watched the roosters for a few hours the first day they showed up and one of them did this little dance where he ran sideways and then opened his wings and turned around in circles. The hens got around him like they were praying to him and the rooster jumped on one of the hens and did some stuff. At first I thought that maybe he was hurting her, but then the other hens lined up and the other rooster did a similar dance and also had a line forming for him.

When my mother added the roosters to our flock, two things happened that she didn't expect. One was that they usually crowed in the mornings. I loved the sound of the roosters waking me up and I'd watch them from my window while they stood on the top of a rock or bucket that made them higher than the other chickens.

My mother hated the crowing and usually threw a shoe or bucket at them. It never came close to the roosters, but the curse words she shouted usually made them run or stop crowing. After a few weeks, my mother traded the roosters in for some hens. It wasn't soon enough, though, to stop something else from happening.

You see, since she didn't collect the eggs, the chickens began sitting on them and they began to hatch. To me, it was amazing the first time I saw a hen walk out with five little chicks following her. I watched the mother hen and her chicks from my window. She walked with her chest stuck out and she clucked at the other chickens when they'd look at her new kids. I sat there for a few minutes staring at them until I heard my mother scream, "Oh my god! What is going on?"

I ran out to the backyard and stood next to my mother. She pointed at the chicks and asked, "How could this have happened? How could they have started reproducing?"

When my father came back from trips, he collected all the eggs that were in the nests and since it takes around twenty-one days for an egg to hatch, this stopped the chicks from being born. I figured out later, though, that one of the hens was laying her eggs behind a bush in the chicken yard.

The morning we found the chicks, my father had already left for work, but when he got home, before he even stepped out of the car, my mother was standing over him shouting. My father grinned a little while she shouted and flapped her arms around. He explained to her what roosters did and she told him, "But we got rid of the roosters a few weeks ago."

My father shrugged and said, "I guess they did their deed before they left."

My mother put her hands on her hips and said, "That's just like a man," and then she went into the house and slammed the door.

Neither my father nor my mother understood the chickens as well as I did. They didn't realize that the rooster was admired for its courage and its morning crow, and because the hen laid eggs, she was a sign of fertility. I looked that word up and it means that she can have a lot of kids. I thought the courage and fertility thing was kind of cool, but the reason I liked the chickens so much was because they made me laugh and listened to me. This was why I wanted to start taking care of them. And I finally asked if I could, two days after my eleventh birthday.

My father had left on a business trip the day before so my mother had to feed the chickens. I went with her because she was scared the chickens would attack her and she needed me to call the police and an ambulance if they did. I didn't mind because I liked watching them get fed and I think watching them was a better present than a Chinese clown or a T-shirt that said, "Kiss Me! I'm 11."

So that afternoon, I stood next to my mother behind our house and looked at the chickens behind the fence that separated them from our yard. My mother was wearing a red bow in her hair, a white pantsuit, and high heel shoes. It was the end of April and it was starting to get hot and so my mother had a bunch of sweat dripping down her face.

"I hate your father," she said, and then she took a deep breath and walked toward the fence separating our backyard from the chicken yard. She threw a fistful of grain over the fence, and one of her red press-on nails flew through the air with the feed. When the chickens started dancing toward her to eat the feed, my mother screamed, "Go away, you nasty rodents!"

Then she dropped the pail, threw her hands up in the air, screamed some more, and ran from them until the heel of her shoe got stuck in some mud. She bent over and started breathing hard and bobbing her head up and down each time she took a breath. The red bow in her hair was flopping back and forth like a chicken's comb. She did this for only a couple of seconds and then stood up and looked at her hand and said, "Oh my god. I lost another nail!"

Then she made a fist and shouted, "I hate you, chickens! You are a feathered curse!"

I laughed because my mother looked like a chicken herself because of the red bow and white suit, so it was kind of like she said she hated herself. My mother scrunched up her face, looked at me, and said, "I can't believe you! I could have been killed and you're laughing!"

I stopped laughing and said, "I'm sorry."

"Well, sorry isn't good enough," she said. "You're punished, young man, so tonight after dinner, I want you to go straight to your room and think about how hateful you are."

That night, right after I ate the boysenberry tart in my Mountains of Meatloaf TV dinner, my mother sent me to my bedroom. My room had a single bed, a desk left over from Uncle Sam, and a wooden toy box I'd won in kindergarten for guessing how many jelly beans were in a jar. The edge of my bed was right by a window, and from it I could see the chicken yard. I sat on my bed and looked at the chickens and laughed again when I thought about how my mother looked like a chicken when she was screaming. That's when I realized that maybe it would be a good time to ask to start taking care of the chickens.

You see, I knew that my mother hated feeding the chickens and that my father wasn't coming back for a few days and so she would probably be happy that I asked to start taking care of them. So I walked over to my door and listened to the television until a commercial came on. This was the best time to ask, I figured, so I opened my door and walked out into the living room. My mother was sitting in her chair watching TV.

"What are you doing out of your room?" she asked. "You're punished."

I looked down at the ground and said, "I," but before I could say anything else, my mother said, "What? You're what? You're sorry for laughing at me?"

I looked up at her, pushed my glasses up on my nose, closed my eyes, and asked, "Can I start feeding the chickens?"

"What?" she asked.

I opened my eyes and asked, "Can I start taking care of the chickens?"

"You want to start taking care of the chickens?" she asked.

I looked up at her and said, "Yes, ma'am."

She looked in the air and then said, "Hmmm. That's not a bad idea. It would teach you some responsibility. Starting tomorrow, you are in charge of the chickens."

I smiled and said, "Thank you. Thank you so much," and I wanted to run up to her and hug her, but *The Carol Burnett Show* came back on and she said, "Sshh, Carol's back on and you're still punished. Go back to your room."

FOUR

I wanted to do a good job taking care of the chickens, so I spent the whole summer learning as much about them as I could. I read every book on chickens I could find and learned that they think chickens came from Asia and that they are older than Jesus Christ. The chickens I mean, not the people.

Anyway, I also learned how to tell the different breeds of chickens. In our flock we had White Leghorns, Rhode Island Reds, White Plymouth Rocks, and a few that looked kind of like they were a mix of all of them. I called the mixed ones Americans because my teacher had said that America was a melting pot and a mix of a bunch of different races. One book said that a bunch of breeds were made by people because they were trying to make a perfect bird. Some people bred chickens for eggs, others for food, and others just to show at county fairs.

I also learned a bunch of other stuff about chickens

that I used to help them. I made sure they always had fresh water and I changed the grain so it had more protein. After a couple of months, a lot of the chickens started growing thick feathers and ran around the yard like the kids at school. Some of them even started laying eggs every day.

The thing I learned that made me a little sad was how chickens can't really fly. They can fly a little bit and I knew this because I'd watched them so much for so many years. But they can't really fly high or far because they're kind of fat and they got that way because people fed them a bunch of food to make them that way so they could eat them. People also bred chickens to make them bigger and fatter. If chickens had stayed small, they'd be able to fly and wouldn't have to stay on the ground and dance.

Every time I learned something new about the chickens, I wanted to tell someone. I'd tell my chickens, but I think most of them already knew this stuff about themselves. I told my father once that chickens were older than Jesus Christ and he didn't look like he cared, so I didn't tell him anything else. It was almost driving me crazy and then something happened and I got to tell a whole bunch of people about chickens.

It was a few months after I had started taking care of the chickens. I was in the fifth grade and I remember it was October because there was a big pumpkin on my classroom's door for Halloween. When I walked into class that day, my teacher, who was writing something on the board, turned and looked at me and said, "Good morning, Don."

"Good morning, Mrs. Forest," I said, and then walked to the back of the class where my desk was and sat and stared straight ahead while the rest of the kids talked to one another. I heard Leon Leonard, the bully who was mean to me all the time, tell this kid Jude, "I'm going to punch John Jefferson because he's a geek. You wanna watch?"

Jude raised his hand in the air and said, "That would be cool, Leon. High five."

After a few minutes the bell rang and Mrs. Forest told us to settle down so we could get started. Then she said, "Please stand, children, so we can say the Pledge of Allegiance."

After we were finished, Mrs. Forest handed out a science test that we'd taken the day before, and when she gave Leon his, she said, "Leon, you need to study for these tests. If you fail another one, I'm going to have to talk to your parents."

Leon said, "Yes, ma'am," and then Mrs. Forest gave Jude his paper and said, "Not bad, but I think if you try a little harder, you can do even better," and Jude also said, "Yes, ma'am."

Then Mrs. Forest handed me my paper and said, "Great job, Don. You got the highest score in the class again."

I took my paper from Mrs. Forest and she walked up to the front of the class. Leon was sitting behind me in the row to my right. He threw a ball of paper at me and said, "Hey, new kid, I'm sure you're going to be real successful in your life as a geek."

Some of the kids in class started laughing and Mrs. Forest asked, "Why are you laughing?"

Nobody said anything and then Mrs. Forest asked, "Did you do something, Leon?"

Leon said, "You're always blaming me," and then Mrs. Forest said, "That's because the laughter came from the back of the class where you happen to be. In fact, every time there's trouble, it's always where you happen to be."

Before Leon could say anything back, someone knocked on the door and everyone jumped. Mrs. Forest opened the door and the principal handed her a sheet of paper and she thanked him and read the paper to herself. Her eyes got real wide and she told us she had two very important announcements to make concerning the upcoming Dairy Festival. The first was that infants who had been fed high-protein milk from a can instead of breastfed couldn't be in the baby contest for obvious reasons.

The kids in the class started whispering to one another and Mrs. Forest said, "Settle down, children, settle down."

The second announcement was the one that gave me the chance to tell people how much I'd learned about chickens. I remember Mrs. Forest's voice was kind of shaking when she told us, "Okay, now listen carefully, students. You need to promise me that you'll stay in your chairs and you won't overreact about this. I'll give you a few minutes to discuss it, but then we have got to go over the science test. Okay, here goes:

'After a heated town committee meeting, it has been decided that the age requirement for the chicken-judging contest at the upcoming Dairy Festival will be lowered to eleven years old.'"

Everyone in the class except me started talking, and Mrs. Forest tapped on her desk with a ruler and said, "Settle down, children, settle down."

Jimmy Jadeau leaned over to me and lifted his hand in the air for a high five, but because he never spoke to me, I kind of backed away because I thought he was going to hit me. But he didn't and he asked me, "Can you believe it?"

Before I could say anything, Leon joined in. "He doesn't care about this." And then he stood up and danced a little jig and said, "He doesn't even know anything about chickens 'cause they only keep theirs for ambience."

He said the word *ambience* real loud and then Jimmy gave the high five to Leon instead of me. A bunch of kids laughed and then he gave them high fives too. Mrs. Forest told us again, "Settle down, children, settle down."

None of the kids knew that I cared about the contest because I didn't really speak to them. It wasn't that I didn't like them. It was that they didn't speak to me, and my mother had always told me not to speak unless

I was spoken to. I guess I got so used to not speaking at home unless someone asked me a question, that I did the same thing at school. And one time, when I was in kindergarten, the teacher found this rubber rat in her desk drawer and she asked the class who it belonged to. I knew it was Leon's because I'd seen him with it that morning. He was in the bathroom when the teacher asked, so I told her that it was his because I figured that he'd want it back. He didn't, though. He was trying to scare the teacher with it, and when he got back from the bathroom he got punished. Brooke Brylee told him that I told the teacher that the rat was his and so during recess he punched me in the stomach and told me that I needed to learn to keep my mouth shut when people weren't talking to me. I didn't want to get punched again, so I listened to him. And after that I didn't talk to anyone unless they spoke to me first.

So during recess and at lunchtime, I usually played by myself on the jungle gym or swing, or read or watched the other kids play games. Except for the few times someone said something about my parents keeping chickens for ambience, the kids in my class left me alone. They had all been friends since before they started school because all of their parents were friends. So even though I had been at school with the other kids in my class since kindergarten, they still called me "new kid."

Anyway, so we're in class that day, and some other kid, Andrew Alkins, said, "That's a good one, Leon. The new kid keeps his chickens for ambience. Give me a high five!"

Mrs. Forest smiled and whispered the word *ambience* under her breath. She saw me staring at her and she said, "Settle down, children, settle down. Don, ignore them. Now let's get back to going over our science test."

Mrs. Forest went over the science test, but all I could think about was the Dairy Festival and the chicken-judging contest. Before that day I had thought about the year that I would be old enough to compete in it. It was something that I dreamed about, but since it was so far away, I could hardly believe that it would ever happen. I thought maybe my mother would finally get my father to move before the next contest or that the age requirement would be raised even higher or that maybe my mother was right and I'd have my eyes pecked out by one of the chickens. But now, here was my chance to be in the contest and maybe win an award to put next to Dawn's dance trophy above the TV, music box, and *War and Peace*.

I had to get permission from one of my parents to be in the contest and because my mother had said a bunch of times that she hated Horse Island festivals and that they were a breeding ground for malaria, white trash, and tuberculosis, I figured I should ask my father when my mother wasn't around.

The teacher made the announcement about the contest on a Tuesday, and my father and I were alone the

Friday after, when my mother went to the beauty parlor. I figured this would be the best time to ask, but I wasn't sure how to do it. Then I realized that my father always signed my test papers on Friday, so I could just put the permission slip in with them and maybe he'd sign it and I wouldn't even have to ask.

So that afternoon, I did my homework on the coffee table in the living room, while my father sat in his chair and read his paper. I watched him out of the corner of my eye to see when he was finished, because this is when he usually asked me if I had test papers to sign. It seemed like he was taking forever and it was so hard for me not to jump up and just hand him the papers. But I figured he wouldn't like that, so I didn't.

When he finally finished reading the paper, he folded it up, scratched his head, wiped his glasses, and asked me if I had any school papers to sign.

"Yes, sir," I said, and then handed him the test papers and permission slip and a pen. My father looked at them and signed each one. The permission slip was the last one in the stack, so I hoped he would just sign it and not ask what it was for.

But he asked, "What am I supposed to do with this?"

"Can I be in it?" I asked.

He looked at the paper again, raised his eyebrows, and then said, "You were fed milk from a can. You aren't allowed to be in it."

"Oh," I said.

He handed me back the stack of papers and I turned

away from him. I looked down at the permission slip and realized that he'd read only the first couple of sentences about the changes at the Dairy Festival. I was trying to think about what to do next when I heard my mother's car in the driveway. I knew that if I wanted to be in the contest I would have to ask my father before my mother got in the house. So I walked back to my father's chair and asked real quick, "I want to be in the chicken-judging contest. Not the baby contest."

"Oh," he said.

I heard my mother's key slip into the lock of the front door and I tapped my foot because I was so nervous.

"Well," he said.

The front door opened and my mother's high heels tapped against the hardwood floors and I heard her yell, "Hello! Is anyone here?"

My father yelled, "In the living room!"

I heard my mother's shoes go toward the kitchen and then heard her say, "I'm coming. Just give me a minute."

So I asked my father again, "Can I be in it?"

I could smell my mother's hair spray getting closer and I thought she'd be in the living room before my father answered.

But then he said, "Yeah. Why not?"

FIVE

One of the first things I bought when I had saved up enough birthday and Christmas money was a book called *The Standard of Perfection*. When I bought it from Mr. Chance Chandler, the guy who owned Chance Chandler's Chicken Chow and Saddle Salon, he told me, "It's the chicken man's Bible. If you ain't got the book, chickens ain't in your heart."

The book was written by the American Poultry Association and it told you everything you'd ever want to know about chickens. It described breeds, varieties, colors, and tons of other useful things. I had read it hundreds of times because chickens were in my heart, and the Saturday morning of the contest, I opened it up to read it again.

I couldn't concentrate, though, because I kept wondering what would happen if I won. Would the other kids start calling me Don and invite me to play games with them during lunch and recess? The boy who had won the chicken-judging contest the year before was Michael Motto, and before he won, not many people talked to him, and after he won, people talked to him all the time and he was always picked first for teams.

I was thinking about all this stuff on the morning of the contest, so I couldn't concentrate on *The Standard of Perfection* and decided to go out to the yard to practice judging chickens.

I pointed at one chicken and said, "You are a White Plymouth Rock, have a reversed main wing feather, and a missing spike."

I spun around and kneeled on one knee and pointed to a different chicken and said, "You are a Rhode Island Red, have a crooked breastbone, and are bowlegged."

I jumped back on two feet, leaned over, stuck my head between my legs, pointed to a young chicken, and said, "You are a female under one year of age, so you are a pullet."

When I had finished judging all of the chickens in my yard, I went into the kitchen and poured myself a bowl of cereal. My mother walked in and said, "You're not making a mess, are you?"

"No, ma'am," I said, and then she asked, "Why are you up so early?"

"I'm going to the chicken-judging contest today," I told her, and she said, "Chicken-judging contest. What's that?"

"We look at different types of chickens and name their breed and rank them on their traits from one to ten, and the person who ranks them the best wins a blue ribbon, and it's really cool because—"

And then my mother cut me off and said, "Don, please, you're giving me a headache. What I think you're trying to tell me is that it's a contest for a bird that can't fly. Why would anyone want to do something as stupid as that?"

I wanted to tell her that chickens could fly. They couldn't fly too high or real far, but they could fly, and the reason that they couldn't fly like a black bird or an eagle was because people had made them that way. I wanted to tell her that if she would just watch the chickens she would know they could fly. Instead, I swung my foot back and forth and listened to my blue jeans rub against the chair leg until my mother told me, "Don! Stop making that sound. It is too early in the morning to be getting on my nerves. Also, don't you think you should have asked my permission before you decided to go and do something stupid like this and risk humiliating the family?"

"Father gave me permission," I told her.

He walked in just then and my mother looked at him and asked, "Did you tell him he could go to some stupid chicken-judging contest?"

"Yes," he said.

"Well, I wish someone would tell me what's going on around here," my mother said. "Who is going to help me do the weekly shopping if he's off at some chicken contest? I cook and clean all day and all I ask for is a little help now and then."

My father looked at me and I thought he was going to tell me that I couldn't go. I felt like I did the day I got stung by a wasp. My eyes started to water, and then I felt like my nose was leaking. My throat felt dry and it was like I couldn't breathe. I got really hot and then really cold. I had cried when that wasp stung me and my mother told me to be quiet because she couldn't hear the TV. So I didn't want to start crying again even though the TV wasn't on. But I could feel it coming, so I thought about running out of the kitchen before I started or before my father told me I couldn't go.

But before I could, my father asked, "Don't they have bag boys at Horse Island Food and Furniture?"

I looked at him, and then my mother said, "Yeah, I guess they do have bag boys and I guess I can get one of them to help me if they're not off at that chicken-judging contest with Don and the rest of the rednecks."

I couldn't believe my father had saved me and I didn't know why, either. Maybe he saw that I was about to cry and didn't want me to give my mother a headache. Or maybe he really wanted me to win that contest so that he could brag to everybody about how smart his son was. A part of me didn't care why he had saved me and I just wanted to run up to him and hug him. But by the time I'd realized what had happened, he had walked to the freezer and pulled out a box of frozen waffles.

I knew that I needed to get out of the kitchen before my mother changed her mind, so I finished my cereal in about ten seconds and then cleaned up after myself, left the house, and headed off to the contest.

It was the last weekend of October so the sun was still shining, and when I peddled to the end of our driveway, I had to cover my eyes a little so I didn't get blinded. After I looked both ways to make sure that no cars were coming, I took a left.

The only people out in their yard were Paul Picard and his wife, Patricia. People called Patricia "Purple Patricia" because she had a purple car, a purple house, and wore purple clothes. When I passed their house on my bike, I turned onto Porcupine Street toward a large hill. I had to get off my bike and push it up the hill because it was so steep. Every time I did this, a stray calico cat would chase me and try to bite my legs. That day a raccoon ran by us, and the cat turned from me and chased it through a ditch.

When I got to the top of the hill, I got back on my bike and took a left onto Armadillo Street. On the right side of the street were trailers, cars on cement blocks, and horse troughs. A girl in my class named Vickie Viceroy lived in one of the trailers there and she was chasing after a dog that had an apple tied to its head. She aimed at it with a slingshot and just before she was about to let go of what I guess was a rock, the apple fell off of the dog's head. Vickie yelled at her brother, Vince, "I told you string wouldn't work. Go get the tape."

I kept going down Armadillo Street and then turned right onto Main. There was a large sign on the boulevard in the shape of a chicken with some words above its head, like the ones they use in comic strips. The face of the white chicken was cut out so anyone could step behind and stick their head in it. The caption read, "Welcome to Horse Island. Home of the Best Chickens and Eggs in the World."

The stray dog and pig that usually ran around the school yard were looking up at the sign. No one knew where the stray dog and pig came from. As long as anyone could remember, they were in Horse Island running around together. They usually came to the school yard about four times a week and a group of kids chased after them trying to catch them. They were both black. The dog was about the size of a golden retriever, and the pig was a special breed called a potbellied pig and was about the size of a cocker spaniel. They watched me peddle past Horse Island Food and Furniture, Connie's Cones, Candies, and Condiments stand, and then to the entrance of the fairgrounds.

The chicken-judging contest was held on the fairground of the Dairy Festival, a big pasture with a few cow pens that the fair committee used for the cattle, sheep, and horse showing. Sometimes they had contests where people had to rope a calf and tie it up or try to catch a greased pig.

When I got to the registration table for the chicken-judging contest, there was already a line of about fifteen people. I got behind them and while I was waiting, I heard this girl, Kelly Kramer, tell another girl that she thought Leon was going to win the contest because she'd heard that he could say the word *chicken* before he could say the word *momma*.

I thought that was kind of cool and tried to think about what my first word was, but before I could, it was my turn at the registration table. My teacher, Mrs. Forest, was there, and she looked up at me and said, "Oh, Don, this is a surprise."

She was sitting between two other ladies and turned her head to each side and smiled and then said, "Well, Don, here's your name tag and your ranking sheet. The contest will start at ten sharp. Until then, you can wait over there in that cow pen with the rest of the contestants."

The cow pen was like all cow pens. I mean it was square-shaped and surrounded by a wooden fence. To get in, I had to walk through a big swinging gate that Leon stood on top of while other kids swung him back and forth. Inside the pen were a bunch of other kids all waiting to compete in the eleven-to-thirteen–year-old chicken-judging contest. Before I got in, though, I heard Leon say, "What do we have here?"

He jumped off of the gate and walked toward me and said, "It looks like the new kid, who keeps his chickens for ambience, is going to enter the contest," and then some other kid said, "That's funny, Leon. Give me a high five."

I walked into the middle of the pen and Leon gave the kid a high five, walked up to me, and said, "Do you really think you have a chance against me, new kid?"

I had thought I did before Leon asked me, but after, I started wondering if I did have a chance of winning against someone who'd said the word *chicken* before the word *momma*.

Since I didn't know what to say I said, "My father made me do it. He thought maybe I could learn some things from you guys that we could use on our farm."

Leon picked up a stick from the ground and waved it around in the air like a baton and said, "Huh. That makes sense. I could school you a little on raising chickens," and then a bull in the next pen made a pie and all the kids held their noses and Leon said, "Somebody had beans for breakfast," and then everyone ran to the gate and left me alone in the middle of the cow pen.

Right after that, Mrs. Forest came into the pen and said, "Excuse me, children, I have an announcement to make, so please be quiet."

After everyone stopped talking, she said, "Okay, listen, children. One of the supervisors of the contest, Mr. Bufford, is going to be a little late, so the contest won't start until 10:45. So you're free to walk around the fairgrounds, but be back here at 10:15 sharp or you will be disqualified."

I didn't feel like waiting in the pen for the contest to

start, so I walked around the fairgrounds. There were big tents, food booths, a roller coaster, and a Ferris wheel. On the edge of the fairgrounds, I found a small open-walled tent with a few machines. One of them would stamp your name on a penny for twenty-five cents, and another one would take your picture with backgrounds of waterfalls, flowers, or a giant chicken leaning over so it looked like it was pecking you on the head. In the corner of the tent was a machine with a glass box and inside there was a white chicken and a small piano. The chicken was real skinny and had lost most of her feathers and she was sitting in the box, staring out into space. She wasn't moving at all, but even if she had wanted to, she couldn't because the box was only about four feet wide and three feet long, kind of like a fish tank.

The sign above the machine said, "Henrietta, the Piano Playing Hen." I'd never seen a chicken play a piano before and it was only twenty-five cents, so I put a quarter in the coin slot. Lights started flashing and then Henrietta got up and went over to the little piano and started pecking on the keys. She played the first verse of "Mary Had a Little Lamb."

After she played, some chicken feed fell into the box from a small hole in the top of it. Henrietta ate the food real fast and then sat down again. It wasn't healthy for a chicken to be in a glass box all day without being able to roll around in the dirt or be in the sunlight. I wanted to let her out of the box and take her home with me so she'd be able to dance around the chicken yard and maybe even fly a little.

I put my hand on the glass and said, "Give me a high five."

She laid her body against it and it felt warm and I really liked it. I think I could have stayed there almost all day just looking at her and talking to her. But I had to go back to the contest. So I told her that I was going to come back and hear her play again and make sure she got some more food.

When I got to the cow pen, Mr. Bufford was there and was ready to start the contest. The way it worked was that professional judges from nearby towns had judged fifteen chickens and ranked them on egg-production qualities and exhibition standards on scales from one to five. We were supposed to do the same, and the person who ranked the chickens closest to the judges would win.

The fifteen chickens were in cages on top of tables inside the cow pen. Since there were so many kids in the contest, we went into the pen twenty-five at a time and had forty-five minutes to judge. The eleven-year-olds went in first and when we did, all the kids crowded around the first cage. I tried to see the chicken, but I couldn't, so I decided to start at the last cage.

It gave me a chance to look at the chicken, which I saw right away was a White Leghorn. I could tell by its size and shank color that it was a good egg producer. I wanted to look at it closer, though, so I asked one of the judges if I could take it out of the cage. He said, "Yes," so I pulled the chicken out real slow, head first, so I wouldn't damage any of its feathers. I checked the eye color and the head for defects and when I didn't see any, I checked the comb quality and the beak color. This was when I noticed that the kids at the first cage were watching me. It made me a little nervous because I thought that I might be doing something wrong. But since the judge had given me permission to look at the chicken and no one was laughing at me, I went along with my ranking. I could still feel everyone looking at me, and I had to put the chicken back in the cage because it made me so uncomfortable and I was afraid Leon would make fun of me and call me stupid.

But no one said anything and so I kept judging the chicken and noticed that one of its toes was really short. Even though it was a small defect, it helped me to forget about the other kids and think about the chicken and look for other faults it might have. It turned out to have a lot of deformities that I hadn't noticed at first. For example, its comb was red and waxy, which meant that it was a good egg layer, but it was so big that the comb fell into the chicken's eyes, and that wasn't a good exhibition standard.

By the time I had ranked the chicken and given it a very low score for the exhibition standards, I had forgotten all about Leon and the other kids. When I moved to the next cage, though, I noticed that Leon pushed the other kids out of the way and pulled out the chicken from the first cage. Soon all the kids were pulling the chickens out of the cages and feeling them and shaking their heads up and down and saying, "Oh, that's not good," or "Uh-huh."

About halfway through, when I was writing down my scores and comments about a Rhode Island Red with one leg longer than the other, I heard someone say, "Huh." I looked up and saw Mr. Bufford standing above me and looking at my ranking sheet. It made me wonder if I'd written something down wrong, so I looked at the chicken again just to make sure that I hadn't missed anything. I hadn't, but just to be careful, I studied it again and even made sure the scales on its legs weren't too dry or waxy.

After I judged all of the chickens and rechecked my answers, I turned in my ranking sheet and walked out of the cow pen. I don't know why but I kind of wanted to run really fast. I had all this energy and I wanted to run and jump and I thought for a few seconds that if I ran fast enough and jumped high enough I'd take off and start flying. I ran a little, but there were so many people at the Dairy Festival I had to stop because I kept bumping into them.

I felt great and I wanted to celebrate like the people on television celebrated when something good happened. On *The Love Boat*, they drank champagne when they celebrated, and on *The Brady Bunch*, they drank fruit juice. I decided to celebrate with a soda I bought from a food booth called "Pops, Pizza, and Pineapple."

But on TV, the people always celebrated with other people. There was no one at the festival that I wanted to celebrate with, though. And then I remembered Henrietta and decided that I could celebrate with her.

The winners of the contest weren't going to be announced for an hour, so I had a bunch of time to spend with her. I wanted to tell her all about the contest and how well I did. But when I got to the glass box with the piano, Henrietta wasn't in it. There was a man standing in the tent watching all the people play the games and so I walked over to him. He was a tall, skinny man, wearing a white T-shirt with yellow sweat stains under the arms. I stared at him hoping that if I kept my eyes on him long enough, he'd talk to me and then I could talk back. My plan worked and he said, "What can I do you for, kid?"

I looked down and said, "There was a chicken in that box this morning. Where is she?"

Then the man pulled a packet of chewing tobacco out of his pocket and asked, "Why? You want to buy that chicken?"

I hadn't really thought about buying Henrietta, but after the man asked me, I realized that maybe I did and so I said, "Yes."

"That chicken was getting too ugly to be Henrietta, the Piano Playing Hen, anymore," he told me. "But I tell you what, kid. If you want, I'll sell her to you for five dollars."

Henrietta was too old for egg laying and also for

meat. I didn't want her for either, but I still knew that five dollars was way too much, and even if it wasn't too much, I didn't have five dollars. I told him that and he looked at me and then spit on the ground, missing my foot by only an inch.

Then he asked, "How much you got?"

I looked in my pocket and showed him that I had only one dollar and he said, "I tell you what, boy. Instead of you standing here wasting my time, why don't you go and look for your parents and ask them for the money to buy that chicken? But you better do it by the end of the day 'cause that's when I'm going to put her up for sale and ain't nobody going to be buying that chicken for the eggs she's going to lay. They gonna be buying that bird for voodoo rituals or alligator bait."

I walked to the bleachers where the judges of the chicken-judging contest were supposed to announce the winners. And then I went up to the last row and closed my eyes. People started sitting down in the bleachers and I started thinking about Henrietta and where I could get the money to buy her so she wouldn't be killed. I knew I couldn't ask my parents and I didn't have time to earn it, either.

While I was thinking about this, the judges came out of the cow pen and went onstage. One of them stepped up to a microphone and said, "Ladies and Gentlemen, we have the results of the chicken-judging contest for the eleven-to-thirteen age group."

I started thinking about Henrietta again and where

I'd get the money to buy her. That's when I saw Leon Leonard's mom, Lucy, sitting in front of me. Next to her was her purse and it was open and inside I could see her wallet. I'd heard people say that the Leonards were rich because Lucy Leonard owned a beauty salon and Lyle Leonard, Leon's dad, worked offshore on one of the oil rigs. I couldn't ask Mrs. Leonard for the money, though, because I knew that she probably wouldn't give it to me to buy an old chicken. But then I realized that I could reach down and grab her wallet without anyone seeing me because no one else was sitting on the last row and everyone was standing and watching the announcer.

Before I could do anything, though, the announcer said, "Third place goes to Ray Reilly!"

I had never stolen anything before and knew that it was wrong but thought that maybe it wasn't that wrong because the Leonards could afford it and they owed me that money because Leon was so mean to me and it would help save Henrietta's life. I thought about that skinny man from the game tent throwing Henrietta into a pond full of alligators and I felt like someone had punched me in the stomach.

"Second place goes to Leon Leonard!"

When I heard that, I felt like someone had punched me in the stomach again. I think it was the first time I ever hated someone and the first time I understood why those crazy women on daytime soap operas threw vases at people. Those women weren't as crazy as I thought they were. They were just mad because someone had been mean to them, beat them in a chicken-judging contest, or something like that.

That's how I felt when I saw Leon get his ribbon. I wanted to throw a vase at him. But I didn't have a vase so I decided that I was going to steal from his family to save a chicken's life. That was kind of like throwing a vase but better, because this way, Henrietta would get to live.

So when Mrs. Leonard stepped away from her purse to get a picture of Leon holding his ribbon, I took a deep breath and put my shoe by her purse. I bent down and pretended I was tying it and then grabbed the wallet.

"Don Schmidt!"

I let go of the wallet and stood up real fast. Someone had shouted my name and everyone in the bleachers was talking low. I started thinking of things to tell my parents when they found out that I was a thief. Then the announcer said, "Does anyone see him? Does anyone know where Don Schmidt is?"

That's when Ray Reilly said, "There he is!"

"Well come down here, boy, and get your award," the announcer said.

I sat down on the bleachers because I didn't understand what was going on. Then the announcer said, "Boy, you need to get down here and claim your blue ribbon or I might have to take it home myself."

Everyone in the bleachers laughed and then I realized that I had won first place. I walked down the bleachers thinking that I was dreaming and that I was going to wake up. But I didn't. I made it to the stage and the announcer handed me my blue ribbon. It was the most beautiful thing I'd ever seen. I put it against my face because it was so soft. It smelled like apple pie and I almost wanted to put it in my mouth to taste it.

I looked up at the crowd and saw Mrs. Leonard walking down the bleachers. Her wallet was sticking out of her purse and it bounced around until it fell on the bleacher floor behind her. I could have waited until everyone left the bleachers and gone up and taken it, but I did something else instead. I ran from the crowd that was around me and straight up to Mrs. Leonard and said, "Mrs. Leonard! Your wallet!"

I bent down and picked up her wallet and she said, "Oh, Lord. Thank you, Don. Thank you so much."

Then someone shouted from the crowd, "He knows how to judge chickens and he's honest! He's like Honest Abe!"

The crowd cheered even more and Mrs. Leonard hugged me while photographers took our picture. I thought it was the best day of my life, but then things just got really weird.

SIX

After everyone left the bleachers, I stood on the stage and stared at my blue ribbon until Mr. Bufford, one of the chicken-judging supervisors, walked up to me. He was about my parents' age and was wearing a light blue suit, a white shirt with red, bucking horses on the collar, and a black cowboy hat. He smiled real big, which showed a gap between his front teeth.

"Congratulations, boy," he told me. "Your parents must be very proud of you. I have a daughter a year younger than you, and I hope that when she gets to compete in this contest she can do half as good as you do. Did? Do? No, did."

He smiled some more and nodded his head up and down when he was sure that the right word was *did*. Then he said, "I tell you, boy, I can't keep up with all these new English rules going on, but I tell you what, I don't think it really matters as long as you get your point across."

I had never met Mr. Bufford, but I knew he was the owner of Horse Island Food and Furniture. My mother and I went there every Saturday and he was always putting food out or helping a customer move a sofa into the back of his truck. Sometimes people gave him a couple of dollars for helping them, and that day at the Dairy Festival, Mr. Bufford gave me a dollar and I thought he might want me to move something. He didn't, though. Instead he said, "Here you go, boy. I want to be the first person to get a couple dozen eggs from you."

I asked him, "What?" and he said, "I want to buy a couple dozen eggs from you and to make sure you don't forget me, I'm going to give you the money right now. Just bring them to school on Monday and leave them with the principal. He's my brother, and he'll make sure the eggs get to me."

I couldn't believe that he'd given me a dollar for two dozen eggs because we'd been throwing most of the eggs we got from the chickens away. I looked at the dollar and then told him, "I won't be able to bring you two dozen by Monday, but maybe I can bring you a dozen on Tuesday and one on Thursday."

He scrunched his face up and stared ahead for a few seconds and then said that was fine and walked away.

I stepped off the stage and looked up at the bleachers and saw Leon walking down real slow. When he got to the bottom, he stood for a full minute and stared at me. I looked around to see if there was an adult I could run to and hide behind because Leon looked mad and like he wanted to hit me. I didn't see any and so I froze and played like I was dead because I had seen on *Wild Kingdom* that some animals do that when they're scared. Leon kept staring at me and so I smiled and then let out a little giggle. This seemed to work because he walked away.

Then Henrietta popped into my mind. I still didn't have five dollars to buy her, but I did have two since Mr. Bufford had given me one. So I put my blue ribbon in my pocket and then walked to the tent with all the games. I found the man I had spoken to earlier and walked right up to him and said, "I have two dollars. Can I buy the chicken that was in the box this morning?"

He looked at me for a couple of seconds and then said, "Is two dollars five dollars?"

I told him, "No, sir," and then he said, "Then I guess that's not enough."

I turned from him and walked away so I could think and that's when I heard, "What chicken are you trying to buy?"

I looked up and saw Mr. Bufford standing in front of me and I told him, "I'm trying to buy the chicken that was in that glass box this morning playing the piano."

He looked at the tent and said, "Well, if you want to buy a chicken, then it must be a pretty good one. Maybe I'll buy it."

Mr. Bufford walked up to Henrietta's owner and asked, "Can I see that chicken this boy wants to buy?"

"Sure," the man said. "It's over here."

I followed the man and Mr. Bufford to the back of a large moving truck. On top of a cardboard box with the word *Popcorn* stamped across it was a cage with Henrietta in it.

Mr. Bufford asked me, "That's the chicken you want to buy?"

I told him, "Yes, sir," and he shook his head a bit and asked, "Why? That bird ain't worth a dollar."

I told him, "I know, but I like her and I don't want anyone to use her for voodoo rituals or alligator bait."

Mr. Bufford looked at Henrietta's owner and said, "You know that bird isn't worth five dollars. Why are you trying to steal from this young boy?"

"Hey," he said. "She's my chicken and I can sell her to whoever I want for how much I want, and I want to sell her to this boy for five dollars."

Mr. Bufford answered back like he was mad. "Well, he isn't going to buy it so I guess you're going to be stuck with it," and then he turned to me and said, "Come on, my boy."

We walked a little ways and Mr. Bufford said, "I'm passing by your house. If you want, I can give you a ride."

"You know where I live?" I asked him.

"Yeah, my boy. I know where everybody in this town lives. Besides, I was good friends with your uncle Sam before he passed."

I had my bike with me so I told him that I didn't

need a ride and he said, "Well you're going to have a hard time riding a bike while carrying a chicken."

I looked up at Mr. Bufford and asked, "What chicken?"

"You'll see," he said, and then told me to meet him with my bike on the northwest corner of the fairgrounds in five minutes. I did like he said because I thought that maybe he was going to buy the chicken for me. I knew that it was a lot of money for a chicken and that he barely knew me and that people don't usually buy five-dollar chickens for people they don't know, but I still thought that he might. When he drove up to me, though, he didn't have my chicken in his truck. He got out of the cab, walked over to me, lifted my bike, put it in the bed, and said, "Get in, my boy. I ain't got all day."

We had been warned in school not to get into auto-mobiles with strangers, but I didn't consider Mr. Bufford a stranger because I knew him. But then he said some crazy stuff and I began to wonder if I'd made a mistake.

It started when he was driving and he said, "Now, Don, sometimes you have to do things that may not seem right at first but are right when you look a little deeper."

I looked at him and he looked back at me and said, "So you have to trust me on this one, Don. What we're doing is right."

I didn't know what he was talking about, and I was beginning to get a little more scared than excited about maybe getting a chicken. So to calm myself down, I started singing "Shake Your Booty" by KC and the Sunshine Band in my head.

Mr. Bufford stopped the truck in the middle of the fairgrounds and put it in Park but left it running. Then he stepped out of the truck, turned to me, and said, "Give me that dollar I gave you for those two dozen eggs."

I handed it over and he said, "Wait here," and then walked away.

I sat in his truck for a couple of minutes trying to figure out what Mr. Bufford meant when he said I should trust him. I wondered if I should leave and just forget about the chicken. But then I saw Mr. Bufford running toward the truck with Henrietta. His clothes were full of feathers and the way he was running with his back bent over made him look like a chicken dancing. When he got to the truck, he opened the driver's door real fast, put Henrietta in my lap, jumped in, and drove off.

"There you go, boy," he said. "A little present. Now don't worry. I didn't steal her. I left a dollar in her cage, which is about all she was worth in the first place. Sometimes when people are trying to cheat you, you have to take things into your own hands, and that's exactly what I did. Even if that man doesn't think that I gave him a fair deal, that's too bad because there's nothing he can do about it anyway. He doesn't know our name and his carnival leaves town tomorrow."

I couldn't understand why Mr. Bufford was being so nice to me. No one had ever been this nice to me. Not even the babysitter, who was paid to be nice to me.

"You gonna thank me, boy?" Mr. Bufford asked.

"Yes, sir," I answered. "Thank you."

Then he told me, "Now, you know I took a big risk to get you that chicken."

"Yes, sir," I said. "Thank you."

And then he told me, "The words *thank you* are nice and all, but I'd really feel like taking the chicken for you was worth the risk if you'd start selling me your eggs every week. You see, Don, I'm a businessman and I know a smart deal when I see one. People told me I was crazy when I wanted to open up Horse Island Food and Furniture. They said, 'Bobby, ain't nobody going to want to buy a kitchen table from the same place they buy their milk.' And you know what I told them, Don?"

"No, sir," I told him.

And he said, "I told them, 'And why not? After all, where do you usually drink milk?'"

"I don't know, sir," I said.

"Now think hard, boy," he told me. "Where are you sitting when you drink milk?"

"On our sofa in the living room," I told him, and he scrunched his eyes up a little and asked, "What?"

"I usually drink milk when I'm sitting on our sofa eating my dinner," I told him

"You eat your dinner on the couch, boy?" he asked.

"No, sir," I told him. "The sofa. We don't have a couch."

He kind of pushed his lips out and said, "Oh, well, your answer of a sofa works too, but it's not the answer I was looking for. Now where was I? Oh yeah, so I told that knucklehead that didn't think my food and furniture store was a good idea that when people drink milk, they sit at a kitchen table, so why not go to a place where you can buy milk and a table?"

I didn't understand why he was talking about milk and kitchen tables. It started to make sense to me, though, when he said, "You see, Don, people respect a good chicken farmer in this town, and you are a good chicken farmer. I saw the answers you put on your ranking sheet, and I tell you, I've never met anyone that knows about chickens as much as you do. I bet those yard birds of yours are producing some mighty fine eggs. Ones that I bet my customers are willing to pay top dollar for. So how about it, partner? How about selling some of those eggs of yours to your good friend Mr. Bufford?"

I stroked Henrietta and thought about what Mr. Bufford was asking. I didn't see why I couldn't sell him our eggs. Except that my mother might think I would humiliate the family by selling our eggs because that would mean we kept our chickens for more than ambience. And then I realized that our chickens gave only about four dozen eggs a week, so I told him that.

He closed his right eye a little and opened his left

one real big and asked, "I thought you had twenty-five chickens?"

"I do," I told him, "but a lot of them don't lay anymore."

He opened his right eye and closed his left a little so they were both the same size and said, "Oh, well I guess you'll have to get some chickens that lay eggs, won't you?"

"I guess," I told him. "I'll have to ask my mother, but she doesn't really like chickens and I don't know if she'll let me have any more."

And then it hit me. I didn't know how I was going to explain Henrietta to my parents. They would never let me have another chicken. I'd have to let Henrietta loose in the chicken yard and hope that my mother didn't notice.

Then I thought about something else and asked Mr. Bufford, "Why do you want my eggs? What about the eggs from the winner of the fourteen-to-seventeen age category or the eighteen-to-twenty-one age category or the adult category?"

He laughed real loud and said, "Well, you are a smart one, ain't you, boy? But I have news for you, Mr. Schmidt. I'm a little smarter and I'll tell you why. You see, I already sell most of those people's eggs. Oh yeah, boy, I'm nobody's fool. Now the reason I want your eggs more than I want their eggs is 'cause your eggs are gonna outsell their eggs. Do you know why?"

His eyes got real big like The Three Stooges' did

when they saw a ghost. Then he asked again, "Do you know why?"

"No, sir," I said.

"I didn't think so!" he shouted. "Well, I'll tell you why!"

Both Henrietta and I jumped and then he said in a lower voice, "Because you're Don Schmidt and the youngest boy—no, person—to ever win a chicken-judging contest in Horse Island. I hope you understand that your life is about to change. Kids that have never spoken to you will suddenly become your best friends. People will beg you to sell them your eggs. Chicken farmers will ask your advice on which grain to use. Chicken knowing is important in this town, Don, and you are the master of chicken knowing."

He scrunched his face together like he was thinking really hard and then he asked, "Have you ever heard of Jonathan Jacobs?"

I knew who Jonathan Jacobs was because I'd seen him on the news almost every day of the week. I'd also heard people in the grocery store talk about him and how he was famous in Horse Island before he became a weatherman because he had won the chicken-judging contest for five years in a row. Since I knew all this, I told Mr. Bufford, "Yes, sir. I have."

Then he asked, "Well, do you know where he is now? I'll tell you where he is now. He is a weatherman in Lafayette. But before Jonathan Jacobs left Horse Island to pursue his dream of studying rain and stuff, his eggs were going for one dollar a dozen. Can you believe that? Everyone else was getting only forty cents a dozen, but Jonathan Jacobs was getting one dollar a dozen. I'll repeat it because sometimes I think things are so incredible that they need to be repeated. One dollar a dozen. One dollar a dozen! Now, no one could ever come close to knowing as much about chickens as Jonathan Jacobs. But I think that he has finally met his match."

I stared down at Henrietta for a few minutes and then Mr. Bufford asked, "So what do you think about being famous, boy?"

I couldn't believe that I would be famous. I was sure that Leon hated me because I'd beaten him in the contest and I was sure everyone else would hate me too.

I looked at Mr. Bufford and told him, "I think Leon Leonard hates me and is going to hit me because I beat him in the contest."

Mr. Bufford started laughing and I looked out of the passenger seat window waiting for him to stop, and when he did, he said, "Ain't nobody gonna hate you. I know that little Leonard boy, and he's a tough one, I'll give you that, but he ain't stupid. If Leon Leonard knows what's good for him, he ain't gonna lay one finger on you. I know for one, his daddy would skin him alive if he did and his momma would be right behind to pour the salt."

When we reached my house, Mr. Bufford turned off the truck, leaned across me, and pulled an instant camera out of his glove compartment.

"Why don't you let me get a picture of you with your new friend?" he asked.

I got out of the truck and Mr. Bufford ran around to my side and took two pictures of me holding Henrietta. He gave me one of the pictures and said, "Here you go, my boy. You keep this and whenever you look at it, I want you to think about all the trouble I went through for you. And I'll keep this one in case you ever forget."

After I got my bike out of the back of his truck and he drove off, I went to put Henrietta in the chicken yard. I watched her a few minutes to make sure she and the other chickens got along. Sometimes chickens fight each other to make a pecking order so they know who the master of the yard is. Even though Henrietta was smaller than most of the chickens, she didn't act like she was scared of them. The other chickens surrounded her and she danced and clucked like she was singing and let them know that she was going to control that yard no matter how small she was. It reminded me of a picture of KC on his album cover. You see, he was dressed up like an Indian chief and he had this hat with all these feathers on it and he kind of looked like a chicken. I imagined him standing in front of the Sunshine Band, dancing like he was the head of the flock, and no one could even come close to being as good at dancing and singing as he was. Henrietta was doing the same thing with the other chickens and so I decided to call her KC.

When I was sure she was safe, I remembered my

blue ribbon and ran into the living room of our house to show my parents. But as soon as I got in, I saw my parents standing up in the middle of the room. My mother screamed, "I hate it here!"

My parents looked at me but didn't say anything. I pulled my blue ribbon out of my pocket and showed it to them. I was going to tell them that I'd won but then my mother said, "Don, go to your room."

"But," I said.

"Don, don't question me when I talk to you. Dick, tell him not to question his mother."

My father closed his eyes and said, "Don't question your mother."

SEVEN

The day after I won the contest, I got on my bike and headed to town so I could get a paper with my picture in it. It was really sunny and our closest neighbor, Mr. Picard, and his wife, Purple Patricia, were in their yard painting a fence. When I passed them they both waved and smiled and shouted, "Congratulations!" and Purple Patricia's purple scarf flowed through the air like an American flag, only purple.

I turned onto Porcupine Street toward the large hill and I saw the stray calico cat sitting on top of a fence post. I had all this energy and for the first time, I peddled right past her up the hill without getting off my bike. She blinked when I passed and then turned and jumped on top of some dog that was walking by.

When I reached the top of the hill, I took a left onto Armadillo Street. Vickie Viceroy and her little brother were running through the pasture chasing a sheep.

When Vickie saw me, she stopped and shouted, "Hey, Don! Congratulations!"

I waved and then thought that maybe Mr. Bufford was right and that I might be famous. And maybe things were going to change and the kids would stop calling me "new kid" and start calling me "Don" and giving me high fives. And that made me really happy and I didn't think I could get any happier that day, until I got to the paper box on Main Street.

That's when I saw the paper with my picture and the headline "Don Schmidt Is Youngest Boy in Town's History to Win Chicken-Judging Contest."

I was about to put a quarter in the box and take one of the papers out when I heard, "Congratulations again, my boy. You're going to be a great man one day if you play your cards right."

I looked up and saw Mr. Bufford. He bent down and put some change in the paper box and pulled out two papers.

"Here you go," he said, and handed me one of them.

I smiled and said, "Thank you," and then Mr. Bufford folded the newspaper and asked me, "So did you think about our arrangement?"

I had thought a little about the arrangement but not a whole lot because I was thinking about how much my life was going to change and how proud my parents were going to be of me.

But I only said, "Yes, sir."

He smiled and asked, "Good. So when can I expect the eggs to start rolling in?"

"Well," I said, "I guess I can bring some to school tomorrow and give them to your brother, if you want."

Mr. Bufford's smile got bigger and then he said, "That would be great, my boy. That would be great. So how many dozen do you think you can get to me a week?"

I told him, "I don't know. Maybe about four or five."

Mr. Bufford stopped smiling and said, "Four or five? That won't do me no good, boy. I thought you were going to talk to your momma about getting some more chickens."

"I forgot to ask them," I told him.

Mr. Bufford squatted down and said, "Forgot? Forgot? Did you forget all I did for you, boy? Did you forget that I risked my good name to get that chicken for you?"

"No, sir," I said.

Mr. Bufford stared at me the way Mrs. Forest stared at Leon Leonard when she wanted him to confess to something. He stood up and said, "Well, you know I like you, Don, and because I like you, I'm going to help you solve this problem of yours. Let me think about this and I'll get back to you. Until then, you keep bringing me all your eggs."

I said, "Okay," and then Mr. Bufford said, "I'll figure this out, my boy, even if I have to take out the big guns."

Mr. Bufford made his hands look like pistols and

then put them at his side and pulled them out like he was drawing guns from a holster. He made a popping sound and pretended like he was shooting me. I jumped back and he started laughing and said, "I got you, boy. You take care now and I'll get back to you next week."

I didn't know what he meant by the "big guns." I wondered if he meant that he was going to shoot me if I didn't give him more than five dozen eggs a week. That seemed kind of weird but I didn't want to think about it, so I got on my bike and peddled back to my house.

When I got home I decided that these big guns probably weren't a good thing and that I should find a way to get some more chickens so Mr. Bufford didn't use them. This is when I got the idea to show my parents the paper because I figured that they'd be so proud of me and give me whatever I wanted and if it meant more chickens, they'd buy me more chickens.

I walked into the house and looked at my parents. They were both in the living room and a basketball game was playing on the television. My mother was gluing on some fake pink fingernails and my father was flipping through the *TV Guide*.

Since my parents were busy, I didn't want to disturb them. But I really wanted to show them the paper. That's when I got an idea to have them ask me about it.

First I went to my room and got my blue ribbon. Then I walked into the living room with it and the newspaper. I sat down on the sofa and put my blue ribbon right next to me. Neither of my parents looked at me, so I opened up the newspaper and shook it a little so it would make a noise. Then I fixed it so that the front page of the newspaper faced out and my parents could see my picture. I sat like that for a couple of seconds and then my mother shouted, "Don!"

Here it was, I thought. She'd seen my picture and now she was going to run over to me and put her arms around me carefully, so she wouldn't mess up her new glued nails, and tell me how proud she was of me.

But she didn't do that. Instead she said, "Don't get any ink from that newspaper on the sofa."

She didn't see the picture or the ribbon so I decided to just tell her.

"Yes, ma'am," I said. "My picture is in the paper because I won the chicken-judging contest. I even got a blue ribbon."

"What?" my mother asked.

"My picture is in the paper because I won the chicken-judging contest," I said.

"Let me see that," my mother said, and I walked over to her and held it out and she told me, "Don, can't you see I'm doing my nails? Hold it up for me."

I stood in front of my mother and held the paper.

"Stop dancing around," she told me. "I can't read it."

She looked at it for about a minute and then said, "You know, it's a sad day when the most exciting news in the town is about a little boy winning some chicken contest. Don't these people care about what's going on in the world?"

I stood in front of my mother for about ten more seconds and then she told me, "Don, you're blocking the television. Don't you have something better to do?"

I folded up the newspaper, put the blue ribbon in my jeans pocket, and went out to the chicken yard and sat on an old tree stump and read the article over and over again to my chickens.

"You see?" I told them. "That's me. Do you want to hear what they said about me?"

They didn't do anything but peck at the ground and since it kind of looked like they were bobbing their heads up and down to say yes, I read the article.

It said:

Yesterday at the Dairy Festival, history was made in Horse Island. After a heated town committee meeting several weeks ago, it was decided to lower the age requirements of the youngest-aged participant category of the chicken-judging contest to eleven years old. Concerns were that eleven-year-olds weren't mature enough to seriously compete. One committee member was quoted as saying, "An eleven-year-old knows as much about judging a chicken as a Yankee knows about baking biscuits."

The committee member was forced to eat his words when eleven-year-old Don Schmidt walked away with the blue ribbon. Not only did he beat out ninety-nine other participants, but several judges said that they'd never seen anyone who knew as much about chickens as this young boy.

The chickens danced around the yard after I read them the article, and so I closed my eyes and made up a song in my head and then imagined the red, white, and brown chickens making a circle around me and dancing until I floated up in the air above them. I flew around the chicken yard until my mother called me in to dinner and told me to make sure I washed my hands because she didn't want me to give her some chicken disease.

EIGHT

The Monday morning after the contest, when I walked out of my front door to go to school, I saw this brown-haired kid on a bike by our mailbox. It took me a couple of seconds to realize that it was Leon Leonard, but when I did, I stopped on our steps.

"Hey, Don," he said.

I didn't know what to say back. I was sure that he was there to hit me because I'd beaten him in the contest, so I stepped back to go into my house. And then I realized he'd called me "Don" instead of "new kid." I was confused about why he would do that if he wanted to beat me up. So I decided that instead of going back into my house, I would risk getting hit by Leon.

"Hey," I said back, and then he smiled and asked me, "You want to ride bikes to school together?"

I wondered why Leon Leonard, the most popular and toughest boy in the fifth grade, wanted to ride his bike to school with me. I thought it might be a trap and that there would be some other kids waiting at the end of the road to beat me up. But that didn't make sense because Leon was big enough to beat me up by himself. I wasn't sure I felt safe riding my bike with him, but I didn't want to tell him no because I thought then he'd beat me up for sure.

While we were riding our bikes side by side and I waited for him to push me over or throw a stick in my wheel, Leon asked me, "Where did you learn so much about chickens?"

"I take care of ours and so I spend a lot of time with them and I read a lot of books about them," I told him.

"Really?" he said. "There are books on chickens?"

"Yeah," I said. "There's a lot in the library."

"Huh," he said. "Who knew?"

Then Leon asked me a few more questions like what types of feed I gave my chickens, how many eggs per week did each one give, and did I think this girl, Susie Sanders, looked like a bird. I answered him real quick and then stopped talking until he'd ask me another question.

When we got to school and walked down the hall toward class, all the kids were looking at me and saying stuff like, "Hey, Don!" and, "Hi, buddy!" and, "How about a high five?"

They did more than just that, though. A lot of them wanted to sit next to me at lunch and girls handed me notes during class asking if I wanted to be their boyfriend. Leon hardly ever left my side and wanted me to do everything he did.

During lunch, Leon stopped me and said, "Hey, Don. Do you want to come watch me hit Jeremy Jones because he's a big geek?"

I said, "No thanks," and then he said, "Oh, okay. Do you want to chase that stray dog and pig around the school yard?"

"Yeah. Okay."

Kids would chase after the stray dog and pig to try and catch them, but no one ever had because they were too fast. I had watched kids chase the dog and pig for years and I'd always thought it would be fun but that I'd never get to do it.

But I did get to do it. That day Leon made a plan and then explained it to about ten of us. You see what we did was make a large circle around them. When Leon nodded his head up and down, we took one step in. We didn't look at the stray dog and pig when we'd step in because we were trying to act like we didn't see them so they wouldn't figure out what we were doing. Some of us would pretend to be tying our shoes or playing in the dirt with a stick or pointing up at the sky. When the circle reached about ten feet from the stray dog and pig, the two of them ran in different directions.

Leon shouted, "Get them!" and half the kids went for the dog and the other half went for the pig. I didn't move because I was trying to figure out which one to chase, but then Leon ran toward the pig and shouted, "Come on, Don!"

I ran as fast as I could and followed him and about three other kids. When the pig turned left, we turned left, and when he turned right, we all turned right. We chased that pig all over the school yard until he ran into the corner of a chain-link fence and turned around and looked at us.

"All right!" Leon shouted. "We got him! We finally got him!"

Then Matt Marceaux asked, "How do you know it's a him?"

"Because a girl can't run that fast," Leon said, and then Kay Kramer said, "Yeah, a girl can."

They kept arguing about it, and while they were, I was looking at the pig and noticed that something pink came out of its stomach. I had seen something similar on dogs and knew what that was, but the thing on the pig kind of looked like a corkscrew so I wasn't sure if it was the same thing. I thought that Leon might know what it was, so I asked him, "Leon, what's that pink thing coming out of the bottom of its stomach?"

Leon bent down and said, "That's the thing that tells us it's a boy."

Kay took a step back and said, "Yuck! I'm not touching him now. That's gross."

Leon said, "I don't care. I want to catch him, so those of you that are man enough to catch him, follow me."

The pig looked at us, and we looked back at it. It put

its head down and then started scratching the ground the way a bull does right before it charges.

"Okay," Leon said. "Let's walk in slowly and jump on him. On the count of three we'll all take a step in. One. Two."

Before he could say three, the dog ran in front of us and the pig followed him.

Matt screamed, "Jump on it!"

We all jumped, and landed on one another on the grass.

"I can't believe this!" Leon shouted.

I started laughing and I think it was the hardest I'd ever laughed in my life. Tears fell down my face, and my side started hurting, and then the other kids started laughing too and we all laid there rolling around until the bell rang.

For the rest of the week, we chased the stray dog and pig if they were on the playground for recess. When I wasn't chasing them, I was answering questions for people. In that week, I had more people talk to me than I'd ever had in my whole life.

NINE

That first week after the contest was awesome because I was the most popular kid in the fifth grade. Maybe even the whole school! Well, not high school, but probably elementary and junior high. Anyway, it wasn't just me that got popular. The Saturday after the contest, my mother got real popular too.

It started when we went to Horse Island Food and Furniture to grocery shop. We always went on Saturdays because my mother told me that the frozen dinners were delivered the night before and so she knew she was buying them fresh.

Horse Island Food and Furniture was the biggest building on Main Street because they needed a lot of space to sell both food and furniture. When you walked in, the first thing you saw was a row of cash registers, and on the other side of those were a bunch of small rooms separated by half walls. There were bedrooms, living rooms, dining rooms, bathrooms, and kitchens. In each room, some of the things in the rooms were used to hold food. There were cases of beer on coffee tables, diapers on top of washing machines, and laundry detergent in bathtubs.

My mother and I walked past all the furniture rooms to the frozen food section of the grocery store. She opened the freezer door and pulled out a dinner and said, "Oh my god! They have a new one here, Don. It's called 'Turkey Ziti Delight.' Dawn would have loved this. I'll get some so you can try it."

At the time I was too worried about running into Mr. Bufford to get excited about the new frozen foods. I had brought eggs to his brother every day, but just like I'd thought, it was only about five dozen and I thought that Mr. Bufford would be mad at me and pull out those "big guns" he was talking about. I still hadn't come up with an idea of how to get more chickens in our yard. My number one idea was to buy some more and hope my parents didn't notice. The only problem was that I needed money to buy some, and I didn't have enough.

Anyway, I walked over to the frozen breakfast section and pulled out a box of waffles. Leon walked up to me carrying a squash and a clock radio and said, "Hey, what's shaking, Don?"

"Hi, Leon," I said. "I like your shirt."

He looked down at his shirt, which was a white T-shirt, and then said, "Look. My mom's talking to your mom."

Leon's mom waved him over to her and he said, "See you later, buddy."

I looked at my mother and she yelled, "Don, come here!"

I walked over slowly and before I got to her, she asked, "What's this about you winning some big award?"

"I won the chicken-judging contest at the Dairy Festival," I told her.

She jerked her head back like she was surprised and asked, "Why didn't you tell your father and me about this?"

"I did," I told her.

Then she shook her head and said, "No you didn't. Are you calling me a liar?"

I wondered if the contest and chasing the stray dog and pig was a dream. I was pretty sure it wasn't so I said, "I showed you my picture in the newspaper and my blue ribbon."

My mother turned her head a little to the side and said, "Is that what that was for? I forgot about that. Anyway, listen, that Leonard lady told me that she runs a beauty salon in town and that if I brought her some of our eggs, she'd give me a free permanent. God, I'm due for a new one. Should I trust her with my hair?"

She passed her fingers through her hair and then said, "Now why do you think she'd want our eggs? I've spoken to her once before and stayed clear of her after that because she really needed a breath mint or mouthwash or something. What did you think of her hair? It looked a little shiny, but I think that look is in style. Oh well, we'd better get moving."

Before she could push the cart any farther, though, another woman walked up to us. It was Mrs. Cameron who owned a flower shop. She looked at me and said, "Good morning, young man. Don't you look handsome today."

My mother looked at the lady, then at me, then back at the lady. Mr. Bufford walked by and I put my head inside one of the standing freezers until he was out of sight.

Then I heard Mrs. Cameron tell my mother, "You must be so proud of your son."

I pulled my head out of the freezer and looked at my mother and watched her say, "Oh yes. Oh yes, I am."

She put her hand on my head and moved it around a little like she was giving me a scalp massage. I flinched a bit and made a yelping sound kind of like a puppy when it's scared. My mother pulled her hand away real fast like I'd tried to bite her.

Then Mrs. Cameron looked at my mother and said, "Listen. I was wondering if you'd be interested in trading some of your eggs for some flowers. I know you've probably gotten a thousand offers for those eggs, but if you have a few left over, I'd really appreciate some."

My mother looked at Mrs. Cameron the same way people looked at her when she said we kept our chickens for ambience. It looked like she was confused. I was right because then she said, "I'm confused."

Mrs. Cameron smiled and said, "Your eggs. They're a hot commodity in this town."

My mother tilted her head and asked, "They are?" and Mrs. Cameron opened her eyes wide and said, "Oh yes, very much so."

My mother didn't say anything and Mrs. Cameron smiled and my mother smiled back at her and then Mrs. Cameron said, "Listen, it was really great catching up with you, but I have to go. Now I want you to promise me you'll stop by the shop and we'll see if we can trade some of those eggs for some lovely long-stemmed roses I got in this morning."

Mrs. Cameron left, and my mother stared after her until she turned the corner. Then she said, "What a strange lady. How does she know who you are?"

"Her son, Clet, is in my class," I told her.

"Clet?" she asked. "Are you sure that's her son's name? That's not a name. That's a noise. Now I don't understand why two ladies in a matter of five minutes would ask me for our eggs. They've never wanted our eggs before and now they're like money to these people. You can't go five feet in this town without having some kind of bird running across the street, so I know they can get eggs from anywhere they want. Why all of a sudden do they want eggs from our chickens? And why is that lady acting like we're best friends? I've only spoken to her once before when she asked me if I wanted to donate something to the bake sale at school. I told her my oven was broken but that I'd give her a couple cans of beets if she wanted. What do you think of her hair? Do you think she goes to that Leonard lady?"

My mother talked to me like this for the rest of the time we were in the store. I think I would have been a little confused too about the ladies wanting our eggs if I hadn't talked to Mr. Bufford the week before or if Leon and all the other kids at school hadn't been so nice to me. I knew that chicken farming in Horse Island was important, but I didn't know that it would be such a big deal to them that an eleven-year-old had won a chicken-judging contest.

Anyway, when we were waiting at the checkout counter, people passed by me and said, "Hi, Don," or, "Congratulations, Don," or just pointed at us and whispered. My mother bent down, grabbed my shoulders, looked me in the eyes, and said, "I want you to tell me what's going on."

"I was the youngest boy to ever win the chicken-judging contest at the Dairy Festival," I told her.

Before I could say any more, the cashier said, "Hi, Don."

Her name tag said "Amelia" and she had on a denim vest with "Horse Island Food and Furniture—Tomatoes, Tables, and More" written in rhinestones on the back. On the front she had a big button that said "Ask me how to save with food-and-furniture combos."

My mother let go of my shoulders, stood up, walked up to Amelia, and asked, "How do you know my son?"

I started taking the groceries out and putting them on the counter and then Amelia said, "Everybody knows Don Schmidt. He's the little boy that won the chicken-judging contest."

My mother stared at Amelia like she was still waiting for an answer, and then the telephone by the cash register rang and Amelia picked it up.

"This is Amelia Angelo."

She was quiet for a few seconds and then said, "Okay."

She handed me the phone and I put it next to my ear and said, "Hello?"

It was Mr. Bufford, and he said, "Don, my boy, turn around and look above you."

"Who is that?" my mother asked.

I turned and saw Mr. Bufford on a platform waving to me and then he said, "My boy. I want to talk to you. I'll meet you at the foot of the stairs."

I gave the phone back to the cashier, and then my mother asked again, "Don! Who was that?"

I wondered if I should tell her the truth; that it was Mr. Bufford and that he had stolen a chicken for me and now wanted to sell my eggs in his store. I looked down at the ground and decided to tell her the half-truth and said, "It was Mr. Bufford, the owner of the store. He wants to talk to me about buying our eggs."

"This is insane and getting out of control," my mother said.

I saw Mr. Bufford at the bottom of the stairs and I didn't want him to come over and tell my mother about KC, so I asked her, "Can I go talk to him? He's right over there."

My mother turned and looked at him, and then let some air out of her mouth and said, "Go ahead while I pay, but don't make any deals with him until I get there."

I walked over to Mr. Bufford, who was wearing a long white coat like I'd seen doctors wear. He rubbed the top of my head and said, "I just wanted to pay you for those eggs you gave me and remind you that I need a lot more than five dozen a week."

I told him, "Yes, sir. I know. I need to buy some more chickens but I don't have the money to."

He smiled and said, "Well, you do now."

He gave me an envelope and inside there was a hundred dollars. When I saw it, I looked up at Mr. Bufford, then down at the money again, and then put the envelope in my pocket real fast.

"Is everything okay, my boy?" Mr. Bufford asked me.

"Yes, sir, but you gave me too much money," I told him.

He smiled and said, "It's an advance, my boy, so you can buy some more chickens and get me some more eggs."

I didn't know how to tell Mr. Bufford that I didn't think I was going to get some more chickens. So I put my head down and said nothing. When I did that,

Mr. Bufford cleared his throat and asked me, "That's your momma over there, isn't it?"

"Yes, sir," I told him.

"Well, let's see if we can persuade her to get you some more chickens," he said. "Leave the talking up to me, my boy."

He closed his eyes a little and pushed his lips out and stood straight up and smiled a little. My mother pushed her grocery cart up to us and said really loud, "Mr. Bufford, I'm Mrs. Schmidt, Don's mother."

Mr. Bufford tilted his head a little and said, "Nice to meet you, Mrs. Schmidt. You must me very proud of your son."

When he spoke to my mother, his voice was a little different. It was deeper, and he spoke kind of slow. I thought it was weird and I think my mother did too because she stepped back a little and said, "Yes."

She said it like she was answering a question she wasn't sure of. Then she said, "I am," like she'd just realized the answer.

The two of them stood for a couple of seconds smiling at each other until my mother cleared her throat and said, "Now what's this I hear about you wanting to buy some of our eggs?"

Mr. Bufford kept using his new voice, and said, "Well, Mrs. Schmidt, I'm interested in selling your eggs in the store."

"Now," my mother said, and then stopped talking for a few seconds. She pushed her shoulders back and then put her hands on her hips and then said in a real slow and soft voice, "You know, Mr. Bufford, we only keep our chickens because we like fresh eggs. We're not chicken farmers."

"Oh yes," Mr. Bufford said, and then he stopped talking for a few seconds and folded his arms and said, "Mrs. Schmidt. I know that you like having your chickens around because it gives your farmhouse a certain cottage feeling, but I think you and I can both agree that it doesn't hurt if they can provide you with a little extra cash each month."

My mother took a handkerchief from her purse and wiped her neck and said, "Well, Mr. Bufford."

He interrupted her and said, "Please call me Bobby."

My mother smiled and said, "Well, Mr. Bufford, I can assure you that my husband and I needn't worry about having extra cash. His career provides more than enough for us."

Mr. Bufford tapped his foot like a chicken did when she was dancing. Then he looked back up at my mother and said, "I'm sure you and your husband are financially stable, Mrs. Schmidt. It's obvious that you enjoy the finer things in life. Anyone in this town can tell that you have a certain style that you find only in the upper class. However, you'd be helping me out a lot by selling me your eggs, and I am very grateful to people who help me out, Mrs. Schmidt."

My mother put her handkerchief back in her purse and then asked, "What are you saying, Mr. Bufford?"

Mr. Bufford smiled and then unbuttoned his long white doctor's coat and said, "What I'm saying, Mrs. Schmidt, is if you scratch my back, I'll scratch yours."

My mother put her right leg forward and asked, "And how can you scratch my back, Mr. Bufford?"

He blinked his eyes and asked, "How would you like your back scratched?"

My mother's face turned red and she giggled a little and then turned her back to Mr. Bufford, but then turned her head toward him.

"Well, I'll have to think about that. Let's get going, Don, before our groceries melt. Oh, and Mr. Bufford. Don't call us. We'll call you."

My mother walked out the door and I followed with the grocery cart. Before the automatic door shut, my mother said, "Unbelievable! Can you believe that man? I think he was flirting with me."

Then my mother laughed a little and said, "How would I like my back scratched? Can you believe the nerve of some people?"

I loaded up the trunk with the groceries and got into the car wondering what flirting was and what Mr. Bufford meant when he said that he would scratch my mother's back. I figured that he didn't really mean that he was going to scratch her back, but something else. I didn't know what, but I was just happy he didn't tell my mother about Henrietta.

My mother sang along to the radio the whole way

home and didn't stop until a chicken ran across the road, right in front of our car.

"You see what I mean?" she said. "There's one right there. A chicken. They're all over the place. Why do people want our eggs? *Our* eggs? Why do people want them? I don't understand."

And then she started laughing again and said, "How would I like my back scratched?"

Then my mother put her foot on the gas again and drove home. When she pulled into our driveway and stopped the car, she grabbed my arm. I jumped a little because it was the third time she'd touched me that day. She squeezed my arm a little and said, "Wait a second, Don. Do you think your winning that bird-judging contest has anything to do with people suddenly wanting our eggs?"

TEN

Every day, the week after my mother and I went to Horse Island Food and Furniture, I'd wake up in the mornings real quick like someone had scared me. I'd be covered in sweat and I was real nervous, and my body felt like the time my babysitter had let me drink coffee. I was that way all morning until I'd find Leon waiting for me outside my house. When I'd see him, I wasn't so nervous anymore, and I think it was because I knew that the day would be okay and that kids would want me to have lunch with them and that we'd chase the stray dog and pig. And then the Saturday after my mother met Mr. Bufford, things started to change and I didn't think things were going to be okay anymore.

You see, that Saturday, a truck from Chance Chandler's Chicken Chow and Saddle Salon pulled up to our house. My father was on a business trip and my mother was in the bathroom, so I was the first one to see it. When I did, I went outside and Mr. Chandler stepped out of his truck and walked toward the front of our house. He took a bandana out of his pocket and wiped his face and then smiled and said, "Good morning, Don."

"Good morning," I told him.

Mr. Chandler pointed his finger at me and said, "Now, didn't I tell you to study the chicken Bible?"

I nodded my head up and down and said, "Yes, sir," and then he asked, "Aren't you glad you listened to me?"

I nodded my head again and said, "Yes, sir," and then he slapped me on the back and said, "I bet you are, aren't you?"

"Yes, sir," I answered.

He folded his arms and said, "Well, good, good. Now, where's your momma? I have some chickens for her."

Before I could answer, I heard our screen door open, and then my mother say, "Mr. Chancler, thank you for coming on such short notice."

Mr. Chandler tilted his head to the side like he didn't understand my mother and then said, "Not a problem at all. I got you seventy-five of the best egg-laying chickens there are. And by the way, ma'am, my name is Chandler, not Chancler."

My mother smiled and said, "Okay. You can just drop them over there in the chicken yard, and I'll get my checkbook."

My mother walked back into the house, and then Mr. Chandler asked me, "Don, you want to help me unload these chickens?"

I nodded and smiled. I didn't know why my mother had ordered all those chickens, but I almost didn't care because it meant there would be seventy-five more hens I'd get to take care of. I realized that I would be able to give Mr. Bufford all the eggs he wanted.

Anyway, after Mr. Chandler and I unloaded all the chickens, my mother came outside carrying a check and said, "Thanks again, Mr. Chandler."

He took the check, told us good-bye, and drove off, and before he even turned onto the road, my mother said, "What a strange man."

She opened up a little makeup mirror and looked at her face and then said, "Okay, Don, I need six dozen eggs by this afternoon, so go collect them."

My mother walked back into the house and I walked to the chicken yard. I knew there was no way I could get six dozen eggs by that afternoon, but I figured I'd collect as many as I could before I told her that. While I was collecting the eggs, I realized something else and that was that our coop wasn't big enough for all the new chickens because it had only thirty nests in it. I didn't want chickens laying eggs all over the yard, so I figured I'd need to build some more nests.

Before I thought about that any more, though, I collected the eggs, which came out to a dozen, put them in a carton, and then walked into our house and into the living room. My mother was sitting down reading a magazine and when she saw me, she put it down and asked, "Well, where are my eggs?"

I picked the carton up so she could see it, and I said, "The chickens only laid a dozen eggs this morning."

My mother stood up from her chair and walked over to me.

"Don," she said. "You mean to tell me that a hundred chickens only laid a dozen eggs? Now I find that hard to believe."

I looked down and said, "The new chickens didn't lay any eggs. These are from the old ones."

"What do you mean the new chickens didn't lay any eggs?"

"They're going to need some more time to get used to the yard before they start laying," I told her.

"Oh, please," she said. "You expect me to believe that?"

I looked up at her and said, "Yes, ma'am."

My mother looked at me and tapped her foot a little and then asked, "Well, how long before we have five more dozen?"

"I don't know," I said

Then my mother asked, "Didn't you win that chicken contest? Why don't you know these things?"

I thought about this for a second and answered, "I can get them to start laying faster if I can build some nests for them but I need some lumber and help."

My mother spread out her arms, kind of like a chicken spreads out its wings, and then she said, "Lumber and help. That sounds expensive. Can't you use something else?"

"Maybe I can make some nests out of cardboard boxes," I told her. "Do you have any I can use?"

My mother said, "Yeah, sure. There's a bunch in the pantry. Take whatever you want."

I walked toward the pantry, but then I really started to wonder why all of a sudden my mother had bought all those chickens, so I turned to her and asked, "Mother, why did you buy all those chickens?"

She looked at me and said, "Don, don't question your mother. Dick, tell him not to question his mother."

We both looked around when we didn't hear him answer, and my mother said, "Oh, I forgot he's not here. Anyway, if you must know, we've had so many offers for those eggs that I decided it's an opportunity we just can't afford to pass up. I mean if we're going to be stuck here in this armpit, we might as well take advantage of the little things it has to offer."

She walked to her room and came back carrying her purse.

"I have an errand to run," she told me. "I'm hoping when I get back, you'll have five dozen more eggs for me."

She took the dozen eggs from me, walked out of the house to her car, and then drove off. I watched her from the living room and then realized when her car pulled onto the road that it was the first time she'd ever left me alone. I took a couple of steps toward the front door to chase after her, but then I stopped because I didn't know why I had to chase her. I wasn't scared and I didn't want to go on her errand with her and I wanted to build some nests for my new chickens.

When I couldn't see her car anymore, I turned away from the window. There was a moth flying around the living room and I watched it until it landed on the music box on top of the bookcase. This made me think of the little ballerina that was inside. Like I said before, when I was a kid, I thought it was a fairy like Tinker Bell and I thought the only way it could fly away was if I wound up the music box as tight as I could and then whispered, "Fly." I never did because my mother was almost always in the living room. But she wasn't there then and even though I knew the ballerina wasn't real and wouldn't fly away like a fairy, I still wanted to wind up the music box.

Before I could do anything, though, I saw my mother's car coming up the driveway from our front window. I walked out into the yard because I thought that she was coming back to get me. My mother stopped the car and got out.

"I forgot something," she said, and then walked past me and went into the house.

She came back outside about a minute later and got in her car and drove off. I forgot about the music box and went back in the house to get some boxes for the nests. I found some in the pantry and then decided to look in the kitchen cabinets for some plastic bowls.

I didn't find any, but I did find something that was

kind of weird. It was an envelope with some checks that were about eleven years old and were made out to a bunch of different places like the grocery store and electric company. They all had the word *paid* stamped on them, so I figured that the people who they were made out to had gotten their money. One of the checks, though, was made out to Ray Munson. He was the man that my parents argued about all the time.

At the bottom of the check near the word *Memo*, it said "Dawn." I didn't understand what that meant because my mother usually used that space to write down what she bought. I wondered if maybe she had bought some dishwashing liquid from Mr. Munson because there was a brand called Dawn and it didn't make sense that she had bought my sister from him. But the check was for two hundred dollars so I knew it couldn't be for dishwashing liquid unless it was for a whole lot of it and I'd never seen a whole lot of it around the house. I thought about asking my parents what it meant, but I figured that my mother would yell at me, so I just put the check back in the envelope and put it back where I found it and then went out to the chicken yard to make nests in the coop.

The coop was a barn with three walls. Inside there were shelves with wooden nests filled with hay. About four hours later, I had built three new shelves from some old planks and seventy more nests. They weren't like the wooden nests that were already in the coop, though. These new ones were made out of shoe and small appliance boxes, wicker baskets, a few casserole dishes that my mother never used, and an old Crock-Pot that didn't work anymore. I filled them with hay, weeds from around the house, leftover Easter egg grass, and old cloth diapers that my mother had never thrown away.

While I was staring at the new nests in the coop and trying to figure out how to make them better, my mother drove up and ran to the fence.

"Did you get me five more dozen?" she asked.

The truth was that I hadn't gotten any more eggs for her because the chickens had watched me all afternoon instead of laying eggs. So I shook my head from side to side and my mother lifted her chin up and asked, "No? Well how many did you get?"

I told her, "None. The chickens need to rest and get used to the new yard. But I made them all nests, so tomorrow we'll probably have five dozen or more. Do you want to see the nests?"

My mother shook her head and said, "No, Don. I don't want to see the nests. I want to see five dozen eggs. I have people who want them. What am I supposed to tell them? That my son can't make our chickens lay eggs?"

I didn't say anything, but my stomach growled because I hadn't stopped building the nests to heat up a TV dinner for lunch.

"Is there any way for people to tell that our eggs are our eggs?" my mother asked.

I wasn't sure what she meant so I asked her, "Ma'am?"

"Well," she said, "if I gave someone an egg I bought at the store, can they tell if it's one of our eggs?"

I shook my head and said, "No, ma'am. Except that our eggs are brown and sometimes the ones you buy at the store are white because their owners feed them different food than we do."

My mother asked, "Really? Is that the only difference?"

"Yes, ma'am," I said. "Except for the carton."

"Why? What do we put our eggs in?" she asked.

"I've been putting them in some old cartons I found in the shed, and Mr. Bufford gave me some to use," I told her.

My mother pointed toward the shed and said, "Go get me five of those cartons."

I went to the shed and got the cartons for my mother and handed them to her.

"Now make sure those chickens start laying eggs by tomorrow," she told me. "You're lucky your mother is as smart as she is to get us out of this mess."

My mother drove off in her car again and I got a little worried that she was going to go to Horse Island Food and Furniture, or a store in Horse Island where everyone knew her, to buy the eggs. I was a little scared that she would get caught and I thought about what would happen if she did. Leon might not ride his bike to school with me anymore or Vickie Viceroy might chase me with a cigarette lighter and a can of hair spray while her brother tried to rope me. I started thinking about how I had won the contest, and how my mother didn't even want me to be in it, and now that she saw how valuable eggs were, she was acting like it was my job to get her eggs, and now she was going to mess it up and get caught trying to trade eggs that she'd bought at the store, and then I wouldn't have any friends anymore. I started breathing fast, and my head started hurting, and I got all this strength, and I felt like I wanted to hit someone, and it scared me because I didn't know what was happening to me, and before I knew it, I was running as fast as I could, and chickens were running all over the yard, and I ran right up to the chicken coop and kicked it with all my might and yelled, "I hate my mother!"

The chickens that were in the coop started running and flying out and danced and clucked around the yard. My head stopped hurting and my breathing slowed down, and I forgot about my mother, and all I could think about was that I had maybe hurt my friends.

"I'm sorry," I told them. "I'm so sorry. I didn't mean to scare you."

I tried to calm them down by petting them, but this only scared them more. Then I got an idea and went to the chicken shed and grabbed some feed for them and threw it on the ground. This calmed them down, and they ran over to the area where I'd thrown the feed and started pecking.

When I saw that they'd forgotten about what had happened, I sat on the old tree stump and put my head between my legs and started crying. I cried like this for a couple of minutes and then I heard flapping and felt something on my head. I picked my head up and then I heard flapping again and I saw KC land on the ground.

I started laughing because I'd never had a chicken fly and land on my head. I put my hand out toward KC and she walked right up to me and I grabbed her in my arms and petted her and laughed some more when I thought about what she'd done. It was like something that you'd see in a movie and I figured that it was a sign that something great was going to happen or that everything would turn out okay. This made me really happy because I thought it meant that my mother wouldn't mess things up for me and that Leon and I would always be friends and that I'd be happy for the rest of my life. Later on, I realized that I was wrong.

ELEVEN

The next few weeks were really cool because a lot of cool things happened. One thing was that my mother was in a good mood and didn't yell at me because she was making a lot of money from selling the eggs and also getting a bunch of stuff by trading the eggs. She even gave me some of the money every week. The other thing that was cool was that Leon invited me to sleep over at his house. I had never been to another person's house to sleep except for the few times I'd slept at a babysitter's. So when Leon asked me, I didn't know what to say because I didn't know what my mother would say.

When I was about eight years old, I asked her to go to the circus because I'd heard some kids talking about it and it sounded really cool. I didn't ask her straight out if I could go because I was kind of scared, so I thought about trying something else. One morning I drew a picture of the circus and put it down next to me on the kitchen table during breakfast. My plan worked because my mother saw the picture and said, "Don, don't waste your colors on doodling. At least try to draw something that people can recognize."

I smiled at my mother real big and said, "It's the circus."

She looked at it again and said, "I hated going to the circus when I was little because of all those animals in that enclosed space. That dust used to make me sneeze and it would take a week for me to get the smell of elephant out of my hair."

"Can we go to the circus?" I asked.

She looked at me and pushed her lips together so they kind of made an upside-down U. Then she said, "Didn't you hear me? I just told you I hate that place. Do you want your mother to go around smelling like animal for a week?"

After that, I didn't really ask my mother for anything. I really wanted to go and sleep at Leon Leonard's house, though, and since my mother wouldn't have to sit in a tent with elephants, I thought maybe she'd let me go. So during dinner on the Thursday before the Friday that Leon had invited me for, I tried to come up with a way to ask my mother. I thought about drawing a picture like I had done for the circus, but since that hadn't worked before, I thought about asking her straight out. I was thinking about how to word the question when she told me, "Lucy Leonard called me today and asked if you could sleep at her house tomorrow night."

I swished my fork around my mashed potatoes and my mother sneezed and then said, "I told her, of course you could go, because I think it's time we make friends with the people in this town. I mean, the better friends we become with them, the more things we can get from them, right? Especially since they're under the impression that our eggs are better than everyone else's. Did you know that Mr. Nichols over at the bakery is selling cakes made with our eggs? I hear he can't keep the angel food cake on the shelf."

I stopped listening to my mother after that because I was going to get to spend the night at Leon's and have a pillow fight or stay up late watching television and learning the songs to the commercials. I thought about this all night and all the next day until that afternoon when Leon and I rode our bikes to his house after school.

When we got there, we did a bunch of stuff like play with his dog and climb trees and collect the eggs from his chickens. When we were finished doing that, Leon's mom stepped out into the yard and yelled at us to come in for dinner. I'd met her a few times before, and every time I had, she had a new hair color or style and sometimes even wore wigs. She had put on a wig between the time she first told me and Leon hello that afternoon and the time she stepped out in the yard to get us for dinner. If Leon hadn't said, "In a minute, Mom," I don't think I would have known who she was.

When Leon's dad stepped out in the yard, the same thing kind of happened. I had seen him before at Horse Island Food and Furniture but he looked different from before because this time he had curly hair instead of straight hair. I thought it might be him but I wasn't sure until Leon said, "Hi, Dad," and then Mr. Leonard said, "Hey, my boy. Go wash your hands and come in and chow."

After we washed our hands, we went to the screen porch and on it there was a table with chairs all facing the chicken yard. Mr. Leonard was sitting in one of the chairs and he reached up and put his hand on my shoulder and told me, "Have a seat, Mr. Schmidt."

I was confused because I didn't know why he'd want me to sit at the table on the screen porch. So I asked him, "Why do you want me to sit here?"

Mr. Leonard started laughing. He was really big and tall and when he laughed, he reminded me of the giant from the brand of canned vegetables called Green Giant. He slapped me on the back and said, "Because we're going to eat here, my boy. This is the best place because we get to watch the chickens while we eat. I swear I can't get enough of watching those crazy birds."

It smelled funny on the porch and it reminded me of the odor from my mother's hair after she'd gotten a perm. Only this smell was a lot stronger and I had to turn my head to my shoulder and hold my nose a little. I guess Mr. Leonard saw me because he asked, "What's the matter, boy?"

I knew it would be rude to tell him that his house smelled, so I said, "Nothing. I just had to sneeze."

"Oh," Mr. Leonard said. "I hope the smell from my new perm isn't bothering you. Lucy just put it in, and the smell can be a little strong."

"No, sir," I said, and then looked out at the chicken yard.

Although the smell from Mr. Leonard's hair was still pretty strong, I was so interested in the dinner that I forgot about it. It was strange for me to hear the sound of my fork hitting a real plate and not an aluminum tray, and I tapped it a couple of times because I liked it. Nobody told me to be quiet when I did it, so I did it again, and then Mrs. Leonard said, "Look at that rooster the way he rules the yard. All the other chickens are scared of him."

Mr. Leonard laughed and said, "Except that one white hen with the reddish streak down her back. She's not scared of him. He's scared of her."

Then Mrs. Leonard smiled and said, "That's because she knows she has what every man wants."

Both she and Mr. Leonard started laughing. I asked Leon what it was that the hen had that the rooster wanted, and he told me he didn't know but that he was sure it was funny.

Mr. Leonard stopped laughing and asked me, "What do you think about that, Don?" and Mrs. Leonard slapped him and said, "Lionel, he's only a boy."

Mr. Leonard lifted his arm up to block her from slapping him again and said, "Oh, come on, Lucy. I'm sure he knows about the birds and the bees."

I didn't know about the birds and the bees although I'd heard people talk about them a lot on television. I didn't know what to say, so I smiled and told Mr. Leonard that I liked his shirt.

"Oh, Leon," Mr. Leonard said. "You have to bring this one over more often. He cracks me up."

Then Mr. Leonard slapped me on the back and said, "You're good people. You know that, Don?"

I didn't know what he was talking about or why he was laughing, so I just smiled and shoved a fork full of yams in my mouth and took a sip of juice. Then Leon said, "Look at that little chicken trying to fly over the fence. It's so funny when they think they're going to make it and smash right into it."

The chicken hit the top of the fence and fell to the ground, and Leon and his parents started laughing. Even though it wasn't the way the Brady Bunch ate, I thought that the Leonards were a normal American family, and that I was having a normal American dinner.

I kind of liked it, until Mr. Leonard asked me, "So, Don, how do you do in school? Do you bring home F's like Leon here?"

I looked at Leon, and he looked like he was a little

mad, and it was the same face he made when our teacher asked him a question he didn't know the answer to or yelled at him for making a bad grade. I didn't say anything because I didn't know what to say, but I didn't have to because Mr. Leonard started talking again. He said, "Yeah, Leon isn't the sharpest tool in the shed. He's lucky that when he gets old enough he'll be able to work on the oil rigs with his old man here because he ain't ever gonna be able to get a job using his smarts."

Leon's face got real red, and he looked down at the ground. I didn't know what to say but I wanted to say something so that Mr. Leonard would stop talking.

"Mr. Leonard," I said.

He smiled at me and said, "Yeah, my boy?"

I was stuck, but then something happened and I thought of something to say.

"Your face is getting really red."

Mrs. Leonard looked at him and screamed, "Oh my god! The chemical must have been too strong. Come on, Lionel, we need to wash that right away."

Mr. Leonard dropped his fork and started rubbing his head and hollering, "My scalp's starting to burn. Ow. Crap!"

Mr. and Mrs. Leonard ran from the table, and I heard Mr. Leonard screaming and cursing in the house. Leon's mad face changed, and he started laughing, and then he ate the rest of the potato salad that was on his dad's plate.

That night, we all watched television. Mr. Leonard sat in a leather recliner like my father did. He had white lotion on his ears and parts of his forehead for the burns from the hair chemicals. Mrs. Leonard sat in an armchair and filed her nails and didn't speak that much. Leon and I sat on pillows two feet in front of the television.

After hours of television, Leon and I went to his room and all I could think about was the pillow fight we were going to have. When we got into his room, though, he jumped into his bed and fell asleep. I had thought that he would start the pillow fight, but when he didn't, I thought that maybe he was waiting for me, but then I thought he might get mad at me and tell his mom to call my mother, who would be embarrassed by her son who went around hitting people with pillows while they slept. I lay awake on the side of Leon most of the night and waited for him to hit me with a pillow or ask me to sneak into the living room and watch television. I eventually fell asleep from being so tired and bored and thought that maybe in the morning we'd have a pillow fight.

The next morning a rooster crowed and woke me up. When I heard it, I got up real fast and ran to Leon's window to watch it. His window didn't overlook the chicken coop, though, and so I had to go out on the screen porch to watch the rooster. By the time I got there, he'd stopped crowing, so I went into the living room and looked around. There was a brown sofa facing a wall with a television, and there were pictures hanging on the walls and sitting on top of end tables and bookshelves. One of the pictures was of Leon and his parents dancing. They were doing weird things with their hands and Leon was wearing a tie. Also in the picture was a woman in a wedding dress and a guy playing an accordion.

While I was looking at the picture, Mr. Leonard walked into the living room and said, "Good morning, Mr. Schmidt."

I smiled at him and said, "Good morning, sir."

He walked up to the window and said, "I couldn't sleep at all last night, my boy, because my head was burning. I get those perms all the time so I don't know why it burned so bad this time. What do you think happened?"

"I don't know, sir," I told him. "I've never gotten a perm."

He laughed and said, "You're good people, Don."

I smiled because I liked it when he told me I was good people. I'd never had anyone tell me that, and I guessed it meant that he liked me, and I liked him too, except when he'd made fun of Leon because he wasn't too smart, but other than that, I liked him a lot. So I told him, "Thank you. I like your T-shirt and shorts."

He smiled and said, "Thank you back, my boy."

I felt really comfortable with Mr. Leonard and wasn't afraid to ask him questions. So I asked him,

"Mr. Leonard, what are you guys doing in this picture with the guy with the accordion?"

He grabbed the picture from me and said, "We're dancing, my boy. It's called the Duck Dance or something like that. It was at a wedding for a partner of mine who I work offshore with. He came to Louisiana from some country in Europe and they used to do that dance there. It's a crazy dance, boy, and to tell you the truth if I wouldn't have been so chock ayed then, I don't think I'd have done it."

I didn't understand what he meant by *chock ayed*, and I think he could tell from my face because he said, "You mean to tell me that you don't know what *chock ayed* means?"

I told him no, and then he asked me, "Don't your parents teach you anything, boy? It means *drunk*."

Mrs. Leonard walked into the living room and Mr. Leonard looked at her and said, "Hey, Lucy, Don here was asking about that Duck Dance we did at my buddy Alex's wedding. You remember him. He's from some country where we get that chocolate from. What's it called? 'Swiss Miss'? Yeah, yeah. 'Swiss Miss.' Where's that again?"

"Switzerland."

"Yeah, yeah," Mr. Leonard said, "that's it. Switzerland. You remember that?"

And then Mrs. Leonard said, "Oh god, yes. That was such a fun dance. How did it go again?"

Leon walked into the living room in a T-shirt and his underwear and asked, "How did what go?"

"The Duck Dance," Mrs. Leonard asked.

"It went like this," and then Leon started humming a song and moving his hands all kinds of ways. First he put his hands up in the air like they were two birds' beaks and flapped them back and forth. Then he put his hands underneath his armpits and flapped his arms like he had wings. Then he shook his butt from side to side and then clapped his hands. Mr. and Mrs. Leonard did the same thing, and then all three of them were humming and turning one another around like they were square dancing. Each one tried to outdo the other one by either singing louder or moving their butt all over the place. Leon got on the sofa, and then jumped off, and flapped his arms in the air like he was trying to fly, and when he couldn't, he landed on the ground and danced.

Mrs. Leonard fell on the sofa and grabbed her stomach and said, "Whew! That wore me out."

Leon and Mr. Leonard sat down next to her and then she said, "You know, the bride told me a funny story about that song. She told me that it was written by this Swiss accordion player back in the fifties. Well, one day this German band played it at some Oktoberfest here in the States and since it was called the Duck Dance, they wanted someone to dance around in a duck costume. Nobody had a duck costume, though, but they did have a chicken costume and so they used that. Well, since everybody saw a chicken dancing around to this song, they started calling it the Chicken Dance."

TWELVE

The next few weeks my mother didn't really talk about Dawn, or Chinese food, or missing Shreveport anymore and instead talked about people in Horse Island and what they were doing. She started acting different too. She sang out loud and spent less time at the house, and one night she started baking pies.

I think it was a Wednesday because of the shows that were playing on TV. My father and I had finished eating our salty food and right before we were about to start eating our dessert, my mother jumped out of her seat and said, "Freeze. I have a surprise for you. Don't move a muscle and whatever you do, don't start eating your dessert. I'll be right back."

She walked to the kitchen real fast and then came back a few minutes later carrying three slices of apple pie.

"Surprise," she said, and then gave my father and me each one.

My father and I both looked at the pie and then looked back at her.

"Well, what do you think?" she asked.

"But there's already a dessert in the TV platter," my father told her.

"I know," she said. "But I thought it might be nice to have a little change."

My father pushed on the pie with his fork like he thought it would move or something, and then said, "Well, if you ask me, it's a waste of the good dessert that's in the TV platter."

My mother picked up some of the pie with her fork and said, "Oh, Dick, you're so boring. You need to live a little."

My father didn't say anything. He only ate his pie and stared at the television, and about every third bite he took of the apple pie, he'd scoop up some of the peach cobbler from his TV dinner and look at my mother like a dog did whenever someone kicked it. She didn't notice him because she was too busy staring down at her pie, smiling. When she finally stopped looking at it, she looked at my father and said, "I think I'll make a cherry one for the dinner party this weekend."

My father was about to take a bite of his pie, but stopped and asked, "What?"

"I invited some people over for dinner this weekend," my mother told him. "Sort of a little Christmas party."

My father put his fork down and asked, "Christmas

party? Why? I thought you hated all the people who live here."

My mother looked at her pie again and said, "I do. Well, I did. But I decided that they're really not bad people and have some very interesting lives. Did you know that Sandy Simon used to live in California? That's right by Nevada. I almost lived in Vegas, you know."

"Yes, Janice," my father said. "We know you almost lived there. Who's coming to dinner?"

My mother ate her last bite of pie and said, "I assure you, it's only going to be people in this town that matter," and then she stood up and said, "That was delicious. I'm going to go get another piece."

That Saturday my mother made my father go buy a Christmas tree. We usually had a fake one because my mother said the real ones gave her allergies. But that year we got a great big real one! And my mother let me help her decorate it. It was really pretty when we finished it. It had red balls and white lights and a silver garland.

When we were finished with the tree, my mother and I cleaned the whole house. She cleaned the tops of light fixtures, which I'd never seen her do before, and made me vacuum underneath the sofa, which she'd never made me do before, and for the first time ever, my mother cleaned the room that she called the dining room but my father called the big closet.

In the room, there was a table and a bunch of boxes

of stuff like old clothes, books, and folders of paper. Sometimes one of them went in there if they were looking for the warranty for the refrigerator or stove, but we never ate in that room, and until the night of the dinner party, I didn't know that we could eat in that room. I also didn't know that there was a box in there with a bunch of secrets about Dawn and me.

I found it when I was helping my mother clean out the room by carrying boxes to a closet in our foyer. When I was picking up the last box, the bottom broke and everything inside fell out. It was mostly papers and bubble wrap, but there was also a metal box that I'd never seen before.

The box was about the size of a cigar box and there was a number dial attached to it like the padlock I used for my bicycle. Whoever had opened the box last hadn't spun the dial to relock it, and so when I pushed on the lid, it popped open. Inside were bills from a company called Munson Detective Agency, but the thing that really caught my eye was a birth certificate with the name Stanley Ronald Schmidt and my birth date, April 19, 1969. Before I could see anything else, my mother grabbed it out of my hands and screamed at me, "What are you doing! This is none of your business! I can't believe you opened that box! Get out of my sight!"

I ran to my room and then heard my father walk into the dining room and ask my mother what was wrong. I was really scared and so I sat on my bed and stared out the window at my chickens to try and calm down. I started wondering who Stanley Ronald Schmidt was and why he had the same birthday as me, but before I could think about it too much, my father walked into my room.

"Listen, Don," he said. "You shouldn't stick your nose in your mother's and my things. Now tell me what you saw."

I lied and told him, "I only saw the birth certificate."

His face got red and he didn't say anything, so I asked, "Who is Stanley Ronald Schmidt, and why does he have the same birthday as me?"

My father's eyes opened wider and he said, "Stanley Ronald Schmidt? You want to know who he is?"

I nodded my head up and down and said, "Yes, sir. He has the same birthday as me. Is he my cousin?"

My father scratched his leg and then folded his arms and said, "No. You're Stanley Ronald Schmidt."

"What do you mean?" I asked.

My father dropped his arms by his side and said, "When you were born, we named you Stanley Ronald. Because . . . that was the name of my uncle."

He stopped there and so I asked, "Why did you tell me my name was Don Fred?"

My father rubbed his feet on the floor like he was a chicken scratching the dirt or dancing, and then he said, "Well, because your uncle—I mean, my uncle Stanley—drank and gambled a lot and owed some people a large amount of money and had to leave the country, and your mother and I didn't want you to have the same name as a man like that, so we changed it."

I thought about this for a second, and then asked, "Why Don Fred? Was that the name of another one of your uncles?"

My father tapped his foot and said, "No. We just liked the name Don because it kind of reminded us of Dawn. And we didn't want you to be called Donald Ronald and your mother really liked that famous dancer Fred Astaire, so we came up with Don Fred."

My father had never spoken to me as much as he did in those five minutes. He also had never sweated as much. Not only was his face covered in sweat, but his shirt was too. And he couldn't stop scratching himself, either. It was like he was standing on an ant pile.

Anyway, then he told me, "Listen, Don, I don't want to talk about this anymore. We changed your name and now it's Don, and from now on don't look at anything that isn't for you. Now wait in here until your mother comes and then I want you to tell her you're sorry for violating her privacy."

I thought it was kind of strange that my parents had changed my name but didn't bother to change it on my birth certificate. I wondered if a lot of parents did that and if there were a bunch of other kids with names different from the ones on their birth certificates. Maybe Vickie Viceroy's name was really Vera or Leon's name was really Larry. I didn't like that my parents could change my name anytime they wanted to because I was worried that they might decide that they didn't like Don anymore and change it. I liked the name Don because before I had won the chicken-judging contest, all the kids had called me "new kid," and so I'd only been Don for a few months. I decided that I wouldn't tell any of the kids my new name if my parents changed it and then I started wondering what the Munson Detective Agency had to do with changing my name.

That didn't make sense because people always hired detectives on television to find someone or to take pictures of someone's husband in bed with another woman. I didn't know who my parents could be looking for and I wondered how I could find out without asking them. Then I thought that maybe they were lying to me and that I wasn't Stanley Ronald Schmidt and that he was a real person and they were looking for him, but if he was born on the same day as me, he would be my twin brother.

When I thought of this, my heart fell like it did when my mother or father had driven really fast over a hill. The more I thought about it, the more the feeling increased. I felt like I had won my blue ribbon all over again, but it wasn't a blue ribbon that I'd won this time. It was a brother. I thought about how he could sit next to me on the sofa and watch television, and help me raise my chickens, and I could introduce him to people and say, "This is my brother. We're best friends."

I imagined how we'd have to share my bedroom and how we could stare out of the window together and talk to the chickens. And late at night we'd have pillow fights, or just lay awake and talk about any and everything that we wanted.

Then I started to wonder where he was. I got a little sad when I thought that maybe he had died. I hadn't even met him, and now he was gone. Since I didn't want to think about him being dead, I made up a story that would make him alive.

My parents had taken my brother and me on a picnic in a park in Shreveport when we were babies. My mother was playing patty-cake with us while my father played a guitar. He remembered that he had a surprise for us and went off to the car to get it. A stray Frisbee flew near my mother and she stopped playing with Stanley and me and picked up the Frisbee and threw it back to its owner. She only had her head turned from us for a minute when the kidnapper grabbed Stanley. My parents looked everywhere for my twin brother, and finally they hired a private detective, Mr. Munson, to find him. My parents kept it a secret from me because they didn't want to upset me.

The story made me happy, and I felt like I was riding fast over a hill again. It explained the birth certificate and Mr. Munson and gave me a twin brother who could walk up to me at any minute.

Any minute, I thought, and then I heard footsteps and I smelled an odor that was kind of like flowers sprayed with glass cleaner. My mother came in my room in a bright red dress that I'd never seen before and had on more makeup than usual.

"You owe me an apology," she said.

I told her, "I'm sorry."

And she said, "Well, you should be. You have no right to go through my things," and then she breathed real hard and said, "When will my family respect me?"

"I don't know," I said.

She scrunched her forehead up and said, "Don, that's a matorical question. You're not supposed to answer it."

I knew she meant to say "rhetorical," because Mrs. Forest had used it two days earlier when she said, "Leon, when I ask you if you're trying to drive me insane, I don't want you to answer me back. That is what's called a rhetorical question. Say it with me class. 'A rhetorical question.' "

I didn't correct my mother, though. Instead I looked down at the floor until my mother started spinning around in circles as if someone were turning her on the dance floor.

"How do I look?" she asked.

"Very nice," I said.

"Very nice?" she asked. "Is that all you can say? I mean, how many women in this town can pull off a dress like this?"

Before I could answer, she walked out of the room and then shouted, "I think I need more perfume!"

She came back three seconds later and handed me a box and some clothes on a hanger. There was a green shirt and some dark blue pants and a clip-on red tie with green dots. When she handed them to me, she said, "I'm tempted not to give these to you because you invaded my privacy this afternoon. You're lucky I'm a nice person. Besides, I want you to look nice in front of the guests and I don't think I should have to suffer because of your rudeness."

She walked out of my room and then shouted, "Now, Don, I want you to take a bath and get dressed and then come in the kitchen and help me cook! Oh, and wear the black shoes and belt that are in the box!"

"Yes, ma'am," I said, and then whispered, "Stanley and I will be there in a minute."

I knew that Stanley wasn't really there with me, but I pretended that he was because I liked it. I could make him listen to whatever I had to say and I could have him answer me back with whatever answer I wanted to hear. Since he was my twin, I imagined speaking to someone who looked just like me. Only he didn't wear glasses and he didn't have freckles covering his body and he was a little taller. His voice was deeper than mine and when he wasn't smiling, his face looked relaxed like he wasn't afraid of anything.

While Stanley and I took our baths, I told him all about what had been going on since he'd been kidnapped. I told him all about the chicken-judging contest and how I'd chased the stray dog and pig.

"Can I be friends with you and Leon and chase the stray dog and pig?" he asked me.

I told him, "Yeah, sure," and that we'd ride our bikes to school together too, because we were brothers and best friends and we would always be together, except that I had to leave him for a few hours to help our mother, but that I'd be back soon. He told me, "Thanks," and then smiled at me and rubbed my head.

After I got dressed, I went to the kitchen to help my mother. She was cutting up some lettuce, tomatoes, and cucumbers, but she stopped and looked at me and said, "Nice, real nice. You're lucky I have such good taste in clothes."

I smiled at her and then she pointed at a bunch of Salisbury Steak TV dinners on the kitchen table and said, "Now put three of those dinners in the oven."

My mother was wearing a long white apron that my father had given to her for Christmas one year and it had big fold marks on it because she had never worn it before because she didn't wear aprons. I thought it looked kind of funny and I was glad I didn't have to wear one but then she picked up another apron that my father had given to her for her birthday once and told me to put it on.

For the next couple of hours, my mother and I heated the TV dinners three at a time. We took them out ten minutes before they were finished and then separated the dinners by what food they were. What I mean is that we put all the steaks in a metal container, all the mashed potatoes into another, and all the cherry pies in the trash can. My mother said they would be too messy to serve, and we'd instead have a frozen apple pie that she'd heat up during dinner.

When we were finished, my mother smiled at the containers and said, "When the guests get here I'm going to put these containers in the oven for the final ten minutes. That way they'll be nice and warm and they won't be overcooked. Pretty smart idea, isn't it?" and then she sat down at the kitchen table and said, "Cooking wears me out. Now you understand what I have to go through every day to feed you and your father."

I told her, "Thank you," and she asked, "What time is it?"

She looked up at the clock and said, "Oh my god! It's six o'clock. The Power Couples will be here any minute."

The *Power Couples* were Mr. and Mrs. Bufford, Mr. and Mrs. Simon, and the Leonards. My mother called them that because she said they were the most powerful people in town and that they could buy and sell anyone they wanted to. Mr. and Mrs. Simon owned Horse Island Shoes and Toys, and my mother said that they controlled what shoes people wore and what toys kids played with, and if that wasn't power, she didn't know what was.

Right after my mother said "The Power Couples will be here any minute," someone knocked on the door, and she let out a little yell, and then said, "Ah, they're here."

She jumped up from her chair and ran from the kitchen through the foyer and into the living room and said, "Dick, turn off that television and go and greet the guests."

Then she came back into the kitchen and told me, "Don, help him."

I took off my apron and walked to the front door, where my father was standing. He was wearing a pair of dark blue pants, a green shirt, and red tie just like me. He looked down at me and then at his shirt and tie and then down at me again. He stared at me for like five or six seconds, and then my mother yelled, "Answer the door, Dick!"

My father took a deep breath, let it out real slow, and then opened the door. All three of the Power Couples and Leon were standing on our porch. Leon was wearing a dark blue suit and a white shirt and a red tie with white chickens holding little American flags. His hair was slicked back, and I almost didn't recognize him until he stuck his tongue out and smiled. I smiled back, and then Mr. Bufford took off his black cowboy hat and said, "Hello, Schmidts. Merry Christmas."

"Please come in," my father said.

Mr. Bufford rubbed my head and asked, "How's Horse Island's newest celebrity doing this evening?"

I told him fine, and then my mother walked into the foyer without her apron and said, "I'm so glad you could all make it."

A couple of the ladies blinked their eyes and Mr.

Leonard sneezed. I think it was because of my mother's hair spray and perfume, because I almost sneezed too. Mr. Bufford didn't sneeze, though. His eyes got real big, and then my mother's eyes got real big too. I looked at all the other people to see if their eyes got big, but nobody else's did. My father's eyes got a little smaller and then he looked at Mr. Bufford and then at my mother. Then she looked at my father looking at her and her eyes got even bigger and she said, "Well, dinner's almost ready. If you want to wait in the sitting room, Dick will fix you all some drinks."

We had never called any room "the sitting room," and when my mother said it, my father peered down through his glasses at her. She gave him a big smile and looked toward the living room. He blinked his eyes and then walked in there.

My mother smiled and said, "I'll join all of you in the sitting room in a minute. Don, show Leon your room."

Leon and I walked to my room, and when we got in there, he looked around and then asked, "Who was that trophy for in your sitting room?"

"My sister, Dawn," I told him, and then I asked, "What's a sitting room?"

He shrugged and said, "I don't know. That's what your mom called it. It looked like a living room to me."

Leon kept looking around my room, and when he saw my blue ribbon tacked on the wall above my door, he asked, "Why isn't your blue ribbon in the sitting room with your sister's trophy?"

"I don't know," I said. "I like it better in here."

Leon pointed to the ribbon and said, "Why did you put it all the way up there above the door?"

I had put the ribbon above the door because any-time someone opened it, the air made the ribbon fly a little, so it kind of looked like it was dancing. I thought Leon might think that was stupid so I told him, "I don't know. I just like it there. It's above everything else."

"That's kind of stupid," he told me. "You can't even read what it says."

"I know what it says," I told him, and he looked up at it for a few seconds and then turned to me like he'd just figured something out.

"Where's your sister now?" he asked.

I told him that she had died and he said, "Oh," and then looked through the drawers of my desk until my mother shouted, "Don, dinner's ready!"

Leon and I went to the dining room/big closet where the grown-ups were sitting. My mother told us that we'd have to eat in the kitchen, so we went in there and sat down at the table and started eating the food my mother had set out for us. Leon cut a piece of the steak and sniffed it and then took a bite of it. While he was chewing he said, "Tina Touchet wants to go out with you. I think she looks like a horse, but some guys think she's pretty."

I told Leon, "She's okay, I guess, but she's a lot taller than me."

"Yeah, you're right," he told me. "You don't want to go out with a girl who's taller than you."

Leon kept talking about different things like who he was going to hit at school on Monday and what girls he'd kissed and who he was going to hit at school on Tuesday. From our seats in the kitchen, I could hear the grown-ups talking in the living room. I heard Mrs. Simon say, "These plates look brand new as if you've never used them."

That's because we had never used them because we'd always used paper plates or ate out of the trays from our TV dinners, but my mother didn't say that. Instead she said, "Well, I only use them for special occasions."

Leon punched me in the arm and asked, "So, what do you think, Don?"

I didn't know what he was talking about so I asked, "What?"

"You hard of hearing?" Leon asked. "Do you want me to start talking louder?" and then he did and said, "I might shave my head 'cause it will make me look tougher. What do you think?"

I told him, "Yeah, it would make you look tougher," and then he said, "Yeah, that's what I thought."

I started listening to the grown-ups again and heard Mrs. Simon say, "Sammy always makes us sit in front of the television when we eat. It's such a treat to sit and talk. You see, Sammy, the Schmidts are civilized people. They don't eat with the television on."

"Well," my mother said, "we think talking is important."

Leon started hitting his fork on the table and then asked real loud, "What's the matter with you? I keep asking you questions, and you don't answer me."

I hadn't heard anything he'd told me and hadn't even realized that he was talking. I put my head down and said, "I'm sorry. I thought I heard my mother calling me."

Leon tapped his fork a couple more times and then asked, "Why do you call her your mother and not your mom?"

"That's what she told me to call her," I told him and then he asked, "Do you call your dad, 'father'?"

"Yeah," I said.

I had always called my parents "Mother" and "Father." When I'd hear other kids call their parents "Mom" and "Dad," I wondered why they didn't call them "Mother" and "Father" like I did. I tried calling my mother "Mom" one day and she asked me, "What did you call me?"

"Mom."

"Don't ever call me that again," she told me. "Call me 'Mother' and your father, 'Father.' Do you understand me?"

Then I asked why and she sent me to my room, and so I never called her "Mom" again.

Leon told me it was strange that I called my mother "Mother" and then said, "Anyway, so on Wednesday, I think I'm going to hit Christopher Chesternut. He's in the sixth grade, but I can handle him."

I tried to listen to Leon because I didn't want to become the guy he was going to hit on Thursday. It was hard for me to listen to him, though, because I could hear the adults talking and I wondered if my parents were going to tell them about my twin brother. Since I was trying to listen to both Leon and the adults, I only caught bits of what they were saying.

Mr. Bufford: "I knew your uncle Sam real well. He told me a lot of things about you before you moved here."

Leon: "I hate our teacher. When the school year is over, I'm going to tell her she's fat."

Mrs. Leonard: "These steaks are delicious. You'll have to give me the recipe."

Leon: "I stuck my finger in a chicken's butt the other day."

When Leon said that, I stopped listening to the grown-ups talking and asked him, "What?"

Leon's face was all red and he said, "I've been trying to talk to you all night and you're not listening. Do you want me to start dancing on the table or something?"

I didn't know what to tell him. I had never had anyone try to get my attention as much as he was trying to that night. I was so scared that I had made him mad at me and he'd no longer meet me to ride bikes to school or invite me to chase the stray pig and dog around the playground, and I'd go back to being the kid I was before I won the chicken contest. I had to make him like me again and so I told him, "I think I have a twin brother who was kidnapped. Can you help me find him?"

THIRTEEN

The week after my mother's dinner party was Christmas vacation so we didn't have school. Leon and his parents went to visit his aunt in Mississippi so I didn't see him until after New Years. As soon as he got back to Horse Island, he came over to my house so we could talk about Stanley. It was our secret, which was kind of cool because I had never had a secret with anyone before, except my chickens, and I liked being able to talk to someone and have him talk back to me.

We went out to the chicken yard so we could talk about Stanley and collect the eggs.

"That's like something you see in the movies," Leon said. "I bet you could get any girl you wanted if she knew you had a brother who was kidnapped."

I heard a car start up, and so I turned and saw my mother driving off. I smiled at Leon and said, "Yeah, I guess so. I wish he was here now, though."

And then Leon said, "He'll be here soon 'cause we're going to find him."

I put down the bucket of eggs I'd collected and told Leon, "I've been thinking about that and I'm not sure we can do it. I mean, my parents had a private detective trying to find him."

Leon looked up in the air like he'd heard a noise and then said, "Well, I saw this movie one time where this guy was trying to find some girl he used to go out with because he loved her, and so he hired this private detective to find her, and anyway, the private detective told the guy he was looking for her, but he wasn't. He was just trying to get money out of the guy. Maybe that Mr. Munson guy is doing the same thing to your parents and not even looking for your brother."

I had never thought that my brother, Stanley, was out there waiting to be found and nobody was looking for him. So I asked Leon, "What do you think we should do first?"

Leon folded his arms and said, "We need to find that metal box that had the detective's name and address."

I hadn't seen the metal box since the day I'd found it and didn't know where my parents had hidden it. Since my father was at work and my mother had just driven off, I said, "Well, maybe we can go look for it now. Can you keep an eye out for my parents?"

Leon rubbed his hands together like he was about to

eat something and said, "This is awesome!" and then the two of us ran into the house.

Leon stood by the front window in the living room, and I went to the dining room/big closet. I put my hand on the doorknob and then yelled out to Leon, "Holler out to me if one of them comes!"

"What do you think, I'm stupid?" Leon shouted back. "I know what to do!"

I told him I was sorry and then opened the door of the dining room/big closet. It was filled again with empty boxes and folders the way it had been before the dinner party with the Power Couples. I didn't know which box to look in first, so I closed my eyes and then spun around and pointed to pick one.

The metal box wasn't in it or in any of the other boxes I looked through, so I looked in the cabinet my mother called an armoire. There was nothing in there, either, and so I thought about looking through the boxes again. But then I heard, "Don!"

I ran to the living room and asked Leon, "Are they here?"

He shook his head and said, "No. Did you find any-thing?"

"No," I told him. "You scared me."

He smiled and said, "Yeah, I can tell. You're pretty funny when you're scared."

"It's not in the dining room," I told him. "Where do you think they put it?"

Leon kind of shrugged his shoulders and said, "I

don't know. They're your parents. Look in their bed-room."

I had only gone into my parents' bedroom a few times because my mother told me that it was her room and that there was no reason for me to ever be in there. When I was younger I had run into my parents' room in the middle of the night because of a thunder and lightning storm. My mother yelled at me and told me that I had invaded her and my father's privacy.

Since then I hadn't gone into my parents' room unless one of them had called me in there. This time was different, though, because I had to find the metal box so I could find my twin brother.

I walked over to my parents' bedroom door, put my hand on the doorknob, and turned it. Before I opened it, though, Leon screamed, "Don!"

I pulled my hand away and ran back into the living room and Leon asked, "Did you find anything?"

I told him not yet, and then I said, "Stop yelling my name. It's freaking me out."

He laughed and said, "Yeah, I can tell. You're pretty funny when you're freaked."

I was really scared to go into my parents' room and because Leon kept calling my name, I was getting even more scared. So I told him, "Don't call my name again unless you see them."

Leon smiled and said, "Okay, I won't. But hurry up. I have to go to the bathroom."

I opened the door this time and walked into my

parents' room and turned on the light. There was a dresser against the wall on the right, a bed on my left, and a small table by the bed. On it was an angel with a lightbulb sticking out of its head.

I walked over to the dresser and started looking through the drawers. I went through every one, but I didn't find anything except clothes, so I went to look under the bed.

There was nothing under there, either, except some pieces of dust, but while I was looking, my foot hit the little table next to the bed and the angel lamp fell. It scared me a lot and I got up real fast and hit my head on the edge of the bed. It hurt so bad and for a few seconds I had a hard time seeing. I blinked my eyes a couple of times and wondered if I'd gone blind, but then I started to see things and I saw the angel lamp on the floor. I had never seen it before, so I thought that maybe my mother had traded it for some eggs. I picked it up and didn't see anything broken, but then I heard something move and I wondered if there was something broken inside of it. So I looked on the bottom of it and saw a small round hole like one in a piggy bank and inside there was a folded piece of paper.

I took it out because I thought it might be Stanley's birth certificate. But it wasn't. It was a hand-written note that said, "Janice, you are my beautiful angel. I can hardly wait to see you and kiss you. Meet me tomorrow. R. B."

I didn't understand what it meant because my

father's initials were D. S., and I didn't think he would write a note to my mother, and I was just starting to realize that my father hadn't written the note when I heard, "Crap! Your mom's here!"

I stuffed the note back into the lamp, put it on the table, turned off the lights, and ran out of my parents' bedroom. Right when I closed the bedroom door, I heard my mother open the front door of the house and yell, "Don!"

I walked into the living room and said, "Yes, ma'am."

"Were you just in my room?" she asked.

I stared at her not understanding how she knew, or what I should tell her, and so to buy some time I asked, "What?"

She put her purse on the sofa and said, "I thought I saw a light on in there when I drove up."

I looked at Leon, who was standing on the side of me with his pants unzipped, and my mother yelled, "Don, answer me!"

Before I said anything, though, Leon stepped forward and said, "It was me. I thought it was the bathroom but when I saw it was your bedroom, I left."

I looked at my mother to see if she believed Leon, because he seemed like he was telling the truth. My mother looked at him for a few seconds and then at me and said, "Oh," and then walked to the kitchen.

I went to my room and Leon followed me. As soon as we got in my room, I closed the door and asked him, "Why didn't you tell me my mother was coming?"

He shook his head and said, "I'm sorry, dude. I had to go to the bathroom and I didn't think she'd come when I was taking a leak. What are the chances, huh?"

My head still kind of hurt and I put my hand on it and felt a bump. I was kind of mad at Leon and I guess he could tell because he said, "Come on, Don. Don't be mad. I covered for you, and I don't think she knows you were in there."

"Okay," I said. "I'm not mad at you."

Leon put his hand out for me to shake and then said, "Good. Now did you find anything?"

I didn't know what to tell Leon because even though I kind of knew what I had found, I wasn't sure. So I looked at him and said, "No. I didn't find anything."

FOURTEEN

The note I'd found in the angel lamp was all I could think about for the next few weeks. I had seen enough soap operas on television to figure out that the note was from a man who was in love with my mother, and that maybe she was doing stuff with him that she probably wasn't supposed to be doing. I didn't know who the man was, though, and I didn't know anyone with the initials R. B. in Horse Island. Every time my mother spoke on the phone, I listened to see if I could hear clues. There were a few times I could hear her whispering, but I could never make out what she was saying. I even looked through the phone book, but there was no one with the initials R. B. Most people's first name began with the same letter as their last name. For example, there was Ross Roberts, Nicolas Newman, Bobby Bufford, and Ashley Aprils. But there was no one with the initials R. B. Then something happened and I was too busy to look for the note anymore.

You see, during breakfast one day, a few weeks after I found the note, my mother told me she was going to pick me up from school. She said she had some errands to run in town and had a surprise for me, and that kind of surprised me because my mother never had surprises for me. Even for Christmas and birthdays, she'd just let me pick out my own gift, or tell me what I was getting before I opened the present.

I was really excited about getting a surprise, but that afternoon when I found out what it was, I realized that I didn't want it. You see her surprise was that she had signed me up for a dance class.

"Can you believe it, Don?" she said. "You're going to be a dancer. Just like me and Dawn. Lucky for you, I was almost a famous dancer in Las Vegas, so I can help you with your homework. Oh, and the best part is, we only have to give them three dozen eggs a week for it. You're not saying anything. Is it because you're speechless? I thought you would be."

I didn't say anything because my mother didn't stop talking. Even if she had stopped talking, I don't think I would have said anything. I didn't want to take a dance class because I didn't want to have to wear a pink tutu and learn to spin the baton or lift one leg up in the air. I didn't know how to tell my mother that, though, and I knew that even if I did, she'd still make me take the dance class. I talked to Stanley in my head while my mother talked about how great dance class was going to be.

I said, "Stanley, what am I going to do? I don't want to take that class," and he told me, "Don, don't worry. You may like it, and all the other kids will think you're cool because you know how to dance and they don't. You might even win a trophy, and maybe Mother will put it up next to Dawn's."

I thought about this and wondered if I won a trophy if it would be a boy trophy, and if it was, if my mother would put it next to Dawn's. I thought she might, and then I thought that maybe taking a dance class wouldn't be so bad.

Well, there were two grown-up ladies and a bunch of girls in leotards about my age, but no other boys. I thought I saw another one but then I realized that I was just seeing myself in one of the mirrors that covered the walls. On those mirrors was a long railing about four feet from the ground, and some of the girls were standing on one leg and had their other one on the railing. I didn't think I could do that because it looked like it hurt. I wanted to run out of the class but this lady wearing a black leotard walked up to my mother and me and said, "Good to see you again, Mrs. Schmidt."

My mother said, "Good to see you too. This is Don, whom we spoke about. He's very excited about becoming a dancer."

The woman looked at me and smiled and said, "Nice to meet you, Don. I'm Ms. Mary and I'm going to be your dance teacher."

I said, "Okay," and then Ms. Mary said, "Well, let's get started."

She clapped her hands together and said, "Girls, let's get started."

All the girls ran over to Ms. Mary and then she said, "Class, we have a new student today. His name is Don Schmidt, and I think we all recognize him as the youngest boy to ever win the chicken-judging contest at the Dairy Festival. Let's give him a hand."

They all clapped, and some of them laughed and whispered into each other's ears. My mother smiled and clapped along with them until the teacher told her that she'd have to leave when the class started.

My mother smiled at Ms. Mary and asked, "May I speak to you?"

Ms. Mary looked at the girls and said, "All right, girls, go and line up in the formation I put you in last class."

She turned to my mother and said, "What would you like to speak to me about?"

My mother leaned toward Ms. Mary and I moved a little closer to them so I could hear. My mother asked, "What if I threw in fifteen dollars cash and an extra dozen eggs a week. Would you let me stay and watch my son?"

Ms. Mary looked up in the air and then said, "Fifteen dollars and two dozen and we have a deal," and my mother said, "Deal," and then the two of them shook hands.

A few minutes later I had changed into some shorts my mother had brought for me. Ms. Mary made me stretch and then said, "Now, Don, since you're joining the class late, I think you and I should work alone so you can catch up. We'll try without music first, and then once you have it down, we'll do it with music. Sylvia, can you work with the rest of the class while I work with Don?"

The piano player nodded her head up and down and then walked over to the girls. Ms. Mary brought me to a corner of the room and my mother followed right behind us. Her heels tapped on the wooden floor and Ms. Mary turned and looked at her and then back at me and said, "Now, Don, all we're going to work on here today is 'kick, step, step, kick.' Now watch my feet. You see how I 'kick, step, step, kick'?"

I watched Ms. Mary kick, step, step, kick a bunch of times, and then she told me to try. I kicked, and then I stepped, and then I kicked again, and Ms. Mary said, "No, Don, kick, step, step, kick."

I tried again but this time I stepped, and then kicked, and then stepped.

Ms. Mary said, "No, Don. Watch me again. Kick, step, step, kick. Do you understand?"

I said, "Yes, ma'am," and then I tried, but I kicked, and then kicked again, and before I took the step, Ms. Mary yelled at me, "Pay attention, Don! I said, kick, step, step, kick," and then my mother yelled, "Come on, Don, I'm paying good money for this. Pay attention!"

As hard as I tried, though, I couldn't get it, and the last time I did it wrong, Ms. Mary yelled, "No, Don! No! Kick, step, step, kick. You were the winner of the chicken-judging contest, so surely you can grasp this."

Then my mother yelled, "If you really want it, you can achieve it," and then she made a fist and shook it.

Ms. Mary let out a couple of deep breaths and then said, "Why don't you watch for the rest of the time today and you can practice at home."

On the way home my mother told me that even though my talent was raw, she was sure she could mold it because she had what people in show business called, "It." Then she told me, "We'll have to work really hard because you have a recital coming up in a month and a half."

I knew what a recital was because of all the times my mother had talked about Dawn's recitals, but I couldn't help asking my mother, "What?"

My mother turned and said, "A recital. You know, normally Ms. Mary wouldn't let anyone start her class in the middle of the session and then dance in the recital, but let's just say that your mother has a way with words and was able to persuade her to let you be in it. Aren't you excited?"

I wasn't excited because I didn't want to dance in front of a bunch of people. Going to class and dancing in front of those girls was hard enough and I didn't think I could do it onstage in front of a bunch of people. But I didn't know how to tell my mother. Then I started thinking about this episode of *The Brady Bunch*. You see, Cindy had a dance recital and she didn't want to be in it, so she decided to pretend that she hurt her ankle so she wouldn't have to. It didn't work because her mother noticed that sometimes she limped on her left ankle and then sometimes on her right. I thought it was a good idea and that if I did it, I would be a lot smarter than Cindy had been and only limp on my right. I figured that my mother wouldn't make me take dance if I had a hurt ankle and so I planned on falling right after dinner that night.

I decided to fall after I finished my dessert and a few minutes before *Three's Company* started, because I liked dessert and thought Janet, Crissy, and Jack were really funny on the show. So I untied one of my shoestrings and moved my tray onto the side of my chair and stood up. Before I could take a step and fall, though, my mother said, "Come on, Don. Let's go to the kitchen."

I didn't know why my mother wanted me to go to the kitchen, and it kind of shocked me, so I forgot about pretending to hurt my ankle and followed her. When we got in the kitchen, she told me, "Now, Don, I think we need to practice those steps. If you want to be a great dancer like me and Dawn, you're going to need to practice every chance you can."

I didn't want to practice the dance steps. I wanted to fall and pretend to hurt my ankle and then sit and watch *Three's Company*. But then I started thinking that it might be better if I fell while I was practicing dancing because my mother would feel bad for making me dance and fall. So I pretended like I really wanted to dance and asked, "Do you want me to stretch first?"

She smiled and said, "That's a good idea, Don!"

I bent over and my mother pushed on my back and then I started to feel funny because the blood started rushing to my head. It was hard for me to breathe, and my legs and back hurt so much that I couldn't take it anymore, and I had to stand up. My mother backed up from me and said, "What's wrong?"

"I felt dizzy," I told her.

"Well, get ready for a lot of dizzy days and nights," she told me. "Dancing isn't easy, you know."

I said, "Okay," and thought about falling then, but then my mother grabbed my hand and squeezed it and said, "This is going to be so much fun."

Her hand was real soft and warm and I kind of liked the way it felt, and I thought maybe if I practiced with her a little that she might grab my hand some more, so I decided not to fall until the end of the night.

My mother let go of my hand and said, "I have a surprise for you," and then she pulled a box out of the kitchen cabinet and gave it to me. It was wrapped in red paper and had a silver bow, and while I looked at it, waiting for my mother to tell me what it was, she said, "Go ahead and open it."

Inside the box was a pair of black shoes, which I wasn't that excited about because I already had a pair of black shoes, but I still told her, "Thanks for the shoes," and my mother said, "Those aren't just shoes, Don. They're jazz oxfords."

They looked like shoes to me, but my mother picked one of them up and bent it and said, "You see how it bends? And there's a low heel so it's easier for you to move. Here, put them on."

After I put them on my mother asked, "How do they feel?"

I said, "Okay," and then she said, "Good. Now sit right there and watch me dance. I want you to pay close attention to the steps I take and then I'll let you try."

I think I watched my mother kick, step, step, kick for like a million times, and then I tried it. I couldn't do it, and so I tried it again and I still couldn't do it, and I didn't think that I'd ever be able to do it, but then my mother did something really strange.

She told me to take off my jazz oxfords and then she took off her shoes and told me, "Come here."

She grabbed me by the shoulders until the back of my head was touching her stomach. Then she said, "Now stand on my feet and I'm going to do the steps with you."

At first I didn't think I'd heard her right so I told her, "I don't understand."

"Step on my feet," she said. "I'll hold you, and I'll do the steps, and that way you can do them with me."

I got on her feet and she held me tight and kicked, stepped, stepped, and kicked. My feet moved along with hers, but the first few times she did it, I was in too much shock to really pay attention. After a few more times, I got used to it and could feel what she was doing. I really thought I could do it by myself, but I didn't say anything because I liked standing on top of her feet and having her arms around my shoulders. I guess her feet got tired because she was the one who said it was time for me to try it on my own.

So I got off of her feet and then tried the dance step that she'd been trying to teach me all night. I thought about how my feet felt on top of hers and I kicked, stepped, stepped, kicked, and then my mother screamed and put her face in her hands and yelled, "That's it, Don! That's it! You've done it! I told you that you could do it, and you did!"

Before I knew what was going on, my mother hugged me. It was the first time I could ever remember her doing it. It was only for a few seconds, but it felt so warm and soft, like when I got under the electric blanket on a really cold night. And during that hug is when I decided that I wouldn't fall and pretend to hurt my ankle.

FIFTEEN

I was kind of nervous about telling Leon that I was taking a dance class, but when I finally did, he just smiled and said, "Dude, that's kind of cool because you get to be around all those girls."

I was real happy that Leon didn't make fun of me, and for the next few weeks I thought that it was really cool that I got to go to dance class on Mondays, Wednesdays, and Fridays and then dance with my mother every night in the kitchen. It made me even happier when I thought about winning a trophy that I could put next to Dawn's. But then the day before my recital, everything changed and I stopped liking to dance and I wasn't happy anymore.

It was a Saturday and my mother and I were at Horse Island Food and Furniture. When we walked in, she told me to go get some paper towels and to meet her in the frozen food section. When I got to the aisle where the paper towels were, I saw Mr. Leonard and Leon.

They didn't see me walk up at first and I heard Mr. Leonard tell Leon, "Now, these paper towels are twenty-five percent off of four dollars. Why do you think it's on sale? You think it's some of that stuff that's used already?"

Leon shrugged his shoulders and said, "I don't know, but I wouldn't risk it to save two dollars."

Mr. Leonard looked at Leon and said, "My boy, we wouldn't be saving two dollars. We'd be saving two dollars and fifty cents. Don't you pay attention in school? Your problem is that you think going to school is useless, but now you see, my boy, you can use this stuff everywhere."

Mr. Leonard shook his head from side to side and raised his voice and said, "You know, I don't even think you try. I mean, it embarrasses me sometimes, Leon, that my son's a dummy."

Leon took a couple of steps away from his dad and then looked at me. I guess Mr. Leonard saw Leon staring at me because he turned toward me and asked, "How you doing, Don?"

I told him that I was okay and he said, "You know, Don. I wish you'd do me a favor. You're a pretty smart boy. I wish you'd tell Leon here that he needs to start paying attention in class. I mean, the boy can't even do simple math."

I didn't know if I should tell Mr. Leonard that I would help Leon study or that I liked his shirt or that he would save one dollar on the paper towels if it was on sale for twenty-five percent off of four dollars. I decided not to say anything and instead just walked over and grabbed the paper towels that we used and hoped that Mr. Leonard would forget that he'd spoken to me. He didn't forget, though, and asked, "Don, what did you get on your last report card in Math?"

I squeezed the paper towels and told him, "I got an A."

Mr. Leonard looked at Leon and said, "Did you hear that, my boy? He got an A and you got an F. I think you need to spend more time studying so you can be more like Don here. Starting today, Leon, you're punished until your grades get better. That means no more television or running around with your friends."

Leon didn't say anything and then Mr. Leonard said in this really loud voice, "You hear me, my boy?"

Leon nodded his head up and down and then looked at me. His face was red and it almost looked like he was more mad at me than he was at his dad. It was kind of weird being there so I took a couple of steps back and tried to walk away without saying anything. But then Mr. Leonard turned and looked at me and said, "Tell your momma and daddy I said hi."

I said, "Yes, sir," and then walked away real quick to the frozen food section to find my mother. She was there with Mrs. Leonard and when I walked up, Mrs. Leonard looked at me and said, "Well, if it isn't Fred Astaire himself. You know, your mother has told me all about your dance classes. I'm afraid I'm not going to be able to go to your recital tomorrow because I'm going out of town for a hair convention. I'm very upset about it because I've heard how hard you've been working. Hey, how about a little preview, Don?"

My mother clapped her hands and said, "That's a wonderful idea. We can do it right here and I'll do it with him."

I didn't want to dance in the middle of the frozen food section of the grocery store because I thought it was stupid. I was already kind of scared about dancing at the recital in front of all those people, but at least they were going there to see me dance. Nobody had come to Horse Island Food and Furniture to watch me dance, and so I didn't want to, but then my mother started singing the song "He's So Shy" and tapping her feet.

"Come on, Don," she said. "Dance."

I stood still and Mrs. Leonard said, "It's okay, Janice, he doesn't have to dance if he doesn't want to."

"Oh, he wants to dance, Lucy," she said. "He's just a little modest, like his mother. Come on, Don. You shouldn't keep talent like that to yourself."

My mother starting singing again and dancing and customers in the store stopped shopping and watched her. My mother stopped singing and yelled out, "Attention, everyone! Don is making his dance debut tomorrow at The Dance Loft's recital. I'm trying to convince him that he should give us a little preview, but he's being modest. Maybe you can help me by cheering him on. On the count of three, everybody repeat 'Dance,' until he does."

People started clapping and yelling, "Dance, Don, dance! Dance, Don, dance! Dance, Don, dance!"

After a few minutes there were about twenty people surrounding my mother and me yelling, "Dance, Don, dance!"

I started to get hot and I thought about running away, but there were a bunch of people surrounding me, and I knew my mother would punish me. I couldn't just stand there anymore because people kept cheering and clapping. I knew they wouldn't stop until I danced, so I closed my eyes, took a deep breath, took a step, and then kicked my leg forward.

The people stopped yelling "Dance, Don, dance!" and started yelling "He's going to do it! Yeah! All right!"

Then my mother said, "All right, everybody, quiet down so I can sing and he can hear the music."

My mother started singing and dancing next to me. We kicked and stepped and kicked and spun around. I kept my eyes closed and felt dizzy and didn't think I'd be able to make it through the whole song. Thankfully after the first chorus, my mother stopped singing and said, "All right, everybody, that's it for today. If you want to see more, you'll have to come to the recital tomorrow."

People clapped and said things like, "Good job, Don. You were great."

My mother laughed and clapped her hands together and looked at me and said, "God, that was fun, wasn't it?"

It wasn't fun. I thought it was the worst thing in the world and that it couldn't get any worse, until I turned and saw Leon staring at us. That's when he said, "Nice dancing," and walked away.

It was the first time since I'd won the chicken-judging contest that Leon had been mean to me and I didn't really know why. It didn't make sense to me because he'd told me that he didn't care that I was taking a dance class. He even said he thought that it was kind of cool because I got to be with all those girls. But at the grocery store that day, when he said, "Nice dancing," I could tell that he thought it was stupid and that's when I didn't want to dance anymore.

I talked to Stanley about it that whole afternoon, night, and the next morning and I still didn't know what I was going to do a few hours before the recital. I decided to talk to KC about it and see if she could help me figure it out. I told her, "I hate dancing. At first I kind of liked it, but now I hate it because my mother made me do it in the grocery store and now Leon doesn't want to be my friend. I don't want to dance and I can't even remember the steps to the song."

KC sat on the ground in front of me and closed her eyes, so I closed mine and imagined Stanley sitting next to me.

"Hey, Stanley," I said. "Can you help me come up with a way to fall in front of Mother so she thinks I really hurt my ankle?"

"Don," he told me. "You know she's going to be mad if you can't dance, and she's going to stop being nice to you."

"I know," I said. "But I don't want to dance, and even if I did want to, I don't remember the steps."

Someone in my house turned on the radio, and the song "Rockin' Robin" by Michael Jackson started playing, and Stanley told me, "That's one of your favorite songs, Don. Why don't you try dancing to it? You knew all the steps before and you used to like dancing."

I told him, "Yeah, a little, but I don't like doing it in front of people, and what about Leon?"

"Well," he told me, "act like there's nobody watching you. Leon's not going to the recital anyway, so he won't see you."

Stanley had a good point, and since I liked "Rockin' Robin," I thought I'd try. I started tapping my foot and Stanley told me, "Get up now, Don. Get up now and dance while no one is around."

"Dance with me, Stanley," I told him.

We both stood up from the stump and tapped our feet in the dirt to the beat of the song and then we moved our hips from side to side. I closed my eyes and swung my arms, and then I imagined all the chickens lining up behind Stanley and me. They made a box and the mixed colors of their white and red feathers looked kind of like pictures I'd seen of snow on fall leaves.

We walked sideways and kicked, stepped, stepped,

and kicked. I was turning, walking backward, and tapping. I didn't even feel like I was trying, but like something had taken over my body and was doing it for me. I imagined my chickens flying on my shoulders and lifting me up in the air like I was the one flying, and then Stanley disappeared, and it was just me.

Then I heard my mother yell, "Oh my god! Don, you're doing it! Oh my god!"

I opened my eyes, and I wasn't flying anymore and the chickens weren't lined up behind me. I saw my mother running toward me and I thought that she was going to open up the gate and come into the chicken yard, but she stopped right before the chain-link fence and said, "That was great, Don."

She started crying and then said, "I am so proud of you. I don't think a mom could be any happier than I am now."

I couldn't believe that she'd said she was proud of me and that she didn't think a *mom* could be any happier than she was. That's when I knew that I couldn't pretend to hurt my ankle and that I had to dance in the recital.

SIXTEEN

My recital was in the auditorium at Horse Island High and right before my dance started, our teacher, Ms. Mary, lined all the kids up onstage behind the curtain. I had to wear this white suit and black shirt like John Travolta wore in *Saturday Night Fever* because my mother liked the movie. The girls didn't have to wear suits, though. They wore these red sequined dresses that Ms. Mary picked out and said would look good for the song we were dancing to. It was the Pointer Sisters' song "He's So Shy," and since I was the only boy, I had to dance in the middle of the girls, and they would turn and point at me and sing, "He's So shy."

I was going over all the steps in my head when the curtain went up and Ms. Mary walked onstage and said, "Ladies and Gentlemen, may I have your attention? Tonight we have a special surprise for all of you. Janice Schmidt will sing the song for this last number. I don't think I need to tell you that the handsome young man in the middle of the stage is her son. So without further ado, Janice Schmidt."

My mother walked out onstage and I was kind of shocked because she hadn't told me that she was going to sing. She had changed from the pantsuit she'd worn to the recital into a red sequined dress like the one the girl dancers had on. When she took the microphone from my teacher, a ray of light shot off of her dress and blinded me a little.

"Hello, everyone," my mother said. "It's so good to have everyone here tonight, and I'm so glad to be able to perform for you. Please join me in thanking Ms. Mary for giving us this great opportunity."

Everybody clapped and then the music started and my mother started singing. Her mouth was really close to the microphone and you couldn't really understand what she was saying, but the girls on the sides of me started dancing. I didn't move, though, because I'd forgotten all the steps. I could see my teacher on the side of the stage waving her arms at me, but that still didn't help me remember them.

I didn't know what to do so I closed my eyes and breathed deeply, and then I pretended that everyone was a chicken. The girls on each side of me were chickens, and the people in the audience were chickens, and my mother was KC the chicken, not the singer. I was the only one who wasn't a chicken, but I wasn't Don. I pretended I was Stanley, and then I started to remember the steps to the song. I tapped my foot and then took three steps forward and three steps back. I kicked my left leg in the air, and then my right, and then I danced just like my mother and Ms. Mary had taught me.

I wanted to see the people in the audience looking and smiling at me while I danced, so I opened my eyes to look at them, but all I saw was my mother's finger pointing at me. She was moving her shoulders side to side and singing and I could see her teeth and there was red lipstick on them. It was kind of scary, so I closed my eyes again and kept them closed until I heard my mother start the last verse.

For the last part of the song, I was supposed to step backward and then kneel down on my left knee and throw my arms up in the air and shake my hands. I was so happy when I started to step backward because it meant the song was almost finished and I hadn't really messed up that much. But when I tried to take the step, I couldn't. Something was holding my legs together. I opened my eyes and looked down at this black ropelike thing around my legs. It took me a second to realize it was the cord from the microphone. I tried to step out of it, but then my mother took a step forward and the cord tightened and I tripped.

My glasses flew off of my face and everything got blurry. I could still kind of see the people in the audience. Some of them were laughing and some of them were clapping. A lot of them weren't doing anything. They were just looking up at me with weird faces like they'd just eaten something sour.

Then the curtains went down and everything went black for a couple of seconds. The stage lights came on and I could see the girls standing around me in a circle and looking at me. One of them told me, "You're stupid."

Then the other girls agreed with her and they all walked off the stage. My mother didn't leave, though. She looked down at me and tilted her head to the side.

"What happened?" she asked.

I found my glasses and put them back on. Then I told her, "The cord from the microphone made me fall."

"Oh," she said. "Wasn't I great? Maybe I should join the church choir."

I didn't really care if my mother joined the choir because I was too busy unwrapping the wire from around my legs. I was kind of mad at her because she'd made me fall. But then I realized that I wouldn't have to dance anymore and I got happy. And I was happy until I stood up and stepped out of the pile of cord. That's when my mother walked off the stage and I realized that because I wasn't dancing anymore, we wouldn't practice anymore. I didn't want to stop dancing on her feet at night in the kitchen because I kind of liked that. So I decided I would ask her on the way home if we would keep practicing. But then my mother walked back onstage.

"Don," she said. "I'm sure a few people want to talk to me, so I'll meet you outside by the car."

"Okay," I said.

She started to walk off the stage again and before I could even think about anything, I heard myself say, "Mother. Are we going to keep dancing in the kitchen at night?"

My mother stopped and turned and looked at me. She shook her head and said, "No. There's no reason to start practicing until class begins again in September. Besides, I think I need to start practicing my singing if I want to be able to hit those high notes."

My mother walked off the stage and I whispered, "Can we practice anyway?"

SEVENTEEN

The next morning when I went outside to go to school, Leon wasn't there. I thought maybe he was running late, so I waited a little while for him. He still didn't show up after around ten minutes and I figured I'd better go to school without him or I'd be late.

Leon was sitting at his desk when I got to school. I thought about talking to him, but the bell rang and the teacher told us to settle down because we had to get started.

All morning long I wondered if Leon was really mad at me. I decided to ask Stanley, "Why do you think Leon didn't stop at our house this morning?"

He told me, "I think he was just late to school and didn't have time."

I liked that answer, so then I asked Stanley, "Do you think it's because he saw me dancing in the grocery store?"

"No, Don," he said. "Leon would never do that to you."

I guess I must have stopped talking in my head and started talking out loud, because Mrs. Forest asked me, "Don, who are you speaking to?"

Everybody turned and looked at me and I didn't say anything until Mrs. Forest said, "Don, answer me."

That's when I said, "I was talking to myself."

All the kids laughed and Leon said, "Geez, what a geek."

Then Mrs. Forest said, "Settle down, children. Don, stop talking to yourself; it's very disruptive."

During recess and lunch, I sat by myself and thought about what to do. Stanley told me that I should try to talk to Leon after school. Since I didn't know what else to do, I listened to him and right after school, I walked up to Leon and said, "Hi, Leon. Do you want to come look at my chickens?"

He made a face and then told me, "No," and so I asked, "Do you want to help me look for my kidnapped twin brother?"

Leon got on his bike and then told me, "Let me explain something to you. You're a dancing geek, and I'm not, so I can't be hanging out with you."

Leon rode off on his bike and I stood alone in front of the school. I didn't know what to say, and even if I did, it wouldn't have mattered because I was alone so nobody would hear. I didn't even feel like talking to

Stanley. I don't know why. I guess because I thought there was nothing he could have told me to make me feel better. My stomach hurt and felt like it did this one time when I ate an expired Beef Pie Surprise TV dinner. And my head felt like it did this one time a dodge ball hit me in the face in fourth grade recess. My mouth got really dry and sweat started dripping down into my eyes. I wiped the sweat away and then I got on my bike and started peddling home.

I felt so tired. Like the most tired I'd ever been in my whole life and I didn't know if I'd be able to make it all the way home. And then I got to a stop sign and I felt a little different. I don't know why. Maybe it was the red color of the sign. But I suddenly wasn't that tired anymore. I was mad.

So I picked up a rock and threw it at the stop sign. I missed it and that made me even madder. So I picked up another rock and threw it and I missed again. Then the calico cat ran out from a field onto the road and looked at me. She hissed and ran toward me, so I picked up a rock and threw it at her. It didn't hit her, but she stopped.

I screamed, "I hate you, cat! I hate you because you're so mean and I never did anything to you and all you ever do is chase me and try to scratch me and I'm tired of it!"

The cat ran away and I watched it for a couple of seconds until it disappeared. Then I felt tired again and started riding my bike back home. I thought about how Leon wasn't going to ride his bike with me anymore and how I'd have to sit alone for lunch again and how I wouldn't get to chase the stray dog and pig anymore. I started crying and thought that it was my mother's fault. And I got so mad that I screamed, "I hate my mother and I wish she'd leave!"

I was peddling up the driveway in our front yard when it came out of my mouth. And that's when I stopped my bike and stopped screaming. I just stood there holding on to my bike and breathing really hard. I couldn't even believe I'd said it. It just came out. My stomach started to hurt again, but I didn't feel like screaming. I just felt like dancing.

So I walked my bike up to the house and then went inside. No one was there, so I put my backpack in my room and went into the kitchen. Then I closed my eyes and imagined dancing on my mother's feet.

EIGHTEEN

For the next couple of weeks, Leon and all the other kids pretty much stopped talking to me, so I went back to sitting alone for recess the way I had before the chicken-judging contest. I watched them play kick ball and chase the stray dog and pig. I kind of wanted to play with them, but none of them asked, so I just sat and watched and talked to Stanley.

One day, I think it was a Tuesday, when I was talking to him, he gave me an idea. We were talking about the Easter break that was coming up the next week and how it was going to be fun because we wouldn't have to go to school for nine days in a row. We decided that we were going to try and build some new nests for the chickens.

That's when Stanley told me, "You know what, Don? That sounds cool, but you know what would be even cooler?"

"What's that?" I asked him.

"If you found me."

I hadn't looked for the metal box with Stanley's birth certificate since the day I'd found the note from R. B. I don't know why. I guess I just got busy dancing for my mother and I kind of forgot about it. Or I just never had the chance to look for it. But I really liked Stanley's idea and so I decided that I would look for the metal box with the birth certificate and the bills from that detective, Mr. Munson. I just had to wait until my parents weren't home.

That Saturday, I had my chance. My father had to go into work and my mother told me that she had to run some errands. I stood in the foyer and watched her drive off and as soon as I couldn't see the car anymore, I started to look for the metal box.

I figured my parents' bedroom would be the best place to start and so I headed toward it. But when I was passing through the living room, I saw the music box on the bookcase and I stopped.

My mother hadn't wound it up and watched the ballerina dance since before I'd won the chicken-judging contest, almost six months before. I mean, unless she was doing it while I was in school, but I don't think so because there was dust on the music box and a spider web connecting it to Dawn's dance trophy. I don't know why, but I still kind of wanted to wind it up all the way and whisper, "Fly," and see if the ballerina would fly away.

I knew I wasn't supposed to touch it, but I really

wanted to and so I asked Stanley, "Do you think it would be okay if I wound up the music box?"

He said, "Sure. What's the worst that could happen?"

Since Stanley said it was okay, I pushed a chair up to the bookcase, stood on top of it, and reached for the music box.

My hand was shaking when I picked it up because it was something that I'd wanted to do for so long and I guess I couldn't believe that I was doing it. The box felt like it weighed a couple of pounds and the wood was soft and smooth. I turned and looked out of our front window just to make sure that my mother wasn't driving up. Since I didn't see her, I decided I was going to do it. I was going to wind the box up as much as I could and watch the ballerina dance and then whisper, "Fly."

But then, when I was about to step off of the chair with it, the telephone rang. It scared me so much that my arms jerked up and the box slipped from my hands and flew and flipped through the air like it was dancing. Right when it hit the floor, I yelled, "No!" and then I stepped back and fell off the chair.

I laid on the ground and stared at the music box while the phone rang. I didn't want to leave it on the ground, but I didn't want to know if it was broken. So instead, I got up off the floor and picked up the phone and said, "Hello?"

Some man said, "Hello, yes, is Mr. or Mrs. Schmidt in?"

I said, "No, sir, they're not here. Can I take a mes-sage?"

"Yes," he said. "Can you tell them that Mr. Munson called?"

I couldn't believe that the man who was looking for my brother was talking to me. I wanted to ask him questions like "Where is Stanley?" and "Are you look-ing for him or just keeping my parents' money like Leon said?"

The only thing I could say though was "Yes, sir."

After he gave me his number and I hung up, I heard a car drive up to our house. I looked out of the window and saw my mother and remembered the music box. I picked it up and turned it over and over to make sure that it wasn't chipped. It was okay, and so I jumped on the chair to put it back, but my hands were shaking and I dropped it again. My heart was pounding so hard, I swear I thought it would pop out of my chest. I got the music box back on the bookcase, though, right before my mother opened the front door.

She walked into the kitchen and yelled, "You know, I went all the way to Cloris Callahan's house to give her some eggs, and she wasn't there! I spoke to her this morning and told her I was coming. Some people in this town need to be careful or I might not do business with them."

She walked into the living room wearing a white shirt and purple pants and asked, "Do these purple pants look good on me? I ran into our neighbor Patricia

Picard and she couldn't stop talking about how much she loved them."

I told her, "They're nice," and then my mother walked back into the kitchen and I went into my room. I sat on my bed and stared out at the chicken yard for a few minutes so I could calm down. I realized that the only way I could find out what Mr. Munson wanted was to tell my mother that he called and then try to listen to her when she called him back. So I took a few deep breaths and then walked into the living room where my mother was watching television.

"Mr. Munson called," I said.

She looked at me and her eyes got big, and then it looked like her face turned as white as her shirt. She blinked and then asked, "What did he want?"

I told her, "He just wants you to call him," and she stood up and asked, "Is that all he said?"

"Yes, ma'am," I said. "He left a number for you."

My mother moved her feet back and forth real quick like she was dancing and then asked, "Where's the number?"

I pointed and said, "It's on a piece of paper by the phone."

My mother walked real fast to the phone and picked up the piece of paper and started dialing the number. She stopped dialing and hung up the phone and then told me, "Listen, I need to make a very private and important phone call, so I need you to get out of the house right now."

I said, "Yes, ma'am," and walked out the front door without saying anything else. Then I had an idea and walked around to the side door that went into the kitchen. I opened it slowly, walked in, slid into the pantry, and then pushed the door open a little. That's when I heard my mother shout, "It's me! Mr. Munson called."

She didn't say anything for a few seconds, and then she said, "I don't know. He just left a number for us to call."

Although I didn't know for sure, I had a feeling she was talking to my father. Whoever it was, she read Mr. Munson's telephone number to them, and then she was quiet for a few seconds, and then she asked, "What? I don't know. He just told me that Mr. Munson called. I doubt seriously that he told him what it was about."

My mother told the person on the other line to call her as soon as he or she found out what Mr. Munson wanted, and then she hung up the phone. I stayed in the pantry since I had a feeling that the person she'd told to call her back would call in a few minutes. I was right, because about five minutes later the phone rang and I heard my mother ask, "What did he say?" and then something about not believing something and, "Oh my god! Tomorrow?" and then she said, "Okay, I'll start packing."

My mother hung up the phone and then yelled, "Don!"

I walked out of the pantry and then out the kitchen door and ran around to the front of the house and through the front door and said, "Yes, ma'am?"

My mother looked at me for a couple of seconds, and then said, "Your father and I are going to New Orleans tomorrow. You're going to be staying with a babysitter."

I smiled because I thought they were going to New Orleans to pick up Stanley and my mother asked, "Why are you smiling?"

"Um," I said. "Because I like going to the babysitter."

"Oh," my mother said, and then walked out of the living room.

I went out to the chicken yard and started collecting eggs and asked Stanley if Mr. Munson had found him. He told me, "Yes, and I'm going to be back home either tomorrow or the next day and we're going to share your bedroom and go to school together and everyone is going to be jealous of us because we're twins."

I couldn't believe that in a couple of days my brother, Stanley, would be helping me collect the eggs for real and not just in my imagination. I pictured us sitting on the sofa together eating our TV dinners side by side, while my mother and father asked us how our day was. I was about to imagine what our birthday parties would be like and if there'd be Chinese clowns, when I heard a car in our driveway.

I looked in our front yard, and I saw my father get out of his car and almost run toward the house. I figured he was going to tell my mother about Stanley, so I went into the house through the kitchen door and got in the pantry again, just in time to hear my mother say, "So tell me what he said."

My father told her, "He said he thinks he may have found her, but he wants us to come and see for ourselves."

"Where?" my mother asked. "Where did he see her?"

"I told you on the phone, he didn't want to tell me. He wanted to wait until we met him in person."

"Oh, Jesus," my mother said, "Why couldn't he have just told you? Why does he have to be that way?"

"I don't know, Janice!" my father said real loud, and my mother yelled back at him, "Don't snap at me!"

I thought that they were going to start fighting, but then I heard my father say, "I'm sorry. It's just kind of hard to believe that it's true, and I'm scared we're going to be let down."

"I don't know, Dick," my mother said. "I think this could be it. I think we've finally found her."

"There's another thing," my father said. "Mr. Munson wants us to bring him. He said it might keep her from running."

My mother asked, "Are you serious? I don't know if that's such a good idea. What do you think?"

"I don't know," my father answered. "I think we should sleep on it," and then my mother said, "Oh my god. I don't know if I'll be able to sleep."

I heard my mother's shoes tap on the floor like she

was running somewhere. When I was sure she wasn't coming toward the kitchen, I walked out of the pantry and out the side door into the yard. I walked back to the coop so I could think about what I'd heard them say. I didn't understand why they kept saying "her."

"He thinks he may have found 'her.' "

"I think we've finally found 'her.' "

"Mr. Munson wants us to bring 'him.' " He said it might keep 'her' from running."

I didn't know who "her" was, and I was really confused. I thought that I might be the "him" that Mr. Munson wanted them to bring. But then I started thinking that maybe the "her" was Stanley and that my twin brother was really a twin sister. It just didn't make sense to me because I'd never heard of a girl named Stanley. So I asked Stanley, "Are you a girl?" and he said, "Don, I'm in your head. I can't answer that."

That night during dinner, my parents didn't tell me anything about why they were going to New Orleans. They acted real strange, though. Like they talked during the TV shows and then didn't say anything during the commercials. My mother laughed out loud a few times and then all of a sudden she started crying. My father even said something, and he never talked during dinner. He said, "Don't you think the Fonz was a little old to be dating all those high school girls?"

Happy Days wasn't even on when he said that.

Anyway, all that night I couldn't sleep because I thought about everything that had happened and everything that I knew. It didn't make any sense to me and I think I got even more confused. I realized that I had to either listen to my parents some more or ask them what was going on.

So the next morning, I lay in my bed until I heard my parents' footsteps, and then I got dressed and walked toward the kitchen. It was Easter morning and so I stopped in the living room and looked for a basket with colored eggs and chocolate bunnies. There wasn't one. There never was one, but I always checked. I'd heard kids at school talk about getting baskets from the Easter Bunny. I had figured out that he wasn't real, but I'd always hoped that there would be a basket of candy waiting for me on Easter morning.

Since there wasn't a basket, I went into the kitchen. My father was sitting at the table eating waffles, and my mother was pouring herself a cup of coffee. I stood in the doorway of the kitchen and stared at them until my mother said, "Come and eat your breakfast, Don. Remember that your father and I are leaving today for New Orleans. You're going to stay with a babysitter for a couple of days until we get back."

I didn't move. I knew they weren't going to tell me anything and I really wanted to know what was going on. So I closed my eyes and said real fast, "I know about Mr. Munson. I know that he's a private detective and that you hired him to find Stanley, my twin who was kidnapped when we were at a picnic and Mother picked up a Frisbee and threw it."

My parents asked, "What?" at the same time and I opened my eyes and told them, "I know about Stanley, and I want to go to New Orleans to get her."

My mother said, "Don, you're out of your mind. What are you talking about?"

"Yeah," my father said. "What are you talking about?"

I took a couple of steps toward them and said, "I saw the bills from Mr. Munson and I heard both of you talking and that's the only way to explain why there's a birth certificate for someone who was born on the same day as me."

My mother stood up from the table and screamed, "You were listening to us? How dare you spy on us!"

I backed away from her because she looked really mad and her face was red and I was kind of scared that she would spank me.

My father stood up and said, "Janice, calm down." Then he pulled a chair out from the table and said, "Come here and sit down, Don. We have to tell you something."

I didn't move and my father said, "Okay, stand if you want. We're not going to New Orleans to pick up your twin brother, Stanley, because you don't have a twin named Stanley. Like I told you, you're Stanley."

He looked down at the ground and then back at me and said, "We're going to New Orleans to pick up your sister, Dawn."

NINETEEN

Our hotel room in New Orleans was in the French Quarter and it had two windows and from them I could see Bourbon Street and a place called Bourbon's Broadway. On top of its door, there was a pair of plastic woman's legs popping in and out of a curtain, which I thought was kind of weird but I also thought New Orleans was kind of weird. There were people running and dancing and singing in the middle of the street. Nothing like that ever happened in Horse Island, so I guess that's why I thought it was weird.

Anyway, after my father had told me that Dawn was alive, I felt weak, like I'd been standing out in the sun all day and hadn't drunk any water. I sat down on a kitchen chair and stared at the ground.

"Are you okay?" my father asked.

"She's alive?" I asked.

"Yes, Don," he told me. "She's alive. And there's something else we have to tell you."

"No, there's not," my mother said. "She's alive and we're going to get her. That's all he needs to know."

"But how?" I asked. "I thought she was dead."

I looked up at my father and he put his hand on my shoulder and I jumped a little.

"It's okay, Don," he said. "It's okay."

"Look," my mother said. "We don't have time to get into this today. We'll explain when we get back."

"No," my father said. "We'll explain in the car. He's coming with us."

My mother crossed her arms and said, "No, he's not."

Then my father crossed his arms and said, "Yes, he is."

My mother jerked her head back and made this surprised-looking face. It was the same face she'd made when this man fixed our air conditioner and told her that she would have to pay him in cash and not in eggs.

"Well, I guess my opinion doesn't count," she said.

"No. No, it doesn't," my father said back.

My mother made the same surprised-looking face and then ran out of the kitchen crying. Then my father told me to go and pack some clothes.

A lot of stuff was going on in my head just then. I was excited about going to New Orleans because I'd never been and I'd heard kids at school talking about how cool it was. I was also kind of excited about meeting Dawn. But then I was a little nervous about leaving my chickens. Leon wasn't talking to me so I couldn't ask him to take care of them. The only person I could think of to take care of my chickens was Mr. Chandler. So I called him and asked him if he could feed them and pick up the eggs and bring them to Mr. Bufford. He told me, "Of course, my boy. I'd do anything for the smartest chicken guy I've ever met."

An hour later my parents and I were in our car driving to New Orleans. My mother had stopped crying by this time but wasn't talking. Neither was my father. He just drove while my mother stared at herself in a pocket mirror. Then my mother pulled a tube of lipstick out of her purse and said, "Okay, Don. Here's the truth about your sister, Dawn. She didn't die. She was kidnapped."

My father turned and looked at her the way he did when she spoke during his favorite television shows. My mother looked back at him, tilted her head and smiled and put on some lipstick.

Then she told me, "You see, the spring break when Dawn was fifteen years old, she went to visit your father's blind mother, who was living with a nurse in Texarkana, Texas."

"But I thought you told me that his parents were eaten by sharks?" I asked.

"Oh," my mother said. "I told you that because they hated me so I hated them back."

She looked at herself in her mirror again and rubbed her lips together.

Then my father said, "My father died of a heart attack before you were born and my mother died of cancer a few months after you were born."

"I'm telling the story, Dick," my mother said while she pulled a nail file out of her purse.

Then she said, "Dawn wanted to stay the week in Texarkana because she didn't think your grandmother would live much longer. Dick, slow down. You're going too fast. I'm filing my nails. Do you want me to stab myself?"

My father turned and looked at my mother and then tilted his head and smiled the way she had done to him a couple of minutes before.

"Because of the cancer?" I asked.

"Who is telling this story, Don?" my mother asked. "Yes, she died because of the cancer. Now you're going too slow, Dick. We'll never get there at this rate. Where was I? Yes, so when we went to pick her up, she wasn't there because someone had kidnapped her."

My mother said they hired Mr. Munson to find her. He was a private detective from Texarkana who looked for Dawn for a year. My father started missing work and spent a lot of money on Mr. Munson. My father got fired because of all the work he'd missed. He didn't have a job for almost a year and my parents got into debt and they lost their house in Shreveport. That's why they had to move to Horse Island and live in Uncle Sam's house, which my father inherited around the same time. They didn't think they'd ever see Dawn again until Mr. Munson called.

I was kind of scared about Dawn coming back because my mother always talked about how good my sister was at dancing and how she could hold one leg in the air and spin a baton with her free hand. But I thought it would be kind of nice if Dawn could come to chicken-judging contests with me and dance for everyone and I could shout out, "That's my sister!" I even wondered what it would be like if we became a brother-and-sister act like Donny and Marie Osmond, and went to parish fairs, and while I was winning chicken-judging contests, she'd be winning dance contests, and then we'd put my ribbons and her trophies on the bookcase in our living room.

I was getting real excited about having a sister, but then I got a little sad because that meant that I didn't really have a twin brother named Stanley because I was Stanley. I wondered if maybe my parents had lied to me about Stanley and so I decided that maybe there really was a Stanley, and because I liked talking to him and being friends with him, I would keep on doing it.

So when I was in New Orleans looking out our hotel window, I asked him, "Do you think she will like me?"

"I'm sure she will, buddy," he told me. "You're a pretty cool kid."

Then my father came and stood next to me and stared out the window. I don't know what he was looking at. Maybe he was looking at the legs popping out of the door above Bourbon's Broadway or maybe he was looking at this man selling hotdogs out of a cart that looked like a hotdog. But he only looked outside for a couple of minutes and then he looked at me and put his hand on my shoulder and rubbed it a little. I didn't know what to do but kind of figured that maybe I should do something back. So I put my hand on his leg. When I did that, my father winked. I had never seen him wink and so I thought maybe he'd gotten something in his eye. It was making me nervous and so I sneezed and then my father looked back out the window. We must have stayed there for like ten minutes just staring at the people in the street. Then, all of a sudden, all of the people who were walking on the street kind of disappeared. So my father and I just stood there all alone in the quiet staring at nothing for like ten seconds until someone knocked on the door.

We both turned and looked. I don't know what my father was thinking, but I was wondering if it was Dawn with a baton in her mouth. And so I followed my father when he walked over to the door and opened it because I really wanted to see her.

"Mr. Munson," he said. "I thought we were going to meet you at the restaurant."

My mother walked out of the bathroom and Mr. Munson said, "Hello, Mrs. Schmidt. It's good to see you again."

"Where's my daughter?" my mother asked.

Mr. Munson was about my father's age. He was kind of tall and had brown hair and blue eyes like the superheroes on all the cartoons I watched. He was wearing jeans and a navy-and-red-plaid shirt. I was kind of surprised by his clothes, because all the detectives I'd seen on television wore dark suits, trench coats, and hats. Well, except for Starsky and Hutch, but they weren't regular detectives.

Anyway, Mr. Munson bent down and looked me in the eyes and said, "Hello, young man. You must be Don."

He stuck his hand out and I stood still and stared at him until my mother said, "Don, he wants to shake your hand. Stop being so weird and shake his hand."

I wasn't used to people putting their hands out to shake mine so I didn't know what to say. But then I remembered something that I'd heard Leon tell my father, so I put my hand out and said, "Nice to meet you."

Mr. Munson squeezed my hand and said, "Nice to meet you, young man."

He stood up and pulled some change out of his pocket and asked, "Can you do me a favor?"

I nodded my head and said, "Yes, sir."

"Could you run down to the lobby of the hotel and buy a soda for me and one for you? I'm really thirsty and I have to talk to your parents for a minute."

I knew that Mr. Munson was only trying to get me out of the room so he could talk to my parents about Dawn. I wanted to hear what he was going to say, so instead of going down to the lobby when I left the room, I stood out in the hall and left a small crack in the door. I heard Mr. Munson say, "The reason I decided to come up to your room to talk to you instead of meeting at the restaurant is because I thought that you'd prefer to hear this in private."

"What is it?" my mother asked. "Is she in a wheelchair and will never be able to dance again?"

Mr. Munson said, "No. She's fine physically and is very much able to dance."

"Oh, thank God," my mother said.

I imagined her grabbing her chest the way she did when she thought that maybe the television was broken when it was only unplugged or that Horse Island Food and Furniture was out of TV dinners when they had more in the stockroom freezer.

Anyway, Mr. Munson started talking again and told my parents that he'd seen a young woman named Liza Pinelli who he thought was Dawn. Two things made him believe that it was her. One was that Liza's face looked like the pictures of Dawn that Mr. Munson had seen. The second thing that made Mr. Munson think that Liza might be Dawn was because of the way she danced. He had seen her at Bourbon's Broadway, the same place where the woman's legs popped in and out of the curtain. That's why Mr. Munson had asked my parents to stay at the hotel we were in.

It was his first time at this place, and when Liza Pinelli came out onstage, Mr. Munson didn't notice how much she looked like Dawn. Even when she started twirling a baton, he didn't realize it was her. He said it wasn't until the next day when he remembered the picture my father had shown him of Dawn in a dance costume that Mr. Munson realized Ms. Pinelli could be Dawn.

When Mr. Munson got to that part, my father yelled, "You're saying my daughter's a stripper! I ought to punch you for coming in here and telling me this bull!"

Mr. Munson answered back real fast, "Calm down, Mr. Schmidt."

Then my mother yelled, "Don't calm down, Dick. Hit him. Make him bleed. He hasn't found Dawn. He's just trying to get more money out of us. Hit him!"

Mr. Munson yelled, "Mr. and Mrs. Schmidt, please calm down! Your daughter is not a stripper and I promise you that I'm not going to charge you anything. I hate it when I can't solve cases, and I have a son, and it would kill me if he was missing and I couldn't find him."

Mr. Munson started telling his story again and repeated that he didn't realize until the next day that the dancer could be Dawn. That's when he did a little more investigating and found out that Liza Pinelli's name used to be Jennifer Joy. He found out that that was a fake name too. He told my parents that Liza Pinelli had changed her name so many times that no one knew what her real name was. Before he investigated any more, Mr. Munson wanted my father to identify Dawn.

I didn't understand why Dawn was dancing in New Orleans if she'd been kidnapped. I thought maybe the kidnapper had let her go, or that she'd escaped, but I didn't know why she hadn't come home. I wanted to ask that question, but I didn't because I wasn't supposed to be listening, and I kind of hoped that my parents would ask him.

But they didn't. Instead, my father asked, "So if Dawn's not a stripper, why is she dancing at that place across the street?"

Mr. Munson said, "It's not a strip club. It's a theater where the girls sing and dance. I think we should go over to the club tonight, Mr. Schmidt, so you can see Liza Pinelli for yourself and figure out if she is your daughter, Dawn. But I'm telling you now, you have to remain calm. We don't want to scare her, if it is Dawn. Do you understand me?"

"I understand," my father said. "I'll remain calm."

Mr. Munson cleared his throat and then said, "Mrs. Schmidt, to avoid arousing suspicion, I think you should stay here. There usually aren't too many female clients at Bourbon's Broadway."

"Why not?" my mother asked.

"Because although it's not technically a strip club," Mr. Munson said, "some of the performances aren't meant for other women."

"What are you telling me, Mr. Munson?" my mother asked.

"Exactly what I just told you," Mr. Munson said. "Women don't go there to watch the show. The performers aren't the best singers or dancers. They're usually young, attractive women who wear revealing costumes and who men like to watch sing and dance."

"Are you saying my daughter is a bad dancer?" my mother asked.

"I'm not going to argue with you about this," Mr. Munson said. "If you want to go over there, then go. But I promise you, you'll have a much better chance of reuniting with your daughter if you do this my way."

Nobody talked for a couple of seconds and then Mr. Munson said, "Also, just be aware that legally there's nothing we can do, because she's over eighteen. Right now, the best we can do is get her to tell you why she left."

"Okay," my father said.

I wasn't sure what Mr. Munson meant about trying to find out why Dawn had left. My parents told me that she'd been kidnapped. And then I thought that maybe she hadn't been kidnapped and that my parents had lied to me.

I didn't have long to think about it, though, because I heard Mr. Munson coming toward the door. I ran down the hall a little, turned around, and then walked back toward our room until the door opened and Mr. Munson stepped out. He looked at me, and before he could ask me why I didn't have any sodas, I said, "The machine was broken. I'm sorry. Here's your money back."

Mr. Munson smiled and said, "Don't worry about it, young man. Keep that money, and when the machine starts working again, you buy yourself two sodas and drink mine for me."

I said, "Thank you, sir," and then he walked away from me to the elevator. I liked Mr. Munson and wanted to follow him out of that hotel. I wanted to follow him and have him tell me about the birds and the bees and throw a baseball to me and have him give me a cool nickname like that kid Beaver. I wanted to follow him so badly, and so I did follow him down the hall a little, and I don't even think I realized I was doing it until I heard my mother say, "Don! Where are you going? Get back over here."

Mr. Munson turned, looked at me, gave me a smile and a wink, and then stepped into the elevator. He waved at me, and just before the doors closed, I told him something I'd been wanting to tell someone all day. I told him, "Today's my birthday."

TWENTY

That night, my mother and I sat at the two windows and watched the club across the street. My mother shook her head and said, "I can't believe you did that. I just can't believe it."

I stared down at the door of Bourbon's Broadway where my father and Mr. Munson were inside waiting for a dancer that might be the sister I thought was dead. Since my mother wanted to keep an eye on the place and wanted me to help her, she told me that Dawn worked there.

"I just can't believe it," my mother said again. "Why didn't you tell us it was your birthday? Why did you shout it out to Mr. Munson? Now he's going to think you wanted a gift from him, and that's just selfish and rude."

I had woken that morning knowing it was my birthday, but I was too busy thinking about Dawn to really think about it too much. I'm not sure why I shouted that out to Mr. Munson. I guess I just wanted someone to wish me a "Happy Birthday." I even imagined Mr. Munson showing up at the hotel with a cake with candles and a present. My parents hadn't given me a present, and I didn't think I was going to get one, either, because my mother said, "I have a good mind to not let you pick out a gift this year. You really upset me, Don, and now is not the time to upset your mother."

She started to cry and I thought about how I had seen the mother on *Eight Is Enough* cry once and her son Nicholas had walked over to her and hugged her and told her that everything would be okay. I wondered if I should do the same. But then my mother stopped crying and said, "What's going on down there?"

I looked out the window and saw my father and Mr. Munson standing by the front door of Bourbon's Broadway. Then my father walked to the door of the hotel and disappeared. My mother stood up real fast and then pressed her hands to her face and said over and over again, "Oh my god. Oh my god. I wonder what happened. I wonder if it's her. I wonder if it's her."

A couple of minutes later, my father came into the room and before he could say anything, my mother asked, "What happened?"

My father looked at me and said, "Don, go downstairs and see if that soda machine is working."

I started to walk to the door, but my mother said, "It's okay, Dick. He knows. He was helping me watch the place."

My father breathed real deep and said, "Oh whatever, I don't even care anymore."

He sat down on the edge of the bed and I leaned against the window. My mother stayed standing.

"So what happened?" she asked.

"She wasn't there," my father said.

"She wasn't?" my mother asked. "Well, start from the beginning and tell me everything that happened after you and Mr. Munson left here."

"I'm not really in the mood, Janice," my father said.

"I don't care if you're in the mood or not," my mother said. "Tell me."

My father took a deep breath and said, "Okay. As you know, I met Mr. Munson in the hotel lobby at ten p.m., and then we walked across to the club and sat at a table and had some drinks. A few girls danced and sang, and then the host guy called out a special performance by Liza Pinelli."

My mother stopped him and asked, "What song was playing?"

"What?" he asked.

"The song. What song was playing?"

My father shook his head and said, "I don't know. Some song about school being out for summer. I think it was Alice Cooper."

My mother scrunched her face up like she'd just eaten something sour and said, "I hate that song."

My father closed his eyes and said, "That's not

important, Janice," and my mother said, "Don't snap at me."

My father opened his eyes, stood up, and said, "An Oriental girl walked onstage," and then he walked out of the room and slammed the door.

My mother and I stood and watched the door for about ten seconds and then my mother said, "Oriental. Dawn's not Oriental. What does that even mean? An Oriental girl walked out onstage. Why did Mr. Munson think Dawn was Oriental?"

After my mother said it out loud again, I kind of figured that it was the wrong girl. I still wasn't positive, though, and I was hoping that my father would come back and tell us what he meant before I had to go to sleep. He didn't, though, and after about an hour, my mother told me to go to bed.

I changed into my pajamas and then got under the blanket of one of the two double beds in the room. I couldn't fall asleep, though, because I wasn't tired, and my mother was walking all over the room. I kept my eyes closed so my mother would think I was sleeping. It must have worked, because after a while I heard her dialing the phone and then whisper, "Hey, it's me. Can you talk?"

I didn't know who she was talking to, but I knew that the person was with a "she," because my mother asked, "Where is she?" and then she asked, "Do you think the phone woke her?"

Then I heard her say, "He's out," and then, "He's asleep."

I started to realize that she was probably talking to R. B., even though she didn't say "R. B." or a name with the initials R. B. Anyway, she told that person about everything that had happened and then said, "I miss you," and hung up the phone and went to the bathroom.

I wondered if my father knew about R. B., or if my father had his own R. B. If he did, it probably wouldn't be a man, and she probably wouldn't have the initials R. B.

Anyway, then I heard a door open. At first I thought it was my mother coming out of the bathroom, but then I heard a toilet flush and another door open and my mother say, "Come here."

The bathroom door shut, and even though it was closed, I could hear my mother screaming, "How dare you storm out of the room like some hysterical chicken with its head cut off!"

My father started crying and said, "Janice! Janice! I'm so sorry. It's just so much to take. Please forgive me. Please, Janice. Forgive me."

My mother lowered her voice and said, "You make me so mad sometimes, Dick. Come here."

I heard a slapping sound like she was patting his back. "Everything is going to turn out okay," she told him. "We're going to find her."

"We need to tell him," my father said.

"Not yet," my mother said. "Let's see if we can find her first. I want her to tell him."

I didn't know what my parents were talking about. I didn't know if I was the "him" that my father wanted to tell something to. I figured that I probably was, but I didn't want to know what he wanted to tell me. It scared me because I thought it was something bad. Why else would my mother not want to tell me? I thought maybe I was sick and was going to die soon. But I didn't understand why my mother wanted Dawn to tell me. Even after my parents came out of the bathroom, turned off the lights, and went to bed, I tried to think about what it was they weren't telling me. I found out later, but it wasn't my father who told me. It was Dawn.

TWENTY-ONE

The next morning we all went to breakfast at a restaurant and my father started to tell my mother and me what had happened after the Oriental girl walked out onstage.

Before he could tell us, though, my mother asked, "What was she wearing?"

"Who?" my father asked.

"The Oriental girl. What was she wearing?"

My father put down his cup of coffee and leaned back and asked, "What? Why?"

My mother leaned back too and said, "I just want to know, Dick."

My father took a breath and said, "I don't know. I think a black sequined leotard, but I'm not sure because it was dark."

"A black sequined leotard?" my mother said. "I hope Dawn doesn't wear that. She never looked good in black."

"Anyway," my father said, "after the announcer called out Liza Pinelli's name, the Oriental girl walked out. So I looked at Mr. Munson and asked him what he was trying to pull because there was no way he could have mistaken Dawn for an Oriental girl. Well, then he told me that the Oriental girl wasn't Liza Pinelli, or at least not the Liza Pinelli he had seen and spoken to."

Then my mother asked, "So why did the Oriental girl say she was Liza Pinelli?"

My father popped the lid off of a bottle of aspirin and then said, "Well, Mr. Munson spoke to one of the dancers and she said that Liza Pinelli was sick but no one had told the host, so he was just reading off of the list he used every night. So we're gonna go back tonight to see if Liza Pinelli is working. I already called into work to let them know that I won't be in for a couple of days. I told them there was a family emergency."

That night, my mother and I were in the same positions by the window as we were the night before, but we were wearing different clothes, and my mother wasn't yelling at me about telling Mr. Munson it was my birthday. My mother was looking out of the window at the people going into Bourbon's Broadway.

"You know," she told me. "I bet it was that Oriental girl who picked that Alice Cooper song. Dawn would never pick a song like that. I think she'd dance to something by the Jackson 5 or the Bee Gees."

I told her, "You're probably right."

I don't know why I told her that because I didn't

really know what song Dawn would dance to. I guess I just told her that because I knew she liked it when I agreed with her.

"Oh, I know I'm right," she said. "I know my little girl and she would not dance to some song by Alice Cooper."

Then she turned and looked at me for a second, smiled, and said, "But thank you for your vote of confidence," and then she turned her head and looked out the window again and said, "Or maybe a song by Elvis, but nothing by Alice Cooper."

Before I could say anything else my mother screamed, "Oh my god!"

I looked out the window at the front door of the theater and saw two big guys push out my father and Mr. Munson. My mother yelled, "Oh my god! What do you think happened?"

My father started shouting and both my mother and I opened the windows and heard my father yell, "It was her! It was my daughter and she didn't even want to see me!"

My heart jumped a little because of what my father had said. First I was excited because it meant that Dawn was alive and not just a picture on the wall or someone my mother talked about. But then I was confused because I didn't understand why she didn't want to see my father. Before I could think about that too much, though, my mother screamed, "Oh my god, my baby's alive!"

She ran out of the room and in about two minutes she was on the street yelling, "Where is she? Where's Dawn?"

Mr. Munson talked to my mother while my father walked up and down the street throwing his hands in the air and cursing. I couldn't hear exactly what Mr. Munson was saying because of all the people in the street. I found out later what had happened, though, from my mother.

You see, my father and Mr. Munson were at the same table as the night before waiting for Liza Pinelli to come out and dance. When she did, my father recognized her right away and jumped up from his table and ran toward the stage screaming Dawn's name. Mr. Munson ran after my father to stop him, but before either one of them could get near the stage, Dawn ran off, and then two bouncers grabbed them and threw them out on the street.

That's when my mother ran down to the street and screamed, "Where is she? Where's Dawn?"

Mr. Munson grabbed my parents by their arms and then walked a little ways up the street. I could hear him say something about a back door, and then he made a hand motion like someone would give to a dog to stay, and then he walked off.

My parents stood in the street staring at the front door of Bourbon's Broadway for over an hour. They spoke a little to each other, but I couldn't hear what they were saying. After a while, I got bored and started wondering what Mr. Munson was doing. I guessed that he had gone to look for a back door on another street. It had been over an hour since he'd left my parents and I was beginning to wonder if he needed something to drink or just someone to talk to. It made me a little sad to think that he was alone and thirsty, so I decided that I should go and find him.

I figured my parents would probably be out on the street for a couple more hours and that I could see Mr. Munson and get back to the room before they did. So I grabbed the extra room key and a map and went through the back door of the hotel to a street named Dauphine.

I looked at the map and then headed over to the street behind Bourbon, which was Royal and where I figured the back door of the club would be. When I got there, I was a little surprised because the street was so different from Bourbon. There weren't any bars or restaurants, and there weren't that many people walking around.

I saw Mr. Munson walking back and forth, smoking a cigarette, but I didn't walk up to him. Instead, I stood at the end of the street behind a big trash can and watched him. After a few minutes, a door opened and a girl walked out. It was an Oriental girl and I figured she was probably the same one my father had talked about. Mr. Munson started talking to her, but I couldn't hear what he was saying and after only a couple of minutes, the girl walked away from him and toward me.

Mr. Munson threw down his cigarette and walked in the opposite direction and I waited behind the trash can to get a closer look at the girl. She was wearing high heels, jeans, and a black tank top, and when she passed by the trash can, she turned her head and saw me and said, "Oh my god. What are you doing out here at this time of night? It's, like, one in the morning."

I didn't say anything and just looked at her.

Then she asked me, "Did the cat get your tongue? Are you lost?"

"Dawn's my sister," I said.

"What?" she asked, and I told her, "I mean, Liza Pinelli is my sister."

"Really?" she asked. "Well, I hate to tell you this, but Liza left. Did she know you were here?"

I shook my head and then she said, "Well, she left because some crazy man tried to attack her tonight."

At first I wondered why she didn't speak with an accent like the Oriental people on TV and then I began to realize that she would tell me whatever I wanted to know because I was a kid and she didn't know that the crazy man was my father.

So I asked her, "Do you know where Liza is?"

The girl kind of frowned and said, "I know where she lives, but the thing is, she snuck out of the theater about an hour ago and said she needed to get out of town right away. I doubt she's still in New Orleans. She said she had some friends in Baton Rouge who she was going to stay with for a while. She used to live there, you know. I think she worked at Bill's Broadway. It's the same guy who owns Bourbon's Broadway. His name is Bill."

Then the girl made a funny face and said, "Oh, you're so cute. What's your name?"

I told her "Don" and she said, "Nice to meet you, Don. I'm Stephanie. You know, Don, it isn't safe to be running around New Orleans this time of night. Where are you staying?"

I pointed down the street and said, "At a hotel around the corner."

She grabbed my hand and said, "Let me walk you there."

When we got to the back door of the hotel I asked her, "Why don't you talk like the Oriental girls on television?"

She smiled and said, "First of all, young man, food and rugs are Oriental. People are Asian. Second of all, I'm from Hawaii."

TWENTY-TWO

My parents and I stayed in New Orleans for a couple more days so they could look for Dawn. Mr. Munson had to go back to Texarkana but said he had some detective friends in New Orleans and that he'd ask them to keep an eye out for Dawn. My father didn't go back to Bourbon's Broadway because they wouldn't let him in. So instead, he walked or drove around the city while my mother watched the back door of Bourbon's Broadway and I watched the front.

I didn't tell my parents about meeting Stephanie, the Hawaiian girl, because I thought they might be mad at me for leaving the hotel room. And even though I thought Stephanie was telling the truth and Dawn had left New Orleans, I guess part of me wanted her to still be there and I thought that if we looked for her, she would still be there and that we'd find her.

But we didn't find Dawn and so we packed up the car and drove back to Horse Island and on the car ride is when my mother stabbed me. You see, she was sitting in the front seat and filing her nails and she asked me to get some nail polish out of her bag in the backseat. I leaned forward and asked, "Which bag is it in?"

My mother said, "In the makeup case."

Then she pointed at it with the nail file and when she did, she hit me in the face.

I yelled, "Ow!" and then grabbed my face and then both my parents looked back at me.

"What's wrong?" my father asked and so I told him, "Mother stuck me with the nail file."

"No, I didn't," she said.

Then my father asked, "Are you okay, Don?" and I told him, "I guess so."

Then my mother said, "I didn't do it on purpose."

My father didn't answer her or even look at her. Instead he drove into the parking lot of a convenience store.

"What are you doing?" my mother asked him.

"You just stabbed Don," he said. "I'm stopping so I can see if he's okay."

"Stop saying that," she said. "I didn't stab him!"

My father turned and looked at me and said, "Let me see. Move your hand."

So I moved my hand and my father said, "It looks like she broke some skin."

"Stop saying that!" my mother yelled. "Stop saying that I hurt him!"

My father and I both jumped back a little because

she'd yelled really loud. We looked at her for a couple of seconds and then my father said, "Okay. But would you mind running into the store to see if they have some bandages and hydrogen peroxide?"

"Oh, Jesus, Dick," my mother told him. "I think you're making too much of this. It's just a scratch. Kids get scratches all the time. It's what they do. You don't see other parents rushing them to emergency rooms."

"Janice!" my father said. "Please! I'm not in the mood."

My mother stared at my father for a couple of seconds and then made a fist with the nail file in it. She picked it up real slow and then screamed, "Fine!"

She got out of the car and slammed the door and walked into the store. Then my father turned and looked at me.

"I'm sorry," he said.

"That's okay," I told him. "It's not your fault."

My father didn't say anything. He just stared at me for, like, ten seconds and then turned back around and looked out the front window. Then he asked, "So how are your chickens?"

My father never asked me about the chickens and so it took a couple of seconds before I knew what he was asking. At first I thought he said, "How are your children?" but then I thought that wouldn't make sense at all. And even though it didn't make sense to me that he was asking me how my chickens were doing, it made a lot more sense than him asking me how my children were doing. So I was about to tell him all kinds of stuff about my chickens, but then my mother got back in the car.

She turned around and looked at me and said, "I'm sorry I hurt you, Don. But I didn't do it on purpose."

Then she turned back around and looked out of the window and said, "I'm really sorry. And I'm sorry I forgot your birthday."

My father looked at her for a couple of seconds like he didn't know who she was. Then she looked at him and asked, "Why are you staring at me?"

"Sorry," my father said.

Then he took the bag from my mother, opened it up, and pulled out a bottle of hydrogen peroxide, some cotton balls, and a bandage and told me to lean forward. He dipped a cotton ball in some hydrogen peroxide and then wiped the cut on my face with it.

"Does it sting?" he asked me.

"Just a little," I told him.

He smiled at me and then put a bandage on the cut. When he was finished, he rubbed the top of my head and turned around real fast. Then he started up the car and turned back onto the road.

I thought that both my parents were acting really weird, but I figured it was because they were worried about Dawn. I couldn't believe that my mother told me she was sorry that she forgot my birthday. She never really apologized for anything and if she did, it never sounded like she meant it. But I really think she did mean it that time. I don't know why my father asked me about my chickens. He never asked me about them. I wondered if my parents were going to say other weird stuff to me on the way home. But they didn't. They didn't talk at all the whole way home and that was almost two hours!

When we did get home, they didn't talk, either. They just unloaded the car and went into the house. My father went to the living room and turned on the TV and my mother went into her room.

Since they weren't going to talk and I missed my chickens, I went out to the yard to see them. Before I even walked through the gate, I felt like smiling and talking and I wanted to pick one of them up and squeeze it real tight. But not too tight because that might have killed it or hurt its wings.

Anyway, when I walked through the gate, most of the chickens didn't move. They just pecked at the ground or sat and stared straight ahead. KC was the only one that noticed me and she ran right up to me and danced around.

I asked her, "Did you miss me?"

She didn't say anything, but I imagined that she said, "Yes, my friend. I did!"

I told her and Stanley everything that happened and how we found Dawn and then lost her and that she'd gone to Baton Rouge and that my mother had stabbed me and my father had asked me about the chickens.

"I'm sorry you lost Dawn," Stanley told me. "But I'm still here."

"Yeah," I told him. "You're still here. And so are the chickens."

But even though they were still there, I kind of wanted Dawn to be there too because she was a real person and she could speak back to me and I wouldn't have to make up what she said to me. My parents were real people but they had never really spoken to me that much, and after the trip to New Orleans, they spoke even less.

That evening, when I went into the house for dinner, there was a note on the table from my mother. It said, "Don, choose whatever TV dinner you want and heat it up. I'm eating in my room tonight and your father isn't hungry."

I thought the note was kind of weird for a few reasons. One is because my mother never ate in her room. And my father was always hungry so that didn't make any sense. But the thing that was the weirdest is that my mother had written me a note to let me know that she was in her room and that my father wasn't hungry. She never left me notes unless she wanted me to do something or if I'd done something wrong. And those notes always had an exclamation point after my name. But this one only had a comma!

Even though I thought that note was weird, I found another one a couple of minutes later that was even weirder. It was taped to my bedroom door and was from my father. It said, "Son, I borrowed your bicycle."

My father never called me "Son" and he never borrowed my bicycle. I didn't know that either one of my parents knew how to ride a bike. I'd never seen them ride one and I didn't know if bicycles had even been invented when they were kids.

They must have been, though, because later that night, after I heard my father come home, I went to check on my bicycle and it wasn't broken. I had been worried that my father might wreck my bike, but after I saw that it was okay, I got more worried that my parents were going crazy and I figured it was because of Dawn. I would be sad too if one my chickens ran away and I didn't know where it went or why it left.

So I was lying in bed thinking about this when it hit me. On TV when someone was kidnapped, someone else usually asked for money. But nobody had asked my parents for money. At least I didn't think anyone had. So then I thought maybe my parents just forgot to tell me that part. But I didn't understand why Dawn didn't come home after she escaped from the man who kidnapped her. Then I remembered one time on *The Jeffersons* when Weezy got hit on the head and forgot everything. The doctor said that she had amnesia. She didn't even know George or Florence or Mr. Bentley. I thought that maybe that had happened to Dawn and that's why she thought Father was a crazy man.

But then I thought that maybe Dawn wasn't

kidnapped at all. Maybe she ran away and that's why nobody asked my parents for money and that's why she didn't want to see my father. I thought that maybe Dawn ran away because she didn't like living in Shreveport or with my parents or maybe she owed some bookies a lot of money because she'd lost a big bet on horses and so she had to get out of town or they'd break both her legs. I'd seen people on TV run away because of that.

Anyway, it was kind of driving me crazy that I didn't know if Dawn really was kidnapped or if she'd run away. I knew I had to find out the truth or that I'd start acting crazy like my parents and leaving notes and not talking. And so I figured that the only way I could know if Dawn had run away and or was kidnapped was if I found her and asked her.

TWENTY-THREE

For the next couple of weeks after we got back from New Orleans, my parents still acted kind of weird. My father came home late at night and my mother ate dinner in her room. A lot of times I would eat dinner in front of the TV by myself, which was kind of cool because I could watch anything I wanted. But it also got kind of boring because my mother wasn't there talking.

Sometimes my mother wasn't home when I'd get back from school. But she'd always leave a note and it would say something like, "Don, I'm out running an errand. Hope you had a nice day at school. If I'm not home and you get hungry, there are TV dinners in the freezer."

When I did see her in the house, she didn't say much. She'd just smile at me and then make this sad-looking face and walk away. The couple of times I saw my father, he did the same thing. It was like they were both sad but they didn't want me to know.

I had thought and thought real hard about how to get to Baton Rouge to find Dawn, but I couldn't think of anything. It was too far away to ride my bike and there wasn't a bus in Horse Island that went to Baton Rouge and I couldn't hitchhike because I saw a scary movie on TV about a girl who hitchhiked and who disappeared. I don't know if they found her because I turned it off before it was over.

But then one day at school, without even trying, I found a way to get to Baton Rouge. It happened when I was walking out of the building to go home and the school nurse stopped me. Her name was Nancy and we called her Nurse Nancy and she wore a white uniform like the nurses on TV.

"Don," she said. "Guess what!"

"What?" I asked.

"This year, for the first time in a long time, the 4-H club is going to Baton Rouge for the chicken-judging contest—because of you, Don. Since you know so much about chickens, we decided that we would be crazy not to go."

"Oh," I said. "But I'm not in 4-H."

"Well," Nurse Nancy said. "You'll have to join."

"Do I need my parents' permission to join?" I asked.

"No," she said. "But you'll need their permission to go to Baton Rouge, of course."

I was real excited when she told me that about the chicken-judging contest in Baton Rouge because it was a lot bigger than the one at the Dairy Festival. I figured that if I won, I'd become popular again and maybe even more popular than when I'd won the Horse Island competition. Then girls would start crying when I wouldn't date them and boys would beat each other up to sit next to me at lunch. Then I realized the best part about going to Baton Rouge was that I could look for Dawn.

I figured that if I found her, my parents would be so happy and maybe even have a party for me, and I could invite everyone in the class. I was sure I could find Dawn and get her to come home if I told her my plan of the two of us traveling to different parish fairs, and she could compete in the dance contests and I could judge chickens, and we'd become known all over the world as the brother and sister "Festival Dynamic Duo."

I was so excited about the contest and looking for Dawn that I forgot something. I didn't know if my parents were going to let me go.

So for the next two weeks, when I wasn't studying for the contest, I was trying to think of a way to ask my parents. I thought about just asking them, but like I told you, since we'd come back from New Orleans, they didn't speak that much and walked around looking really sad and tired.

Then the Saturday before the contest, when I was out collecting eggs, my mother walked outside and up to the fence of the chicken yard.

"Don," she said. "Can you come with me to do the shopping at Horse Island Food and Furniture?"

Since we'd gotten back from New Orleans, she had

been going shopping by herself, so I was a little surprised that she'd asked me, but glad that she had. I figured that it meant she was starting to be happy again.

While we were driving to Horse Island Food and
Furniture, I got an idea. I decided I would ask her if I
could go to the chicken-judging contest when we were
in the store because she always seemed like she was
happier there than when she was at home. I guess she
liked shopping or something.

I figured that it would be better if I waited for her
to talk to me before I asked her just so she didn't yell
at me, "Don! Don't speak to adults unless you're spoken to!"

I didn't think she'd do that, because like I said, she
seemed a lot different since we'd gotten back from
New Orleans. But I didn't want to take any chances.

I figured it would be easy to get her to talk to me
because she'd always tell me stuff when we were in
the store, like, "Go get a cart," or, "We need some toilet
paper," or, "It's hot in here."

So when we walked into the store, I was all ready
for my mother to tell me to get a cart, so I could ask
my question. But right when she pointed at them and
opened her mouth, Mr. Bufford walked up with a cart
and said, "Here you go, ma'am."

My mother smiled real big and said, "Thank you."

He smiled back and said, "You're welcome."

My mother just stood there for a few seconds looking at Mr. Bufford and smiling. It was the most I'd seen

her smile in a long time. I thought it might be a good time to ask her if I could go to the chicken-judging contest, but then one of the cashiers said, "Mr. Bufford, your wife is on the phone."

When Mr. Bufford walked away, my mother stopped smiling and started to look sad again. But then her face kind of changed from sad to mad and she turned and looked at me and said, "Let's go, Don."

She pushed the cart real fast to the back of the store where all the food was, and I followed behind. We walked through the furniture section, and my mother stopped at a sofa that was the same orangey color as her pantsuit. She looked at the sofa, and then at her jacket sleeve, and then back at the sofa, and let out a noise that sounded like *urrr*.

Then she took off again until we got to the frozen food section. My mother put a bunch of dinners in her cart and then looked at her shopping list. I'd seen toilet paper on the list and I knew that she'd ask me to go and get it because one time somebody had spilled some juice and she'd slipped and fallen and refused to go down that aisle ever again. I was wondering if I should ask her about the chicken-judging contest when she asked me to go and get the toilet paper.

But then someone said, "Hello," and we both stopped thinking about toilet paper.

"Hello, hello," I heard again.

I turned and saw Leon's mother push her cart up to my mother and me. My mother smiled a little but not a whole lot, which surprised me, because she needed a perm and I figured she would be excited to see Mrs. Leonard.

"Where have you been hiding yourself, Janice?" Mrs. Leonard asked.

"I've just been busy," my mother answered.

"I know how that is," Mrs. Leonard said. "Hey, did you hear about Betty Bufford? She has chicken pox. Both she and her daughter are covered from head to toe in a rash. It's a shame because they are both going away next weekend to Betty's mother's house in Mississippi. They'll be fine by then, but they'll be covered in spots."

My mother's eyes opened up a little, and she didn't look as sad and mad as she had right before. She smiled a little and said, "Oh, really?"

Then Mrs. Leonard said, "If I didn't know any better, Janice, I'd say you look kind of happy about it."

My mother stopped smiling and said, "No, oh no. I'm not happy about it at all. I'm just a little surprised and sometimes when I'm surprised, it looks like I'm smiling."

Mrs. Leonard said, "Oh, well, that makes sense."

"So, do they know how long she's going to be sick?" my mother asked. "Is the rash going to leave scars?"

Mrs. Leonard said she didn't know, and then said, "Well, if you'll excuse me, I have to go back and change this toilet paper. I got all the way to the checkout and realized that I picked up the wrong one. Lyle likes the kind that smells."

My mother looked at the toilet paper and said, "Well, isn't that a coincidence. That's the brand I use, and we need toilet paper. Do you mind if I take this one?"

Mrs. Leonard said, "No, not at all."

She handed the package of toilet paper to my mother and then said, "You guys have a nice weekend."

She started to push her cart away, but then turned and said, "Janice, I have a wonderful idea. Since the boys will be away next weekend, why don't you and Dick come over to my place for dinner and board games?"

My mother looked at Mrs. Leonard like she didn't understand the question, but I know she must have because she said, "I'm afraid Dick is going to be out of town for a convention next week, so we won't be able to make it."

Then Mrs. Leonard said, "Oh, well, you don't want to be all alone in that big house, so why don't you come over anyway?"

My mother looked at me like she'd just asked me a question and was waiting for an answer. I figured she was wondering what Mrs. Leonard was talking about, but since she hadn't really asked me anything, and I didn't like her staring at me, I bent down and untied one of my shoes and retied it.

My mother watched me do it and then asked Mrs. Leonard, "What do you mean that the boys will be away next weekend?"

"Have you forgotten?" Mrs. Leonard said. "They're going away to the chicken-judging contest in Baton Rouge."

"What chicken-judging contest?" my mother asked.

"Don," Mrs. Leonard said. "Didn't you tell your mother about the contest?"

I didn't know what to say. I didn't know if it was a good thing that Mrs. Leonard had brought up the chicken-judging contest or not. I had the chance to ask if I could go, but I kind of felt like I'd been caught doing something wrong. I thought about this for a couple of seconds and realized that I hadn't done anything wrong, so I stood up from the ground.

"Not yet," I said.

Then Mr. Bufford walked up to us and said, "It's such a pleasure to know that two of the most beautiful women in Horse Island shop at my store."

Mrs. Leonard laughed out loud and said, "Oh, Bobby!"

My mother smiled a little and then kind of looked off into space like she was thinking about something. She made that face like those people on TV make when they're thinking about something and a lightbulb pops above their head like they just got an idea. But no lightbulb appeared above her head.

"It's true," Mr. Bufford said.

"Oh, I know." Mrs. Leonard laughed.

Mr. Bufford laughed too and then said, "Let me know if you ladies need anything."

Then he walked away and Mrs. Leonard said, "He's such a card."

My mother smiled a little and turned to me and asked, "So you're going to this contest next weekend in Baton Rouge?"

"Can I?" I asked.

"Yes," she said. "I think that's a great idea."

"Well," Mrs. Leonard said. "It's settled. You'll come over to our house."

My mother smiled and said, "You know, Lucy, thank you so much for the offer, but to tell you the truth, I don't think I've ever been alone in that house for an entire weekend, and I think I'll just stay in and enjoy the peace and quiet."

Mrs. Leonard nodded her head up and down and said, "Well, I can certainly understand where you're coming from. To tell *you* the truth, I'm a little jealous. I never have a second to myself. But if you get a little lonely, give me a call."

My mother said, "I definitely will. Have a great day, Lucy," and then Mrs. Leonard turned around and pushed her cart down the aisle.

My mother walked over to the door of the refrigerator with frozen sausages and looked at her hair. I didn't know why my mother went from sad to mad to glad, but I didn't care because she was going to let me go to the chicken-judging contest. I started talking to Stanley in my head and told him how great it was that we'd be able to go to Baton Rouge and find Dawn, and he told me, "I know. It's going to be great. We really need to thank Mother for letting us go."

I said, "Okay. I'll go thank her right now," and then Stanley told me, "Don't tell her thank you. Tell her something else, like how beautiful she is."

I had never thought to tell my mother she was beautiful, but it sounded like a good idea. So when she said, "I should get my hair permed soon," I said, "You don't need to perm your hair because you're beautiful."

My mother turned and looked at me and her face turned red the way it did the first time she met Mr. Bufford.

"What?" she asked.

"You don't need to perm your hair," I told her.

"No," she said. "The part about me being beautiful."

"You don't need to perm your hair because you're beautiful," I told her.

My mother put her hand on her chest and said, "Oh my god, Don, that's the nicest thing you've ever said to me."

Then she started to cry and dug around in her purse and pulled out a tissue and wiped her eyes.

"I'm sorry," I told her. "I didn't mean to make you cry."

She looked at me and smiled and said, "Oh, Don, thank you. Thank you for appreciating how much work I do to make myself look this good every day. It means a lot."

"Okay," I said.

Then my mother pushed the cart toward the front of Horse Island Food and Furniture and started talking the way she had before the trip to New Orleans. She talked about people in the community, stuff she'd read in the paper, and how she was excited about being alone the next weekend.

Then she stopped walking and asked me, "You ever notice how all the people in this town have the same letter for their first and last name? You know, like Taylor Touchet, Jessica Jaubert, Julia Jay. I can understand naming your kids with the same letters, but even the married women have the same first letter of their first name as the first letter of their husband's last name. Not every one of them, but most of them."

Stanley told me to answer her and so I did. I said, "Maybe it's a law here that women can only marry men whose last name has the same first letter of their first name."

My mother laughed and said, "That's pretty funny, Don."

Then I said, "Maybe you and Father are breaking the law and you'll have to get a divorce or go to jail."

My mother laughed harder and pulled a tissue out of her purse again and wiped her eyes and said, "Oh, that was funny, Don. That's exactly what I needed. A good laugh, and you gave me one. You know what, I don't think we ever got you a gift for your birthday. What do you say after we drop these groceries off at home, we go over to Horse Island Shoes and Toys and pick something out for you?"

That afternoon my mother and I went shopping, and she bought me a book about a little boy who grew up on a chicken farm and sheets with chickens on them. Then my mother told me that we needed to buy me some new summer clothes.

I couldn't believe how happy my mother was just because I had told her she was beautiful and had told her a joke. I liked it and wished I had told her she was beautiful a long time ago. The whole day was great, but then it got really weird during dinner that night.

My father was home because it was Saturday and my mother said she was going to eat with us instead of in her room that night. So my father and I sat in front of the television set and waited for my mother to cook us dinner. It was the first time my father and I had been alone together since New Orleans.

"How has school been?" he asked me.

"Okay," I told him.

I wasn't sure why he was asking me that, but like I said, he'd been acting weird since New Orleans.

"And your chickens?" he asked.

"They're good. Some of them are getting old and don't really lay that many eggs anymore, but they still have good feathers."

Then my mother walked into the living room carrying the three dinners on a tray. I took mine, and my father took his, and then my mother put hers on her television tray. She didn't sit down in her love seat like she usually did, though. Instead, she moved her television tray by me and then sat next to me on the sofa. Both my father and I looked at her until she asked, "Why are you staring at me?"

My father raised his eyebrows and said, "I've never seen you sit on the sofa for dinner."

My mother picked up her knife and fork and said, "I just thought it would be nice for a change. Besides, Don and I spent a wonderful afternoon together and I want to be close to him. He said the funniest thing. Tell him what you said, Don."

Before I could speak, my mother said, "You know. What you said about women in this town only marrying men whose last name begins with the same letter as their first name and that your father and I must be breaking the law and might have to get a divorce. Tell him."

I opened my mouth, but then my mother said, "Never mind, I'll tell him. Dick, Don said—"

My father cut her off and said, "I heard what he said," and then he turned his head back to the television.

My mother took a bite of her food and said, "Don't you think it's funny what he said about you and I breaking the law and that they may make us get a divorce? Wouldn't that be funny?"

Then my father said, "That would be hilarious," and he turned the volume up on the television.

My mother looked at me and said, "Your father has no sense of humor. Not like my little Donny here."

She leaned over and kissed me on the forehead. It was the first time I ever remembered her giving me a kiss. I thought I might be dreaming, but then I looked in the mirror that was on the wall and I could see a pair of red lips on my face.

TWENTY-FOUR

I couldn't really sleep the night before we left to go to the chicken-judging contest in Baton Rouge because I kept thinking about Dawn and the contest. I probably would have thought about this until the morning if I hadn't heard a noise in our living room around one in the morning. I thought it was strange that one of my parents would be up, but I figured that they were in the bathroom or something. I heard a noise again, though, so I got up and walked over to my door and opened it a little. My parents' door was closed and I could see a light on in the living room, so I walked down the hall and took a look.

My father was standing by the bookcase and looking at one of his accounting books. He was in his white pajamas and slippers, and in the light, he looked kind of like a ghost. He put the book back on the shelf and then took off his glasses and rubbed his face with his hands a bunch of times. Then he put his glasses back on and took a deep breath.

All of a sudden, a dog barked, which was really weird because we didn't have a dog. My father looked out of the living room window for a couple of seconds and then he walked toward the kitchen. I stepped back into the hallway and then I heard the kitchen door that led outside open and close.

I went into my room and looked out of my window and I could see his white pajamas standing on the steps outside the kitchen door. He was holding something in his hand like a pot or a pan and was shaking it.

And he was yelling, "Get out of here, dog! Go home!"

I didn't see the dog, so I don't know who it belonged to. I figured it was probably a stray and that I should get up early the next morning and make sure there weren't any holes around the fence of the chicken yard that he could get into. He'd really scared my chickens and they were clucking and running all over the yard.

My father stood on the steps for a couple of seconds and then walked up to the gate of the yard, opened it, and went in. This freaked me out a little because he never went into the chicken yard anymore and I didn't know if he was going to hurt them. I didn't know why he would, but I didn't know why he'd been doing a lot of the stuff he'd been doing since we got back from

New Orleans. So I figured that I had better go and make sure that he wasn't hurting my chickens.

When I got to the yard, I heard a bunch of the chickens clucking and running out of the coop. I walked up to the side of the coop and looked through a small hole in the wall and saw my father standing there. He was holding a chicken and she was moving and clucking and I thought about running into the coop and yelling, "Let go of my chicken!"

But then my father said, "Shhhhh. It's going to be okay."

The chicken calmed down and my father walked over to a bucket and turned it upside down and sat on it. He petted the chicken for a couple of minutes and then started talking.

He said, "You know, you have a good life, chicken. All you do is sit around all day and lay eggs. You don't have to worry about getting married or having children or finding the perfect job."

The chicken clucked a little like she understood and my father laughed and then said, "I see why Don likes you so much. You're a good listener. I wish I'd known you before I made the biggest mistake of my life. You could have talked me out of it."

My father stopped talking for a couple of minutes and I tried to think about what the biggest mistake of his life could be. I knew he was sad that he wasn't an accountant but wasn't sure if that's what he was talking about. Before I could think of anything else that might be the biggest mistake of his life, my father started talking again.

He said, "At the time, it seemed like the right thing. There was a baby coming, so I had to marry her. But now my daughter's gone and my wife is being unfaithful."

Then my father closed his eyes and said, "I could have been an accountant. I could have married a woman I loved. I could have been happy. But I messed up and not only have I ruined my life, I've also ruined the boy's life. He's a good kid and has had to put up with our misery his whole life. Something has to change."

My father started shaking his head and asked, "What am I going to do, chicken? What am I going to do?"

I felt really sad for my father because he looked like he was about to cry. I kind of wanted to go up to him and hug him, but before I could, he kissed the chicken on the top of the head, put it back on the ground, and said, "Good-bye, my friend," and then went back into the house.

After I snuck back into my room, I lay in my bed thinking about all the stuff my father had said. I figured that my father had married my mother because of Dawn, and because they got married, he had to drop out of accounting school and my mother couldn't go to Vegas to be a dancer. And I figured that I was the boy he was talking about. So then it made sense to me why my father was asking me questions about my chickens and school. It was because he was sorry because he thought he'd made me miserable.

When I fell asleep, I dreamed that my father kicked down a hotel room door. My mother was in the room and she was wearing a sheet. She screamed and then some man ran into the bathroom. My father walked up to that door and started kicking, and right when it flew open, I woke up. I knew it was a dream, but I really wanted to know who was in that bathroom. I found out the next day.

TWENTY-FIVE

The chicken-judging contest was at Louisiana State University on a Saturday, but a bus was going to take all the 4-H kids from the parking lot of Horse Island Elementary the Friday afternoon before. My mother drove me there and as soon as she parked, she got out and went to speak to some of the other parents who were dropping off kids.

Leon and his dad were standing in front of the bus and Mr. Leonard told Leon, "I know you ain't no genius, boy, but it would do me proud if you brought us home a trophy."

Leon didn't say anything, but Mr. Leonard saw me and said, "Hey, Don. If you have some time, would you mind teaching Leon here a few things about history? I thought he only had a problem with adding and subtracting, but the boy didn't even know that Abraham Lincoln was the first president of the United States."

I didn't tell Mr. Leonard that George Washington

was the first president of the United States because my mother had told me never to correct adults. I just put my head down and then Leon asked his dad, "Can I get on the bus now?"

Mr. Leonard said, "You sure are in a hurry to get out of here."

"I just want to get a good seat. That's all," Leon told him.

"Well, go ahead then," Mr. Leonard said. "I'll see you and your trophy on Sunday."

Leon got on the bus and walked to the back and didn't look out until Mr. Leonard had walked away. My mother came over to me and asked me, "Now, you're not going to be back until Sunday afternoon around five, right?"

I said, "Yes, ma'am," and then I heard, "Don't come back unless you bring a first-place trophy with you, boy."

I looked up and saw Mr. Bufford smiling. My mother looked at him too and said, "Oh, Robert, you scared me."

He took off his black cowboy hat and bowed and said, "Well, I'm sorry. I would never scare a lady on purpose."

My mother slapped Mr. Bufford's shoulder and said, "Oh, Robert. Stop acting so stupid."

Mr. Bufford laughed and said, "Now you make us proud, boy. I don't want you coming back here with anything less than first place, you hear me?"

"Yes, sir," I told him, and then I got on the bus.

When the bus was pulling out of the parking lot, I realized that my mother had called Mr. Bufford, "Robert." His first name was Bobby, and everyone called him that or Mr. Bufford, and although I knew that Bobby was a nickname for Robert, it seemed weird to me that my mother had called him that.

I began thinking that maybe everyone called him "Bobby" because if they called him "Robert," the first letter of his first name wouldn't be the same as the first letter of his last name like everyone else in the town. "Or maybe," I thought, "Mr. Bufford thinks 'Bobby Bufford' sounds better than 'Robert Bufford.'"

I started saying "Robert Bufford" over and over again in my head trying to figure out if I liked it better than "Bobby Bufford." Then I realized that Robert Bufford's initials were R. B. and that the initials of the man who had sent my mother that love note were also R. B. and so that maybe Mr. Bufford was the guy who had sent my mother the love note! It explained why I saw him going to our house sometimes when I was going to school and why my mother's face turned real red when she looked at him and why she got so mad that time in Horse Island Food and Furniture when the cashier told Mr. Bufford that his wife was on the phone.

All during the two-hour bus trip, all I could think about was the two of them kissing. I thought about my father and I wondered if he knew that R. B. was Mr. Bufford. I wondered if he and my mother were going to get a divorce. I thought that if they did, I would have to live with my mother and Mr. Bufford and start working at the grocery store. Then I thought that I might have to leave my chickens with my father and I got scared.

But then I remembered how happy my parents looked when they thought that they had found Dawn. And so I figured that if I brought her home, maybe my mother would stop having the affair with Mr. Bufford and my parents wouldn't get a divorce and I wouldn't have to work at the grocery store and I wouldn't have to leave my chickens. So that's when I knew that I really had to find Dawn or everything was going to change.

I still didn't know how I was going to find Dawn. I guess I just thought I could walk around Baton Rouge and see her somewhere. But when the school bus pulled onto this big bridge that crossed the Mississippi and I saw how big Baton Rouge was, I knew it wouldn't be that easy. I knew that Baton Rouge was the state capital, but I didn't know that it would be so big. It looked almost as big as New Orleans.

Anyway, when the bus pulled onto the bridge, Leon bet this kid Braxton that he could spit out the window and hit this boat that was going down the river. When he spit, though, it hit the windshield of the car behind the bus. A bunch of kids laughed and then Mrs. Forest, one of the chaperones, yelled, "Leon Leonard, shut that window and sit down! I can see that the two of you want to cause trouble so you leave me no choice but to split you up. Do you agree, Mrs. Broussard and Nurse Nancy?"

Mrs. Broussard, another chaperone, said, "That's a good idea. Leon, tonight you're going to share a room with Don, and Braxton, you're going to share a room with Joey."

Leon stood up from his seat and said, "Ah, great. I won't be able to get any sleep because the dancing machine is going to keep me up all night with his ballet."

Then Mrs. Broussard said, "Leon, do you want me to call your parents?"

Leon sat down and said, "No, ma'am."

"Then shut it," Mrs. Forest said.

I couldn't believe that I'd get to share a room with Leon. It was my chance to show him that I wasn't a dancing geek, but that I was the same boy he used to ride his bike to school with. I got a little happy because of this and was starting to think about how I was going to find Dawn again when we pulled into the hotel parking lot.

The 4-H club usually stayed in the dormitories on campus, but that year because of a fire, there weren't enough dorm rooms for us. Nurse Nancy told me that they almost canceled the trip, but then the 4-H club was able to find a cheap hotel that had just reopened after being shut down by the health department and needed the business, so they gave the 4-H club a really big discount.

As soon as we pulled into the parking lot, we saw a man and a woman having a fistfight. The bus driver jumped out of his seat and ran up to them, but by the time he got there, the woman had knocked the man to the ground and was kicking him. Mrs. Forest yelled at us, "Look the other way, children! I don't want you seeing that!"

None of us listened, though, and we all watched the woman spit on the man and then walk into the hotel.

Mrs. Forest said, "Oh dear. What a nice hotel," and then Mrs. Broussard said, "Yes. Very nice. Now, kids, before we go to our rooms, I want to make sure that none of you come outside without adult supervision. Do you all understand?"

We all said, "Yes, ma'am," and then Nurse Nancy said, "Well then, let's get off this bus and go to our rooms."

When Leon and I got to our room, he threw his stuff on the bed closest to the door and went into the bathroom. I put my stuff on the bed by the window and looked around. The walls were this kind of gray color that was the same color as the frozen food section at Horse Island Food and Furniture. My mother always said she thought that color made it look like a jail cell. I thought maybe I should tell that to Leon and see if he thought it was funny, but when he came out of the bathroom he asked me, "Where's the remote?"

I got up from my bed real fast and started looking all over the room. I looked under the bed, on the desk, behind the television, and finally in the drawer of the nightstand. As soon as I saw it, I yelled, "Here it is!"

I held it up to Leon with a big smile on my face and he said, "What are you so excited about? It's just a remote."

He walked over to me and grabbed it out of my hands. But before he could turn on the TV, Mrs. Forest knocked on our door and said, "Come on, children, it's time to go to dinner."

Leon threw the remote on his bed and then walked out of the room. I was about to follow him, but I saw the open drawer of the nightstand and went to close it. This is when I saw the phone book and realized that it would be the best place to start looking for Dawn.

So after dinner, when we got back in our rooms and Leon grabbed a pack of playing cards from his suitcase and left, I opened the drawer of the nightstand. There was a Bible, the yellow pages, the white pages, and a map of Baton Rouge. I pulled out the white pages and dropped it on the bed. It was so big that it bounced around. I opened it to the S's to look for Dawn Schmidt, but there was nothing. I turned it to the P's and looked for Liza Pinelli and again, there was nothing. Then I realized that if she'd just moved there, her name wouldn't be in the phone book. And if her name was in the phone book, she'd probably have a different name because she didn't remember what her name was because of the amnesia. There was no way I could call every person in the phone book and ask them if they had run away from Shreveport of if they were kidnapped and then got amnesia but remember running away from a crazy man at Bourbon's Broadway in New Orleans.

Then I noticed the Bible in the drawer and thought about praying because it seemed to work for people when they did it on television. But then I saw the yellow pages and pulled it out and dropped it on the bed to see if it would bounce like the white pages. It did and even bounced right off the bed. When I picked it up, I saw an advertisement for a movie theater. That's when I remembered that the Hawaiian girl told me that Dawn used to work at Bill's Broadway in Baton Rouge.

So I pulled out the white pages and found Bill's Broadway and called the number. It rang a bunch of times and then this man answered and said, "Thank you for calling Bill's Broadway. It's like the real Broadway, but you don't have to get on a plane."

I was about to ask for Liza Pinelli or Dawn Schmidt, but then I realized again that Dawn might have changed her name and that she might get suspicious if someone called asking for a name she wasn't going by anymore. She might think it was my father, or if she had really been kidnapped, the man who had done it. And then she might run away again and I'd never find her. So I hung up the phone and decided it was better if I went to Bill's Broadway and looked for Dawn. Because if she saw me and found out who I was, she might not run.

Then I pulled the map of Baton Rouge out of the drawer and found Tom Street, where Bill's Broadway was. It didn't seem like it was that far from the hotel, so I figured I could probably walk there. It was about nine o'clock when I found it on the map, though, and since the chicken-judging contest was the next morning, and I needed to study a little more and get some sleep if I was going to win, I decided to wait until the next night before I looked for Dawn.

TWENTY-SIX

All through the night I could hear people laughing and running up and down the hall of the hotel. I don't even know what time Leon came back to the room, but he was in his bed when Nurse Nancy knocked on the door the next morning and told us to wake up.

About twenty minutes later, all the kids were on the bus to go eat breakfast and then to head to the chicken-judging contest. It was on a Louisiana State University farm and they had tons and tons of land with barns and pens and fields. The barn that the contest was held in was bigger than any building I'd ever been in. The outside was white and made of tin and the inside had a dirt floor and big windows on the ceiling. There were all these tables in the middle of the barn and on top were cages with chickens. Along most of the walls, there were pens with either cows, sheep, or pigs.

When we walked in Mrs. Forest brought us over to a section of the barn that had a bunch of folding chairs and told us, "Now sit down, children, and we'll get this started."

There were about five hundred kids from all over southwest Louisiana who were in the age category of eleven to fifteen. Each school came at different times and judged different chickens. After the kids from my school sat down in the folding chairs, a man I'd never seen before came over to us. Mrs. Forest cleared her throat and said, "This is Mr. Andre, and he's going to go over the contest rules with you."

Mr. Andre said, "Good morning, Ladies and Gentlemen."

Some of us said good morning back, and then he said, "You don't seem too full of energy this morning. What's going on?"

"That's because most of them were too busy running around the halls last night, but that's not going to happen tonight, I can guarantee you," Mrs. Forest told him.

Mr. Andre looked at Mrs. Forest and then back at us and said, "Oh no, that's not good. Well, anyway, I guess we should go ahead and get started."

He gave a stack of papers to one of the girls in my class, Andrea Apple, and asked, "Can you pass these around for me?"

While she was handing out the papers, Mr. Andre went over the rules of the contest. It was a lot like the Horse Island chicken-judging contest, so when he asked, "Any questions?" no one asked anything.

"Okay," he said. "Let's get started."

When I walked up to the first cage, I took a deep breath and then I forgot about everyone and everything around me. All I saw was the chicken. It was a Brown Leghorn, which are known to be good egg producers. They look like they have the basic black-breasted, red color pattern on the jungle fowl and some scientist people think that that's where chickens come from. They think the first one in America was brought from Leghorn, Italy. I was a little excited because although we didn't have any at my house, it was one of my favorite breeds—mostly because of its color. It was a brown color that was kind of the color of the bottom of a magnolia leaf. I had to give it a low score, though, because it was dirty and it had poor feather growth.

The rest of the chickens were all different kinds of breeds, but I knew them all and I knew exactly what was wrong and right with each one. The best one out of the bunch was a Rhode Island Red. It was clean, had nice feather growth, and its comb wasn't too big.

When I finished judging all of the chickens and double-checked my work, I walked over to the table where I was supposed to hand in my ranking sheet. Nurse Nancy was standing there and asked, "How do you think you did, Don?"

I told her, "Okay, but I'm not sure," and she said, "Well, as long as you did your best. That's all that matters."

I smiled and then she asked me, "Don, can you stand here for a minute? I have to go to the bathroom and I can't find anyone to take my place. All you need to do is stand here and collect people's ranking sheets."

I told her okay and then I went around to the back of the table. When she walked away I picked my paper back up to check my answers again. When I did this I saw Leon's sheet sticking out of the stack of papers, and even though I knew that I shouldn't look at it, I did anyway. I didn't really agree with a lot of his answers, and I could tell from his sheet that he probably wasn't going to place.

I thought about what Leon's dad had told him about not being a genius and I felt a little sad for him. I wondered if his dad would yell at him for not bringing home a trophy. This made me think about the time I'd gone to his house for dinner and his dad made fun of him because he wasn't doing too well in school, and about that day in the grocery store when his dad yelled at him because he couldn't figure out the discounted price of paper towels. I remembered how each time Leon's face got red and he looked like he was really mad and really sad.

I didn't want Leon to be mad and sad and I wanted him to win so his dad would stop teasing him. I thought about changing some of his answers, but I didn't know if I'd have time, and I thought the different handwriting would be kind of obvious. Then I got another idea. I thought that I could write his name on my ranking sheet, and then write mine on his, and that way he'd have a better chance of winning. The only problem was that I wouldn't have a chance of winning. I wouldn't be able to go home with a trophy and I wouldn't become popular again at school. Then I thought I could tell Leon that I switched our names and he might become friends with me again because of it, but then I thought he might get mad at me because he thought that I thought I was smarter than him.

Since I couldn't figure out a way to help Leon win and not make me lose, I asked Stanley, "What should I do? If I change the names, I'm going to lose, and I don't want to lose, and Leon's been so mean to me lately that I don't know if I want to help him."

Stanley told me, "Would you help him if he hadn't been mean to you?"

"Yeah," I said. "I guess so."

"Then help him," Stanley told me. "You have school smarts and chicken smarts. Leon doesn't have either."

I thought about what Stanley had said and erased my name off of my ranking sheet and wrote Leon's. Then I saw Nurse Nancy walking back toward the table. I had two papers with Leon's name on them and I didn't know which one to erase. I closed my eyes and Leon's sad face popped in my mind. I didn't want to see that face anymore so I erased his name off of his ranking sheet and wrote mine.

Right when I finished, Nurse Nancy got back to the table and said, "Sorry it took so long. There was a line at the bathroom. I guess chicken-judging makes people have to go."

I said, "I don't know," and Nurse Nancy said, "I was joking."

So then I told her, "Oh. I'm going to wait by the bus."

I sat in the front of the bus while some of the kids played tag, and others talked, and others tried to hit a sign with rocks. While I was waiting, I asked Stanley, "What did I do? I lost the contest."

He threw a rock and hit a sign and told me, "You don't know that. You could still win."

"No, I can't," I told him. "I saw Leon's answers and a lot of them were wrong."

"Maybe you were wrong," Stanley told me, and I said, "That's even worse. That would mean I don't know anything about chickens, and that would also mean that I would win and Leon would lose, and I don't want that."

Stanley threw another rock and hit the sign again and told me, "That would have happened if you hadn't changed the names."

After Stanley told me that, I was kind of glad that I'd changed the names, and then I was kind of sad, and then I was glad again. I was glad that Leon's dad would stop making fun of him and then I was sad that I wouldn't have any friends. I kept changing my mind all afternoon until that night when I found out that I'd have to dance again.

TWENTY-SEVEN

After the chicken-judging contest, the Horse Island Elementary 4-H Club went to lunch, toured the LSU farm, ate dinner at one of the school's cafeterias, and then got on the bus and went to the hotel. Before we were allowed to get off the bus and go back to our rooms, Mrs. Broussard told us that she had to talk to us. She said, "Now listen carefully, students. I didn't say anything this morning, because I didn't want to distract you from the contest. The thing is, Mrs. Forest, Nurse Nancy, and I are not at all happy about your behavior last night. Those of you, and you know who you are, who ran around the hall all night laughing and talking loudly obviously have no consideration for the rest of us. So to ensure that it doesn't happen again tonight, all of you must stay in your assigned rooms and not leave them until tomorrow morning."

All the kids started talking and saying things like,

"Ahhh," and, "That isn't fair," and then Mrs. Broussard said, "Settle down, children. I'm not finished."

Everyone got quiet and then she said, "There's something that I didn't tell you before because I wanted to surprise you. Now I'm not so sure because I don't know if you deserve it. However, I don't want those of you who behaved yourselves to have to suffer for those of you who acted like animals, so I'm going to give you your surprise. What I want you to do now is go back to your rooms and get washed up and change and then meet me in the hall in forty-five minutes. Then we're all going to the 4-H dance!"

All of the kids except for me started talking at once. Some of them clapped and some of them yelled, "All right!" They gave each other high fives and then some of them jumped in the aisle of the bus and did a little dance. Mrs. Broussard smiled real big and then said, "Okay, let's get moving."

I couldn't believe that I'd come to Baton Rouge to find Dawn and to win the chicken-judging contest so I could become popular again and so kids would forget about when I'd danced, and I wasn't going to win and I couldn't leave my room that night to look for Dawn and I had to go to a dance.

I got really sad and thought I was going to start crying in front of Leon while we were getting dressed. I really didn't want him to make fun of me, so I thought about good stuff like my chickens and the day I won my blue ribbon and the first time we chased the stray dog and pig. And while we were on the bus going to the dance, I thought about my father and I looking out the hotel window in New Orleans and how he'd put his hand on my shoulder. And when we got to the dance and then walked off the bus into this big building, I felt a little sad again. So I thought about all the nights in the kitchen that I'd danced on my mother's feet and she'd hugged me and told me how proud she was of me.

That made me smile a little, and so when we walked into this big room with loud music and a bunch of people dancing, I wasn't that sad anymore.

Nurse Nancy walked up behind me and said, "Wow, this is a big room, isn't it?"

"Yes, ma'am," I said. "What do you think it is?"

"I think it's just a room they have for events like this," she said.

She walked away and after, like, two seconds I couldn't see her anymore because there were so many people. I don't know how many people there were, but I bet if I had counted them, I would have counted, like, seven hundred people or maybe even more. I didn't count them, but I did walk around a few times and look at them because I didn't know what else to do. That got kind of boring after a while, so I went and sat down in a chair along the edge of the wall.

I guess I was sitting there for about an hour when this girl walked over to the chairs and sat down not too far from me. She had red hair, and wore glasses, and was wearing a light blue dress, and she kept looking over at me and smiling. I looked around, but there was no one else by me, so I knew that she was smiling at me. I asked Stanley, "Why do you think she's smiling at me?" and he said, "Maybe she likes you. Go and talk to her."

I looked at her and thought she looked nice and might be a good person to talk to. I was so scared, though, and I didn't know what I'd say to her if I did go talk to her. She stood up, and I thought she was going to walk away, and I was a little sad that I hadn't talked to her, but then she walked over to me and said, "Hi. I'm Rhonda."

I stood up and said, "Hi. I'm Don."

I was real nervous and started thinking about which KC and the Sunshine Band song I should sing. Then Rhonda smiled and said, "Nice to meet you, Don."

"Nice to meet you, Rhonda," I said back, and then she told me, "I like your shirt."

I decided that "Get Down Tonight" might be a good song to sing to myself. Rhonda put her hands behind her back and twisted her body back and forth without moving her feet. Then she asked, "Do you want to dance?"

I didn't answer and instead started to sing to myself, but even though I'd chosen "Get Down Tonight," I heard "Boogie Man."

Then something really weird happened and Rhonda said, "I love KC and the Sunshine Band."

I couldn't understand how she knew I was singing a KC and the Sunshine Band song in my head. I thought maybe she was psychic and so I took a step away from her. Then I realized that I wasn't singing the song in my head. It was really playing.

So I said, "Yes."

Rhonda asked, "Yes, what?" and I said, "Yes. I would like to dance."

We walked to the area where people were dancing and I took a deep breath, sneezed, and then danced. It was so cool to see Rhonda a few feet away looking at me, smiling, and I didn't care if anyone was watching. I guess it was because everyone else was dancing, so I didn't have to worry about anyone making fun of me.

I closed my eyes and thought about KC and the Sunshine Band singing and dancing. Then I imagined that I was dancing in front of them. I danced some of the steps I'd learned for my recital and I did some that I'd seen on *Soul Train* and *American Bandstand*. I was having a great time and I couldn't believe that something like dancing could be as much fun as learning about chickens. But it was and I think I could have danced the whole night but the song ended. When it did, I decided I was going to ask Rhonda if she wanted to dance again. But when I opened my eyes, she wasn't the only person a few feet away looking at me.

There was a bunch of other kids looking at me. None of them were dancing. They were just standing there and staring at me like I was a television set or a rooster crowing. There was Leon holding some blond girl's hand, and some other kids from my class, and a whole lot of others I didn't know at all. I turned around and ran out of the room and to the bathroom. Then I sat on a toilet in one of the stalls for about an hour, until the dance was over.

TWENTY-EIGHT

We got back to the hotel about eleven thirty that night and before we got off the bus, Mrs. Forest reminded us that we couldn't leave our rooms until the next morning and that the chaperones would be watching the hall. When Leon and I got back to the room, he didn't talk to me. We both put on our pajamas and jumped into our beds, and then Leon turned on the TV.

He changed the channel on the TV and I turned my back to him and lay on my side. I felt so stupid for dancing and I thought Leon would never be friends with me again. I thought about Dawn and wished that she were there with me so she could tell Leon to be nice to me. For some reason I thought she might be outside, so I got up out of my bed and looked out of the window. I didn't see her, but I did see a soda machine. I pretended to be Samantha from *Bewitched* and wiggled my nose a little and waited for a soda to slip out of the soda machine and fly across the parking lot into my hands. And then I thought how great it would be if I could fly down to the parking lot and go find Dawn.

I was only staring out of the window for, like, a minute when Leon asked, "How did you do today?"

I turned around from the window real fast and looked at him because I couldn't believe that he was talking to me. He turned his head toward me, and I figured that he *had* talked to me.

"I don't know," I said. "My mind went kind of blank and I forgot a lot of stuff."

"Oh, yeah," Leon said. "That's too bad. I thought it was harder than an armadillo's shell. I don't think I'm going to place."

I sat down on my bed and said, "I'm sure you did okay. You know a lot about chickens."

Leon turned his head and looked at the television again and then said, "That dance you did tonight was pretty cool."

I wasn't sure I'd heard him right, but just in case I had, I said, "Thanks."

Leon turned his head toward me again and asked, "Do you think you can teach me how to dance like that?"

I really couldn't believe that Leon was asking me to teach him how to dance. It made no sense to me because he'd picked on me for so long about dancing, and now he wanted me to teach him. I didn't know why he wanted me to teach him, but I didn't care. I was just happy that he was talking to me again and being nice to me, so I told him, "Yeah, sure, I can teach you."

Leon got out of his bed and then pulled a piece of paper out of his pants and said, "Here. That girl you danced with wanted me to give you her address so you can write to her."

I couldn't believe that Rhonda wanted me to write to her. I thought that she thought I was stupid because of the way I danced. But I opened the piece of folded-up paper and saw her address, so I knew it was true.

Anyway, Leon walked in front of the bed and said, "I like the way you spun around," and then he tried it and fell on the floor. I wanted to laugh, but I didn't because we'd just become friends again. But Leon laughed, and so after I saw that he was laughing, I did too.

Leon got up from the floor and laughed and said, "I guess we can't all be a dancing machine like you."

He sat down on his bed and stopped laughing and then looked at the floor and said, "I'm sorry, dude. I've kind of been a jerk to you. I don't care that you danced. I just got mad because you're so smart and my dad is always talking about how smart you are and asking me why I can't be more like you."

I had thought that that night was going to be the worst night of my life, but then, all of a sudden, it changed, and it kept getting better and better and weirder. I couldn't believe that Leon was mad at me because of his dad. I felt bad and wanted Leon to know that I wasn't mad at him, so I said, "That's okay."

Then I walked over to him, smiled real big, and pushed him on the shoulder and said, "But don't let it happen again or I'm going to have to whip your butt."

Leon looked up at me, and when he saw I was smiling, he smiled too and then he stood up and said, "Oh yeah?"

Then he grabbed me and threw me on the ground and hit me with his pillow. I tried to grab the other pillow, but Leon was holding me down, so all I could do was laugh. We wrestled for only a few minutes before Leon jumped off of me and raised his arms in the air and danced around and said, "I am the champion, and the champion wants a soda for his prize."

I got up from his bed and walked over to the window and said, "It's too bad we can't leave the room, because there's a soda machine outside."

Leon walked over to the window and looked outside and said, "We're going to get a soda."

"But we can't leave the room," I told him. "Mrs. Forest is in the hall."

Leon reached out and opened the window and said, "Ta da," like a magician who had just pulled a rabbit out of a hat. I looked at the open window and asked, "You're going to climb out of the window?"

"No," he said. "*We're* going to climb out."

I backed away from Leon and said, "What? No. What?"

Then Leon said, "Listen, how often are we in a big city by ourselves? I want to tear this town apart and have a good time."

I was scared but didn't want Leon to know, so instead of telling him that I was about to pee in my pants, I asked, "How are we going to get down there?"

Leon looked around the room for a few seconds and then said, "Well, the first thing we need to do is strip the sheets from the bed. Then we need to turn off the television so the chaperones think we're asleep. Then we'll take the pillows and tuck them under the covers so it looks like we're sleeping. Then we'll tie the sheets together and use them to lower ourselves out of the window. We're only on the second floor, so the sheets will be plenty long enough."

I was kind of amazed. Leon couldn't name the first president of the United States but he knew exactly what to do to get us outside.

"I'll go down first," he said. "That way if you fall, I can catch you."

I wanted to tell Leon that since we were about the same size, I would probably kill him if he tried to catch me. I couldn't tell him, though, because I couldn't speak. I watched Leon turn off the television and pull all the sheets off of our beds. Then he told me, "Change into your regular clothes and then put the pillows underneath the covers so it looks like someone's sleeping under them."

I did what he said, and by the time I was finished, he'd tied all the sheets together so that they made one long sheet. Then he tied that to the frame of my bed and lowered the sheet out of the window. He got dressed and put on his backpack and then went to the window and grabbed part of the sheet. He looked at me and said, "Here goes. Watch how I do it so you can do it the same way."

Leon sat on the windowsill and then pushed himself up on his feet. He held on to the sheet with both hands and then let himself fall back slowly. I went to the window and watched him walk down the side of the hotel like it was no big deal, and like that was the way he left his house in the morning to go to school. He got all the way to the ground without slipping or anything. I was happy that he had gotten on the ground safely, but then I was freaked because it was my turn. I couldn't move, but then Leon made a birdcall and I was able to move my eyes and see him whisper the words *Come on*.

I backed away from the window and sat on my bed. I didn't know if I could climb out of the window or not, and I didn't want Leon to know that I was scared. I stood up and looked out the window again and I could see Leon at the soda machine. Then I heard a knock at the door and Mrs. Forest say, "It's me, Mrs. Forest. Open the door."

I jumped up from my bed, grabbed the sheet rope and pulled it up, threw it under the bed, and then closed the window. Mrs. Forest knocked again and said, "Don and Leon. I know you're not asleep because you just turned off the TV ten minutes ago."

I took off my shirt and pants and pulled one of the pillows out from underneath the covers of my bed, messed up my hair a little, and then opened the door. Mrs. Forest looked me up and down and said, "My God, Don. Why are you in your underwear?"

I jumped back a little behind the door so only my head stuck out and then I said, "Sorry."

"Where's Leon?" Mrs. Forest asked.

"He's asleep," I said.

"Already?" Mrs. Forest asked. "You guys just turned off the television."

I had to think fast so I just opened my mouth and the words fell out. "He went to sleep a while ago. I was the one watching television. He's really tired because he stayed up late last night studying."

TWENTY-NINE

After Mrs. Forest told me that she had a hard time believing that Leon studied anything besides ways to make her crazy, I closed the door. I had goose bumps all over my body, but I wasn't cold so I guess it was because I was excited. I felt like James Bond or something and even though I was still a little scared, I knew that James Bond wouldn't be and that he'd climb out of that window and look for Dawn. So I decided if I was going to be like him, that I had to climb out that window and look for her.

So I got dressed again and grabbed the map of Baton Rouge and the address to Bill's Broadway. Then I opened the window, threw the sheet rope out, and looked at the parking lot. I didn't see Leon, but I knew he couldn't be too far away and that he was waiting for me. I took a few deep breaths and sat on the windowsill the way Leon had and then got up on my feet.

I was so nervous that I held the sheet rope tighter

than I'd held the side of the chair when I was getting a polio shot. I knew I had to do it, though, so I closed my eyes, counted to ten, and then leaned back. Before I could straighten my legs out, though, my feet slipped off the windowsill and my body fell. I slid down the rope until my hands hit the knot where two of the sheets were tied together. I was about halfway down, which was about ten feet from the ground, but it felt like a thousand feet. I yelled, "Stanley! Help me!"

He told me to calm down and I told him back, "But I'm going to fall. I'm going to fall and die," and Stanley said, "No, you're not. Just do like Leon did and put your feet on the wall and walk down."

I tried to do like he said, but I couldn't and I didn't feel like I could hold on much longer, so I yelled, "Stanley, I'm falling."

"Dance!" he yelled at me.

"What?" I asked, and he yelled, "Kick, step, step, kick."

I didn't know if it would work, but I thought I might as well try or fall. So I stared at my left foot, and then kicked, and then stepped and it landed on the wall. The next move that I should have done was to step again, but that didn't make sense to me so I kicked again, but this time with my right foot. Then I stepped, and it landed on the wall too, and I was standing on the side of the hotel. It felt kind of cool, but I wanted to get down, so I put my left hand below the knot, and then my right, and then walked backward all the way to the ground.

When my feet touched the grass, I felt dizzy but kind of excited because I felt like James Bond again or Batman, even though I think they both probably would have jumped from the second floor. But I still thought it was cool and wanted to tell Leon all about it, so I went and looked for him.

I didn't see him at first, but then he walked out from behind some bushes, drinking a soda, and said, "I thought you'd chickened out."

"Actually, Leon," I told him. "Chickens can be very brave animals when they need to be."

He said, "Whatever. What took you so long?"

I told him about Mrs. Forest and how I'd climbed out of the window, and he said, "No way. Good going, Don. That means we have the whole night to tear this town apart."

I looked at Leon and said, "Leon, we're twelve years old. How are we going to tear this town apart?"

"I don't know," he told me. "Come on, let's walk around."

"Leon," I said. "Can you help me find someone?"

He took a sip of soda and said, "Sure. Who?"

I didn't like lying to him because, besides my chickens and my make-believe twin brother, he'd been the closest friend I'd ever had. I wasn't ready to tell him the truth, though, so I told him, "My cousin. I think she's a dancer at a theater called Bill's Broadway."

Leon pulled his head back like someone had scared him, and said, "All right. I knew you were a little too goody-goody to be real. Who would have guessed that the family who keeps their chickens for ambience has a relative who's a dancer?"

"I don't know," I said, and Leon laughed and said, "Dude, that was rhetorical question."

I said, "Oh," and Leon asked, "So where is this place?"

I pulled the map out and opened it up, and then looked at the street in front of the hotel, which was Lobdell Boulevard. I figured that we needed to go left, so I pointed and said, "I think it's that way."

Leon started walking and said, "Let's go."

Then I asked him, "Leon. Are you scared?"

He took his backpack off, opened it up, and said, "Don't worry, man. I have a flashlight, a knife, and some Mace in case anyone messes with us."

Leon pulled a flashlight and a small can out of the backpack he'd been carrying. He handed them both to me and said, "Here, you can hold these."

"What's in this can?" I asked him.

"It's Mace," he said. "Like policemen carry. My uncle is a cop and he gave it to my mom, in case someone tries to steal her purse."

That didn't make any sense to me so I asked, "What does it do?" and he said, "If you spray it in someone's eyes, it burns and blinds them for a few minutes."

I thought to myself that I was real happy that his mom hadn't caught me trying to steal money from her purse at the Dairy Festival chicken-judging contest, because I don't think that I would have liked it if she had blinded me. I didn't tell Leon that, though. I just smelled the can and he told me, "Don't spray it unless you have to, though. I don't want to use too much because I don't want my mom to find out that I took it."

Then Leon pulled a box out of his backpack, opened it, and pulled out a big hunting knife.

"I had this in my backpack when I went hunting last week and forgot about it," he said. "I'm glad I brought it, though. We might need it in case someone messes with us."

I was a little worried about Leon and that big knife, but then I was kind of glad that he was with me. Although I didn't want him to stab anybody, it made me feel a little better to know that we had protection. Especially when we started walking down Lobdell Boulevard, which was kind of dark and spooky. I started talking to Stanley in my head and he told me that someone should bring Benjamin Franklin to this street so that he could introduce it to electricity. I thought that was pretty funny so I told Leon.

"Someone should introduce this street to Benjamin Franklin."

"Who?" he asked.

"Benjamin Franklin," I told him. "He discovered electricity."

Leon looked at me like I'd asked him what time two trains would meet if they left in opposite directions at fifty miles per hour.

"He's the guy who was flying a kite and got struck by lightning," I told him.

"Oh, yeah." Leon smiled. "That's pretty funny."

Then we heard a noise and Leon swung his knife around and almost hit me.

"Be careful," I told him. "You almost jabbed me with it."

"I know what I'm doing," he told me. "Don't worry."

A few minutes later we turned onto Tom Street. The buildings seemed a little older and more run down than the ones on Lobdell Boulevard, and there were a few people walking down the sidewalk talking really loud. Most of them walked by Leon and me like they didn't even see us, but this one guy stopped and asked, "What are you kids doing out here?"

He looked like he was about my dad's age, but he had all his hair and it was long and blond. Leon and I didn't say anything because the man was really big, and I guess we were surprised that he was talking to us. He leaned toward us and asked, "What are you, deaf? Answer me. What are you doing out here?"

I was waiting for Leon to say something and I guess he was waiting for me to say something because neither one of us talked. The man stood up straight and burped, and when he did, it smelled really funny. Then he said, "I think you boys snuck away from home and your parents don't know where you are."

We still didn't say anything, and the man said,

"Give me some money and I won't tell them that I saw you out here."

I was going to give him the ten dollars I had in my pocket, but before I could, he grabbed Leon by the shoulders and said, "Give me your money, boy."

I thought Leon was going to stab him with the knife, but he just stood there while the man shook him. It looked like he was hurting Leon, so I hit the man in the head with the flashlight, and then with the can of Mace. The man screamed and let go of Leon, and then came toward me, so I took the can of Mace and pointed it at him, and then sprayed him in the eyes. The man screamed and cursed and grabbed his eyes.

Then Leon grabbed my arm and said, "Let's go!"

We ran away from the man and kept running for what seemed like forever, but I think it was only five minutes. I'd never run so fast in my whole life, and I thought my side was going to fall out of me because it was hurting so bad. I had to stop, and when I did, I turned, but I didn't see the man anywhere near us. Leon stopped a little bit in front of me and we both leaned over and took deep breaths for a few seconds. Then Leon stood up and pointed and said, "Look! There it is! There's Bill's Broadway!"

THIRTY

Bill's Broadway was a small brown square building with a parking lot on the right side of it with about ten cars. When Leon and I were standing in front of it, we stared at it like Dorothy, the tin man, the lion, and the scarecrow had stared at the Wizard of Oz. Even when Leon asked me, "What's her name?" he didn't stop staring at it. But when I said, "I don't know," he looked at me and asked, "You don't even know her name?"

"No," I said. "I'm not even sure if she still works here. I guess it's going to be kind of hard to find her, isn't it?"

"Yeah," he said. "It's going to be hard, but we're going to have a good time looking for her," and then he slapped me on the back and walked to the front door. I followed him and asked, "Why are you talking like that?"

"Like what?" Leon asked.

"I don't know," I said. "You're just saying things that

grown-ups would say. I don't know which grown-ups, but I know you're not talking like a twelve-year-old."

Leon shrugged his shoulders and said, "We got cable and I've been watching a lot of Rated R movies when my parents go to bed."

I said, "Oh. Okay," and then looked at the knife in Leon's hand and said, "Maybe you should put that knife away so we don't scare anyone."

He said, "Yeah, you're probably right."

He put it back into the box and into his backpack while I walked to the sidewalk and looked down the street to see if the man I'd sprayed with Mace was coming. I didn't see him, so I walked back to the front of Bill's Broadway and saw Leon looking at a board with a bunch of pictures on the wall next to the front door.

"What are you looking at?" I asked him, and he told me, "It's pictures of the dancers. Maybe we can find your cousin. You know what she looks like, don't you?"

I said, "Of course," even though I didn't, really. I knew what Dawn looked like twelve years before because of pictures, but I didn't know what she looked like now. I started to look at the pictures, but then we heard a siren.

"Come on!" Leon shouted, and we ran to the back of the building.

It was really dark back there and so I couldn't see anything, but I know that there was a doorknob because I hit my elbow on it and it kind of hurt. I didn't say anything, though, because I didn't want anyone to hear us. Although I don't think the policeman could have heard me over the siren.

Anyway, when we couldn't hear the siren anymore, Leon turned to me and said, "It's so dark back here. Someone should bring Benjamin Franklin here."

I laughed even though I didn't think it was as funny as when Stanley had said it. And then Leon said, "I never understood what he was doing with that kite."

I told him, "I'll tell you later. Right now, let's go back and look at those pictures."

When we got to the front, I looked at the pictures one by one so I didn't miss Dawn. I had only looked at a couple of them when Leon asked, "Do you see her?"

"No," I said. "But I think Dawn just started working here so they might not have her picture up yet."

"Who's Dawn?" he asked

I froze because I remembered that I had lied to him. I tried to cover myself, though, and said, "Uh. She's my, um, cousin."

"Don't you have a dead sister named Dawn?" Leon asked.

I said, "Yeah, I do. She and my cousin have the same name."

"That's a little strange," Leon told me.

"Yeah," I said. "I guess it's strange, but don't you have a cousin and an aunt that both have the name Laurie?"

"No," he said. "My cousin's name is Laurie, L-a-u-r-i-e, and my aunt's name is Lori, L-o-r-i."

I said, "Oh, sorry," and started looking at the pictures again.

Some of the pictures on the board had the dancers' names underneath them. The first three were Trudy Garland, Marilyn Monthroe, and Candy Grand. The last one had a candy cane in her mouth and was winking her left eye. I was about to ask Leon why a dancer would take a picture with a candy cane in her mouth, when he said, "That's a stupid name for a girl. Curly Temple. That's a Three Stooges' name. And who wants to see a girl with a baton?"

"Where do you see that?" I asked him.

He pointed to the picture and underneath it was written, "Featuring Curly Temple and Her Baton."

I looked at the picture, and even though she was older and had curly blond hair, I recognized Dawn right away because she looked so much like my mother. I was so shocked to see her that I yelled, "That's her! That's Dawn!"

Leon put his face closer to the picture and said, "No way! That's your cousin, dude? That's so cool! So let's go in."

I took a step toward the door, but then remembered what Mr. Munson had told my mother in New Orleans about the theater not having too many women customers. If they didn't have many women customers, they probably didn't have many kid customers, either.

"They won't let us inside," I told Leon.

Just then an old man walked out of the front door.

He looked at us for a minute and then walked over to a truck, got in, and drove off. Leon grabbed my arm and said, "We have to do something before someone sees us and makes us leave."

I thought about what we could do and then I remembered that I'd hit my elbow on a doorknob when Leon and I had run to the back of the building. So I told Leon to follow me and we went to the back again and I turned the flashlight on and shined it on the doorknob. Leon grabbed it and turned it, but it was locked.

He looked at me and said, "Don't worry about that," and then he pulled a small knife out of his backpack.

It was a Swiss Army knife and it had a spoon, a fork, a corkscrew, and a metal toothpicklike thing. I couldn't figure out what he was going to do with it, but before I could ask he said, "Hold the flashlight on the knob and watch."

He stuck the metal toothpicklike thing in the lock of the door and moved it around a little.

"What are you doing?" I asked.

"I'm picking the lock," he said. "I saw a guy do it on one of the Rated R movies on cable I told you about and I've been practicing on the doors at my house."

"That's so cool," I said. "When we get back to Horse Island, can you teach me how to do it?"

"Yeah, sure," he told me.

Then he looked at me and asked, "Hey, what are you going to tell your cousin if she's in there?"

I didn't know what I was going to tell her. I mean, I

kind of had an idea, but I didn't know the exact words I was going to use. I was going to tell her that I was her brother and that I wanted her to come home with me and that the two of us could travel to different parish fairs and she could compete in the dance contests and I could compete in the chicken-judging contests and we'd become famous like Donny and Marie. I didn't tell Leon that, though, because I thought that he'd think it was stupid.

So I told him, "I'm going to tell her, 'Hi,' and ask her how she's doing."

"That's it?" Leon said. "You came all this way just to tell her 'Hi'? That's kind of stupid."

"Yeah, you're right," I told him. "Maybe I'll tell her that I'm her cousin and that I want her to come home with me and that the two of us can travel to different parish fairs and she can compete in dance contests and I can compete in chicken-judging contests and we can be like Donny and Marie."

"I doubt you'll become famous like Donny and Marie," Leon told me. "But it would be cool if you told her that." Then Leon pulled the pick out of the doorknob and wiped it on his shirt. Then he looked at me and said, "Wait a second. Donny and Marie are brother and sister, not cousins."

I started to realize that maybe I should tell Leon the truth about who Dawn really was. I didn't know if he'd get mad at me, but I figured that he would find out sooner or later if Dawn came home with me.

So I told him, "Dawn's not my cousin. She's my sister, and my parents said she was kidnapped when I was a baby, but I think she might have run away."

Leon turned and looked at me and asked, "Was she kidnapped with your twin brother?"

"Oh, yeah," I said. "I was wrong about having a twin brother. It was my sister the detective was looking for. I found this out over Easter break."

Leon said, "Wow! Your life is like the ones on TV."

I didn't know what television programs Leon was watching, but I'd never thought that my life was like *The Brady Bunch* or *The Waltons* or *Eight Is Enough*. The more I thought about it, though, it was kind of like *Soap* or *Dallas*, but I didn't ever remember seeing chickens on either one of those shows.

Anyway, then Leon said, "Got it!"

He shook the doorknob and turned it and opened the door. We saw this big room with mirrors and tables and chairs and racks with clothes hanging from them and on the tables there were brushes, hair spray, perfume, and makeup.

Then we heard another police siren, and Leon said, "Go in there and find her so I can meet someone who ran away or was kidnapped or maybe both. This is going to be so cool."

I looked at Leon and asked, "Aren't you going to come with me?"

"No," he said. "It's better if one of us waits out here

in case something happens. If you're not out in fifteen minutes, I'll go in after you."

I handed him the flashlight and Mace, but he said, "Keep them. You might need them."

I said, "Okay," and then walked into the room and closed the door behind me.

There wasn't anyone in the room, but all the lights were on. I didn't hear anybody talking, but I could hear music coming from behind this big red door. I thought about opening it and seeing where the music was coming from, but I was getting a little scared. I thought about getting Leon to come with me, but then I heard something that really freaked me out. You see, I heard the song "Rock Around the Clock" playing, and that was the song Dawn had danced to when she won her ballerina trophy.

THIRTY-ONE

When I heard "Rock Around the Clock," I wasn't scared anymore and I got kind of brave and felt like James Bond again and I walked up to the door where the music was coming from, opened it, and then went through.

I was in this dark room with a few chairs in it, and there were these two big curtains hanging, and a little light was coming through where they met. There were stairs that led up to them and since I didn't see anyone, I walked up the stairs to the crack in the curtains and looked through it.

That was the first time I saw Dawn in real life and I felt like I was seeing a superhero, or one of the Partridge Family. Dawn even looked kind of like a superhero because she was wearing this red sequined shirt and a big puffy pink and red skirt, and red high heel shoes that were all shiny. I don't know which superhero she looked like because I don't remember any of them wearing high heels, but Wonder Woman had shiny red boots and Dawn kind of reminded me of her, except that instead of a rope, Dawn had a baton.

Dawn was dancing the same dance that had won her the trophy. I knew this because I'd seen my mother do the dance for so many years. Only my mother never took off her clothes when she did it and Dawn was. First she took off her shirt and danced around in a red, shiny tank top and then she took off the big puffy skirt and spun it around in the air, and then threw it, and the bartender caught it. I put my hand over my eyes because I didn't want to see my sister's butt. I wanted to watch her dance, though, so I lifted my eyes up and only looked at the top of her. She did a couple of flips, and I saw that she was wearing red, shiny shorts that matched her red, shiny tank top.

When the song was almost over, Dawn held up her left leg with her left hand and twirled the baton with her right hand and then threw it up in the air, cut a split, and held her arms up and caught the baton in her mouth. My mother never did that part when she danced, but she always explained it and told me it was one of the most amazing things in the world and that if you asked people what was more amazing, the Grand Canyon or Dawn catching that baton in her mouth, they'd definitely say Dawn, unless they were crazy or on drugs.

My mother was right. The dance was amazing and all the men in the theater stood up and clapped really hard. There were only like ten or so people in the place but it sounded like there were at least fifteen. The place didn't look like a theater to me, though. It didn't have rows and rows of seats like at the movie theater. It looked more like some of the bars I'd seen on TV. It had tables and chairs and a bar where you could get drinks.

I didn't have long to look at it, though, because I felt someone tap me on my shoulder a couple of seconds after Dawn's dance was over. I turned and saw a woman in a red and white striped dress. Then I remembered that she was the woman who had taken a picture with a candy cane in her mouth.

"Who are you?" she asked.

Before I could answer her, Dawn walked through the curtains and ran right into me and I fell down the stairs on the ground and landed on my butt.

I looked up at Dawn and she said, "Oh my god! Are you okay?"

Her voice was scratchy and deep, and didn't sound anything like my mother's.

"Candy, is he yours?" Dawn asked.

"No," Candy said. "I don't know who he is. He was looking through the curtains at you, so I thought he was yours."

Dawn folded her arms and said, "No, the little pervert isn't mine."

"Well, you figure it out, because I have a number to perform," and then Candy stepped over me and walked onstage.

Dawn walked down the stairs, put one of her shoes on my shoulders, pushed me to the ground, and said, "Who are you, kid? Does your mom or dad work here or something?"

I didn't know what to say or do and part of me thought about spraying her with the Mace so she'd get her shoe off of me. But then I realized that I'd dropped it when I'd fallen, and so I thought about talking to her. I didn't know what to say to her, though, and usually when I didn't know what to say to people, I told them that I liked their shirt and they always smiled.

So I said, "I like your red, shiny tank top."

She didn't smile though. Instead she pushed a little harder and said, "Who are you?"

"You're hurting me," I told her. "Can you take your shoe off of my shoulder?"

"Not until you tell me what you're doing here," she said.

"I'm your brother," I told her.

She took her shoe off of me and scrunched her face up and said, "I don't have a brother."

I sat up and touched the part of my shoulder that she'd hurt with her shoe and I said, "Yes," but it came out like a whisper, so I cleared my throat and tried again and said, "Yes. Yes, you do."

"No. No, I don't," she said.

I pushed myself away from her because I was scared she'd hold me down with her shoe again, and I said, "Yes, you do. I was born after you were kidnapped or ran away. I'm Don Schmidt. My real name is Stanley, but Mother and Father changed it to Don because they said Stanley was an uncle who gambled and drank a lot. But anyway, Father tried to find you in New Orleans, but you ran away, and I guess it's because you didn't recognize him because maybe you had amnesia or didn't want to see him. Were you kidnapped, or did you run away?"

Dawn closed her eyes a little, and then opened them wider, and then closed them a little again and asked, "How do you know my last name?"

"Because I'm your brother," I told her. "Your real name is Dawn, and Janice and Dick Schmidt are our parents."

Dawn's eyes got bigger and bigger this time, and she asked me real slow, "How old are you?"

"Twelve," I said, and then she asked me real quick, "When's your birthday?"

I told her "April nineteenth," and then her body started shaking. She walked back and forth in front of me, and then grabbed her face and said, "Oh my god," over and over again.

Then she sat down on the steps that led up to the stage and put her head between her legs and started breathing really, really hard.

"Are you okay?" I asked her.

She looked up at me and her face was all red and her eyes were real puffy. She looked like my mother did when she had to feed the chickens or when "the

Curse" was in town. Since I didn't see any chickens for Dawn to feed, I figured that she was all red because of "The Curse."

So I asked her, "Are you at that time in your menstrual cycle?"

But she didn't answer me. She looked at me and blinked her eyes a couple of times and then stood up from the steps and pointed and asked, "Who is he?"

I turned and saw Leon walking toward us.

"Wow," he said. "Is she your sister, Don?"

"That's Leon," I told Dawn. "He's my friend."

Then a guy walked into the room and said, "Curly, what's going on back here? You can't have these kids in here."

Dawn looked at him and started crying and the guy said, "I don't know why you're crying, but I don't care. You need to get these kids out of here right now."

She screamed at him, "All right! I'll bring them in the dressing room!" and the man said, "No! I want them off of the property now!"

Dawn took a deep breath and said, "All right, I'll bring them out the back," and then she walked to the door that went into the dressing room and said, "Come on, Don. We need to get out of here."

I got up from the floor, and Leon and I followed her. When we got to the dressing room, Dawn put on some jeans and a T-shirt and said, "Let's go outside."

When we got outside, we all stood in front of the back door in the grass. The moon had come out so it wasn't as dark as it had been before. At first it was hard to see her face and all I could see was the outline of her body. She looked like she was about the same size as my mother, which was taller than me, and if I had to guess, I'd say was about five feet and a few inches.

Dawn lit a cigarette and then looked around.

. Then she asked, "Are Mom and Dad here?"

"No," I told her.

Dawn looked at me right in the eyes and asked, "What are you doing here?"

"I want you to come home," I told her.

She started crying again and Leon asked me, "Why is she crying?"

"I don't know," I said. "I guess she's sad because she has amnesia."

Dawn looked at me and stopped crying. She scrunched up her forehead like she was thinking and bent down beside me and asked, "So Mom and Dad told you about your older sister, huh?"

I said, "Yeah, but only last month. They told me you were dead at first, but then Mr. Munson saw you in New Orleans, so they told me you'd been kidnapped."

Dawn asked, "Mr. Munson?"

"Yeah," I told her. "He's a detective they hired to find you."

Dawn took another puff on her cigarette and asked, "They've been looking for me for twelve years?"

"Yeah, I guess," I said. "I think they had stopped

looking for a while, but then Mr. Munson saw you by accident at Bourbon's Broadway."

Dawn stood up and said, "So that's how Dad knew where I was."

"Yeah," I said. "But if you knew it was Father, why did you run away? And were you really kidnapped when you were in Texarkana, or did you run away then too?"

Dawn put her hand on her hip and then looked up at the sky. I looked up too, but I didn't see anything, so I asked, "You weren't kidnapped, were you?"

Dawn didn't say anything, but she shook her head no.

"Why did you run away when you were in Texarkana visiting Grandmother?" I asked.

She stopped looking up at the sky and looked at me and said, "I'm afraid you probably wouldn't understand."

There were a bunch of things that I didn't understand, like why my mother and father had told me that Dawn had been kidnapped or why my parents had changed my name or how Dawn could catch that baton in her mouth without breaking any teeth. But I figured that I'd understand those things when I got older. So I told Dawn, "I want to know anyway."

Dawn looked up at the sky again and said, "I ran away because I was tired of dancing."

Then Leon asked, "What do you mean? You're still dancing."

Both Dawn and I looked at him. He shrugged his shoulders and said, "Well, she is."

Dawn threw her cigarette on the ground and said, "He's right. But at least now I'm not doing it for her."

I didn't say anything because I knew "her" was my mother. It was weird because I'd always thought that Dawn was the luckiest person in the world, I mean except for having scarlet fever. I didn't think she was lucky for that, but I thought she was lucky because she could dance so well, and my mother talked about her all the time like she was a movie star or something. I thought Dawn loved dancing, but when she said at least she wasn't dancing for my mother, I knew that I was wrong, and Dawn wasn't as lucky as I'd thought.

"Are you going home with Don?" Leon asked.

"No," she said. "I'm not. Listen, Don, please don't tell them where I am. They can't make me come back because I'm twenty-seven years old. But I don't want them to start following me. I can't take them right now."

I didn't know what to say. I really wanted her to come with me, so I decided to tell her my plan and hope she might change her mind.

"But if you come home we can travel to parish fairs together and I can win chicken-judging contests and you can win dance contests and we can become famous like Donny and Marie!"

"Well," Leon said. "Not as famous as Donny and Marie."

Dawn looked at me like she didn't understand what

language I was speaking. Then she smiled and shook her head from side to side. I knew then that she wasn't going to come home with me and there was nothing I could do. I decided that I wouldn't tell my mother and father about her, because I wanted to help her, because she was my sister and was nice to me.

"I won't tell them where you are," I told her. "I promise. But how can I find you again?"

Dawn walked over to me and grabbed my hand and said, "I tell you what. If I move, I'll let you know."

"But you don't know my phone number or address," I told her.

Dawn bent down so our heads were the same height and she asked, "Are you guys still at the same house in Shreveport?"

I told her, "No, we moved to Uncle Sam's farmhouse in Horse Island because father got fired from his job because he missed a lot of work to look for you and so we didn't have a place to live until Uncle Sam died and left us the house in his will."

Dawn scrunched up her face and then asked, "Uncle Sam? Was he the one who lived on that chicken farm?"

Leon said, "Yeah," and then Dawn rubbed my shoulders for a few seconds and said, "Listen, I'll find you if I move."

She tilted her head to the side and then asked, "Don, how did you get here? Are you in Baton Rouge with Mom and Dad?"

I shook my head and said, "No, I came to Baton Rouge with the 4-H Club to go to a chicken-judging contest."

"How did you know where to find me?" she asked.

I told her, "Because when we were in New Orleans, I met Stephanie, and she told me that you had come to Baton Rouge and that you used to work at Bill's Broadway."

Dawn said, "Stephanie. Stephanie? You mean the Oriental girl I used to work with?"

"Yeah," I told her. "But she's from Hawaii, and she told me that food and rugs are Oriental, not people."

Dawn stood up and then asked, "Where are you staying while you're here?"

"We're staying in a hotel on Lobdell Boulevard, and Leon and I walked here from there," I told her.

Dawn lit up another cigarette and asked, "You walked all the way over here at night?"

"Yeah," I said. "But don't worry 'cause Leon has a knife."

Dawn took a step back and said, "Oh. Well, let me give you guys a ride in my car."

I said, "Okay," and then Dawn said, "Let me just get my keys," and then she walked back into the building.

I gave Leon the flashlight because I was tired of holding it and I didn't think we needed it anymore. While he was putting it in his backpack I started to wonder if Dawn was going to run away. I grabbed Leon by the arm and said, "Come on. Let's go to the front and make sure that she's not running away."

We ran to the front, but we didn't see her, so I told Leon, "I'm going to go to the back, and you stay here, and if she comes out, yell to me."

Before I could walk to the back, I felt a hand on my shoulder. Both Leon and I turned around and saw the guy that I had sprayed with the Mace. He grabbed both our arms and we screamed and he said, "You little creeps are going to pay."

I didn't have the Mace anymore to spray him, so I tried to hit him, but he kicked my legs out from under me and I fell. Then he did the same thing to Leon. He bent down and put one of his knees on my chest, and the other one on Leon. He must have weighed like six thousand pounds because he was so heavy, and I thought he was going to crush me.

I really thought I was going to die, so I closed my eyes and told my chickens, "Good-bye. I'll miss you."

Then I heard Dawn scream, "What the hell are you doing?"

The man yelled back, "Mind your own business," and then I opened my eyes and saw Dawn hit him in the face with her fist. The man jumped up and swung at Dawn, but she ducked and then kicked him in the privates and the man fell on the ground.

Dawn grabbed Leon's and my arms, and pulled us up and said, "Come on, let's go!"

Then we ran to a blue car in the parking lot of Bill's Broadway and all jumped in. Dawn started it and backed out and drove toward the road. The man she'd kicked had gotten up and was running after us. He slapped the back of the car just as Dawn pulled it out on the road. I didn't look back to see if he was following us because, if he was, it would have scared me. So I just closed my eyes and pretended like he turned around and just walked in the other direction. I opened my eyes back up, though, when Dawn started crying.

"Who the hell was that?" she screamed.

"Some guy that tried to take our money," Leon said. "We don't know who he is."

Dawn hit the steering wheel with her hand and screamed, "Geezum Pete!"

Nobody said anything until we got to the traffic light at Lobdell Boulevard. That's when Dawn asked, "Which way is your hotel?"

I pointed left and she turned and then asked, "Are you guys okay?"

"Yeah," I said.

"You have to promise me that you'll never go out alone at night again," she told us. "There are a bunch of crazy people out there, and you never know what they're going to do."

I told her, "Okay" and then Leon said, "You were like one of Charlie's Angels when you kicked that guy."

Dawn didn't say anything for a few seconds. Then

she asked, "Where is your hotel?" and Leon pointed and said, "There on the right."

Dawn turned into the parking lot, shut off the car, and then we all got out and walked to the front of the hotel. She bent down and hugged me and kissed me on the forehead and said, "Be careful."

Dawn kissed me again, and turned back and walked to her car, got in, and started driving away. I was really sad to see her leave because I thought she was real nice, and a good dancer, and I thought it was real cool that she'd kicked that man in the privates for me. I was praying that she'd come back and then all of a sudden, her car stopped, and then backed up to the front of the hotel again. Dawn got out and said, "I love you."

"I love you too," I told her.

She smiled and hugged me really tight and said, "I'm glad you found me."

Then she let go and got back in her car and drove away. I prayed again that she'd come back, but she didn't, and when I couldn't see her car anymore, I knew she wouldn't.

THIRTY-TWO

I could barely sleep the night Leon and I found Dawn. I guess it wasn't really the night, though, because we got back to the hotel after midnight, so I guess it was really the morning of the next day. Anyway, at first I couldn't fall asleep at all and thought about everything from the chicken-judging contest to the dance to the man that I had sprayed with Mace to Dawn. When I did fall asleep, I dreamed about everything that had happened. I think I was dreaming about Dawn's foot on my shoulder when Nurse Nancy knocked on our door and told us to get up because we had to go to breakfast and then to the awards ceremony.

The awards ceremony was in this big auditorium and it was for the chicken-judging, pig-judging, and good-grooming contest and so it was filled with kids from all over Louisiana. I thought about counting all the kids, but I didn't, because I was too nervous and wanted to make sure I didn't miss when they announced the winners of the chicken-judging con-test. Leon was sitting next to me and he fell asleep when the man onstage announced the winners of the pig-judging and good-grooming contest, but I woke him up when the man on the stage said, "And now we're going to announce the winners of the fourteen-to-eighteen–year-old category in the chicken-judging contest."

When I tapped Leon, he pushed my hand and said, "Stop it."

"But, Leon," I told him, "they're about to announce the winners of the chicken-judging contest," and he told me, "So? I didn't win anyway, so I don't want to hear. I want to sleep."

"Maybe someone in our class won," I told him, and he said, "I don't care."

Then Mrs. Forest said, "Boys! Stop talking. You're being rude."

Leon sat up straight but closed his eyes and put his head down again. When the announcer said, "Now for the ten-to-thirteen–year-old category," I tapped him again. He picked his head up and looked around.

"Third place goes to Leslie Pounds," the announcer said.

Leon made a mean face at me and then closed his eyes again. But then the announcer said, "Second place goes to Leon Leonard," and he opened his eyes up real big.

Leon looked around like he didn't know where he

was and when I jumped up and clapped, he looked at me like he'd seen a ghost.

"You won, Leon!" I told him. "Go get your trophy!"

Leon turned white like he *was* the ghost, but then he stood up and walked to the stage. I sat back down thinking that I was really happy that I'd switched our names. But then the announcer said, "And first place goes to Don . . ."

He stopped and squinted his eyes and looked closer at the paper. I couldn't believe that I had won because I'd tried to do a good thing by switching my and Leon's names, and if I had won, I hadn't done a good thing at all, because Leon had judged better than me and I'd made him get a second-place trophy.

"Forgive me if I get this last name wrong," the announcer said. "Schi, Schi, Schi."

I couldn't believe it. I felt so bad and I wondered if I should tell Leon the truth because I wanted him to know that he'd really won first and that I was only trying to help him. I didn't know what to tell him but decided I would figure something out after I got the trophy. I stood up and started walking toward the aisle, but then the announcer said, "Schickram."

I thought maybe he'd said my name wrong, and I kept walking. But then a boy in the front row stood up and walked toward the stage while all the kids at his school clapped. I watched him walk up and then realized that I must have looked kind of stupid because I was walking up to the stage to get a trophy that I hadn't won. So I kept walking and stopped by Nurse Nancy and told her that I was going to the bathroom.

I stood in the back of the auditorium and watched Don Schickram get his trophy. I couldn't understand why he had beaten me. Then the announcer said, "Ladies and gentlemen. I would like to add that Leon Leonard, the boy who placed second, and this young man here were neck and neck. I have never seen two boys who knew so much about chickens in my entire life. The only reason that we selected Don as the winner was because he drew pictures of all the chickens that he judged."

I couldn't believe that they had chosen him because of that, because there were no instructions for us to draw pictures of the chickens. I was kind of mad, because even though I couldn't draw very well, I didn't think it was fair that he'd won. Then the announcer said, "One picture in particular captured all of the judges' hearts. It was a large picture of a chicken flying through the air like an eagle."

I looked at Don Schickram when the announcer said this and I swear he was looking straight at me like he wanted to tell me something. It kind of freaked me out and I had to put my head down. When I did, though, I was happy that he had won, because he understood that chickens could fly and he wasn't afraid to tell everyone that they could and I thought that was so cool and I decided that if anyone ever said that they couldn't fly, I wouldn't be afraid to tell them, "Yes. They can."

What was really weird is that I got my chance an hour later, on the bus ride home.

You see, I was sitting by Leon, and he was holding his trophy in his lap, talking about where he was going to put it, and that his dad was probably going to build a special case for it. The trophy was about two feet tall and the body was red and on the top of it was a gold chicken. Leon was rubbing the chicken when Mrs. Broussard walked up to us and said, "I can't believe it, Leon. We're almost home and you sat here the whole trip and behaved yourself. I thought for sure you'd be dancing in the aisles causing trouble. I should give you a trophy with a bird that can't fly every day."

Leon smiled and said, "If you want, I can hit someone."

Mrs. Broussard didn't smile back. She said, "No, Leon. I prefer you like this," and then she walked back to the front of the bus.

She was right. Leon wasn't doing the things he usually did, like call people names or make sounds with his armpits. I kind of liked him the way he was with the trophy and it was all because of the chickens and so I stood up and screamed across the bus, "Mrs. Broussard! Mrs. Broussard! They can fly. They can't fly very high or far, but they can fly."

She looked at me like I'd scared her or something and then she said, "Okay, Don. Now sit down and be quiet until we get to the school."

Leon smiled and said, "That was funny," and then

he asked, "Do you want to hold the trophy until we get to school?"

I said, "Sure," and I held it and it felt nice and I never wanted to let it go. I felt like it said my name on it and even though it didn't, I didn't want it to because I don't think I could have loved it as much as Leon did.

When the bus pulled into Horse Island Elementary, Leon grabbed the trophy and ran off. I looked through the window of the bus and watched him dance around with his trophy in front of his parents. His dad grabbed it out of Leon's hands and looked at it, and then smiled, and then handed the trophy to Mrs. Leonard. Then Mr. Leonard picked Leon up and swung him around in the air.

I got Leon's and my suitcases and walked off the bus. Then I went over to the Leonards, put Leon's suitcase down by him, and said, "Hi, Mr. and Mrs. Leonard."

Mr. Leonard smiled at me and said, "Well hello there, my partner," and Mrs. Leonard said, "Don, we're going to that new ice cream parlor called, "Fifteen Fabulous Flavors" to get some ice cream for Leon here. I hear they have twenty flavors. Would you like to come with us?"

"Thank you," I told Mrs. Leonard. "But I have to wait for my mother."

After they left, I waited for my mother for almost fifteen minutes and then Nurse Nancy opened up the school office and called my house. She stood with the phone by her ear for a few minutes and then hung it up.

"Nobody answered," she told me. "They must be on their way."

We waited about fifteen more minutes and then Nurse Nancy called my house again. Nobody answered again.

"I tell you what, Don," Nurse Nancy said. "I'll drop you off at your house. I'll leave a note here on the front door of the school in case one of your parents shows up. I'm sure everything is fine."

When Nurse Nancy dropped me off at my house, I found out that everything wasn't fine.

THIRTY-THREE

Neither one of my parents' cars were at our house when Nurse Nancy pulled into the driveway.

"Do they let you stay home alone?" she asked.

"Yes, ma'am," I told her.

"Are you sure?" she asked. "Because I don't want to get into any trouble for leaving you alone."

"No, ma'am," I told her. "I'm home by myself all the time."

"Okay," Nurse Nancy said. "Take my number and call me if you need anything."

I wasn't sure if my parents would be mad if Nurse Nancy left me alone. They had been kind of nice to me since we'd gotten back from New Orleans, so I figured they wouldn't be. I didn't think about it too much, though, because I was thinking more about my chickens. I wanted to make sure they were okay and tell them about everything that had happened in Baton Rouge.

So after I put my suitcase in my room, I went out to the chicken yard. KC ran up to me and danced around and the others just rolled in the dirt or pecked at the ground. I picked KC up and said, "KC! Guess what? I found Dawn!"

Then I told her almost everything that had happened. But before I was finished, I saw my father's car, and then right behind it, my mother's car. They were both driving really fast and I thought for a second they might drive right into the house!

But both cars stopped a few feet in front of the house. First my father got out of his car and slammed the door and then my mother got out of her car and slammed the door.

Then she yelled, "Are you crazy? What are you doing?"

My father didn't turn and look at her. He went into the house and she screamed at him again, "What are you doing?"

I'd seen my parents fight a lot, but I'd never seen them almost drive their cars into the house. I didn't know if they were fighting about Dawn or Mr. Bufford or because my mother couldn't find a decent Chinese restaurant in Horse Island and wanted to move.

I put KC down and ran to the side door of the house. Before I even opened it, I heard my mother scream, "Will you answer me? Are you crazy?"

I opened the door and went into the kitchen and then I hid in the pantry. Even though I closed the door a little, I could still hear my father yell, "Am *I* crazy? I catch you in our house with a guy who sells tampons and tables for a living and you ask me if *I'm* crazy?"

"You tried to kill him!" my mother yelled.

"I didn't try to kill him," my father said. "I just followed him. I didn't know what I was doing. I was in shock!"

"What is wrong with you?" my mother yelled. "You're crazy!"

"You're right!" Father yelled. "I was crazy to stay here with you even though I knew what you were doing. I just didn't think you'd do it in my house."

"Your house?" my mother screamed.

"Yes!" my father said. "My house!"

"I want a divorce!" my mother screamed.

"Fine. Great. Fantastic," my father said. "But where are you going to live? In the stock room of Horse Island Food and Furniture?"

"No," my mother said. "I'm going to live here. And you're going to have to move."

My father laughed but not like he laughed when Jack Tripper did something really funny on *Three's Company*. He laughed like mean people on soap operas did right before they did something really mean to people.

"Oh, no," my father said. "You're not going to live here. Because there's not going to be a here."

"What are you talking about, Dick?" my mother asked.

"I wasn't at a business convention this weekend, Janice," my father said. "I was in Baton Rouge meeting with Uncle Sam's lawyer. I guess you've forgotten because you've been so caught up entertaining the town grocery boy, but it's been ten years. So we don't have to live here anymore. We can sell the house. And that's what I'm going to do!"

Nobody talked for, like, thirty seconds and all I heard were footsteps. I figured that my mother had forgotten that it had been ten years and maybe she was counting in her head. I had forgotten too. I guess I didn't want to move so I didn't want to think about it.

"You're speechless," my father said. "Well, I guess I've just witnessed a miracle."

"Shut up, Dick!" my mother screamed.

"Don't worry," my father said. "I'll give you half of what I sell the house for. And all of the furniture, including the love seat and sofa. I'll even give you every pot, pan, and cooking utensil in that kitchen, even though you've never used them."

Then my father coughed and said, "But I want something in return."

"What is it, Dick?" my mother asked. "You've already taken my youth and my career from me. What more could you possibly want?"

"Don," he said. "I want Don."

"No," my mother yelled. "No. No. No. No. No. No. No. He's staying with me. A child belongs with his mother."

My mother kept yelling no over and over again. I tried to count how many times she yelled it, but lost my place after about the tenth or eleventh time. Then I started to think about what my father had asked her for. It sounded like he'd said he wanted me. But I couldn't understand what he wanted me to do.

"You're not his mother," my father told her.

"Shut up, Dick!" my mother screamed. "Yes, I am."

I didn't know what my father meant when he said that my mother wasn't my mother. That didn't make sense at all to me and I started to think that maybe my mother was right and my father was crazy.

"He's staying with me!" my mother screamed. "I'll get a lawyer. He's staying with me."

"Why?" my father asked. "Because you hate me? Is that it, Janice? You know that having Don come with me will make me happy and you can't stand the thought of it."

"Because I love him, Dick!" my mother yelled. "That's why. Because I love him."

"Oh please," my father said. "You can't even remember his birthday."

"Neither can you," my mother shouted back. "So don't get all high and mighty like you're the parent of the year."

"You're right," my father said. "I was a horrible parent because I was too busy thinking about how miserable I was. But I want to make it up to him."

"I do too," my mother said.

I couldn't believe my parents were saying all this stuff to each other. I just couldn't believe that they were going to get a divorce and sell the house and that they were fighting over me. I never thought my parents hated me but I guess I never thought that they'd fight over me.

"Well, I guess there's only one thing we can do," my father said. "I don't want to fight over him in court. So I think we should let him decide."

"No," my mother said. "He's only a child. He can't make decisions like that."

"Where's Don right now?" my father asked.

"He's in Baton Rouge," my mother said.

"What time does he get back?" my father asked.

"I don't know," my mother said. "I think at five."

"Jesus," my father said. "It's after six. Oh yeah, you care a lot about him. You can't even remember to pick him up."

"Shut up, Dick!" my mother screamed. "Shut up!"

"Janice," my father said. "Either you let him decide or I'll tell everyone about Bufford. Which means you'll be run out of this town. And also, I won't give you a cent from the sale of this house."

"I hate you!" my mother screamed. "Get out! How dare you threaten me!"

"Don't worry," my father said. "I'm leaving. And don't worry about Don. I'll pick him up so he knows that at least one of us cares about him."

"Shut up, Dick!" my mother screamed. "I'm going to pick him up. I'm not going to let you brainwash him."

"If you think I'm going to let you go and pick him up right now, you're crazy," my father said.

Then I heard a bunch of stuff like people running, the front door open and close, and my parents' cars drive off. I got out of the pantry and went to the front door and watched my parents' cars going down the road really fast, side by side like they were racing.

I didn't know what to do, so I went back to the chicken yard and sat on a tree stump and watched my chickens. I thought about what my father had told them a few nights before when I caught him out there talking to them. He'd told them that they had a good life because all they had to do was sit around all day and lay eggs and they didn't have to get married or have children or find the perfect job. But in a way, it wasn't true because some of them had children. And they had jobs, but they weren't the ones that got to choose them. Chickens couldn't even decide where they wanted to live. And they couldn't do fun stuff like chase the stray dog and pig. So I guess I decided then that I was kind of glad not to be a chicken because I had a choice about where to live. I figured it was better than if I didn't have a choice at all.

Then I realized that my parents would probably come back to the house after they found the note from Nurse Nancy at the school. I didn't really want to see either one of them because they were acting so crazy. And I didn't want them to ask me who I wanted to go and live with. I loved both of my parents even though they were really different from each other. I knew I would have to decide, but I wanted to think about it some more.

So I went into the house and got a pen and paper and wrote a note to my parents. I wrote, "Mother and Father, nobody picked me up from school and nobody was here when Nurse Nancy dropped me off and she didn't want to leave me alone so she said that I had to go and sleep at Leon's house. I brought my stuff so I won't come home until tomorrow after school."

I figured that because they were fighting over me, they wouldn't be mad at me about going to Leon's house. But I didn't really go to Leon's house. I just wrote that so they wouldn't try to talk to me. I figured that I'd hide in my room that night and leave early in the morning.

After I put the note on the front door, I sat in the living room and looked out the front window. About ten or fifteen minutes later, I saw my parents' cars driving real fast toward our house. That's when I went into my room and closed the door. Then I remembered the notebook that I used to write all of my parents' fights in. I hadn't used it in a long time because they hadn't fought in a long time. But I wanted to write down this new fight so I pulled it out. As soon as I found a clean sheet of paper, I heard my father yell.

"Great! Now he thinks we don't even love him enough to be here for him."

"Shut up, Dick," my mother said.

"Okay. Whatever. Fine. Listen," my father said. "I'm going to leave and stay in a hotel tonight. It's probably best that Don's not here. We've both been through a lot today and we should probably calm down before we talk to him. I'll leave work early tomorrow and come here and you and I can talk about what we're going to do. And when Don gets back from school, we'll talk to him."

"Talk to him about what?" my mother said. "There's nothing to talk to him about. He's staying with me and we're getting out of this God-forsaken town."

"Just promise me that you'll let him spend the night at Leon's," my father said.

"I'm not promising you anything!" my mother screamed.

"I can't talk to you like this," my father said. "I'm leaving. But just know that I'm not scared of you and I'll fight you on this if I have to."

"I hate you!" my mother yelled.

For the next few minutes I heard noises like stuff was being thrown against a wall and my mother screaming and crying. I wondered if I should go out and talk to her. I was kind of scared, though, that she'd hit me with one of the things that she was throwing or that she'd yell at me about lying about sleeping at Leon's or that she'd beg me to go and live with her instead of my father. I wasn't ready to decide, so I just sat by my door and listened to my mother throw things.

THIRTY-FOUR

I guess I sat by that door for an hour or so and listened to my mother. I think she was by herself, but I could hear her shouting things like she was fighting with my father. But nobody ever answered her back. I still wrote down the things she said in my notebook even though it wasn't really a fight with my father.

At first she just said a lot of curse words, but I didn't write the exact word down. I just wrote, "curse word," so the fight my mother was having with herself sounded like this.

"He can't take Don away from me!"

"He forgot his curse word birthday too!"

"I can be a good mother."

"I'm going to be a great curse word mother."

"I don't want to be alone. Curse word. I just don't want to be alone. Why is this curse word happening to me?"

Then my mother didn't say anything for, like, about

ten minutes. She didn't throw anything, either. She just cried. I put down my notebook and stood up and put my hand on the doorknob and twisted it a little. I wanted to go and see my mother. I wanted to tell her to stop crying. So I opened the door, but before I took a step out, my mother started talking again.

"Maybe he's right. Maybe I can't be a good mother. Maybe that's why Dawn left. That's why he's leaving. Because I'm a bad person."

After my mother said that, I closed the door and sat back down on the ground. My mother said a few other things that I couldn't make out so I didn't write them down. After a while she didn't say anything at all. I could see out my window that it was starting to get dark outside and I had to go to the bathroom.

I decided to open my door and walk out into the hallway to see what my mother was doing. It was dark in the living room except for this night-light we kept on all the time. I didn't see my mother so I walked to the end of the hall and got a better look at the living room. My mother was lying on the beanbag chair and wasn't moving and looked like she was sleeping.

I backed out of the living room and went to the bathroom. Then I went into my room, put on my pajamas, and got into my bed.

When I was lying there, I thought about who I should go and live with. I wondered where my father and I would live if I went with him or where my mother and I would live if I went with her. I wondered if we'd stay in Horse Island and if we did, if we'd have chickens. I didn't want to leave my chickens and so I thought about running away and living with Dawn in Baton Rouge until my parents sold the house, and then maybe coming back and living with the people who bought it. And then I thought that maybe Dawn could buy the house and the two of us could live here together.

I don't know what time I fell asleep, but I know that I kept waking up because I was having dreams about falling and those always really scare me. I guess it was about the third time I woke up that I heard my chickens clucking a lot more than they usually did. I wondered if it was that stray dog again and so I moved to the end of my bed and looked out my window.

I didn't see a dog, but I saw someone in our yard carrying a flashlight. I wondered if someone was there to steal my chickens, and I got a little nervous. The person didn't go to the chicken yard, though. They stayed in our yard and pointed the flashlight at the house. The light hit me in my eyes, and I backed away from the window and got under my bed. Then I heard someone at the window whisper, "Don! Don, is that you? It's me, Dawn."

I was a little confused, and it took me a couple of seconds before I got out from under my bed and looked out the window through the screen and saw Dawn. She held the flashlight underneath her face, which was kind of spooky, and then she turned it off and said, "Come outside for a minute. I want to talk to you."

I told her to come inside, and she said, "I don't want to wake Mom and Dad."

I told her, "Father isn't here, and Mother is passed out so she won't hear you."

Dawn tilted her head to the side and asked, "Don, why can't you come out here?"

"I can," I told her, "but I want you to see my room and the blue ribbon I won for the chicken-judging contest at the Dairy Festival."

Dawn smiled a little and said, "Okay. Go and open the front door for me."

I got out of my bed and walked real quiet to the front door and opened it. There was Dawn standing with her shoes in her hand. She was wearing jeans and a pink tank top, and there were mosquitoes all over her arms and she was swatting them with her free hand. I grabbed her arm, pulled her in, closed the door, and then the two of us tiptoed back toward my bedroom.

Dawn stopped right before we left the living room and looked at my mother lying on the beanbag chair in the dark. Dawn stared at her for a couple of minutes, and then my mother moved a little and Dawn turned and followed me into my room. After I closed the door and turned the lights on, Dawn bent down and hugged me and kissed me on the forehead, over and over again until I asked, "What are you doing here?"

She grabbed my head in her hands and looked at me for a few seconds, and then said, "Listen, Don. I need to tell you something. Your name is not Don. It's Stanley."

"I know," I told her. "Mother and Father changed it when I was little because they didn't like Stanley anymore because Father had an uncle named Stanley and he gambled a lot."

"Well," Dawn said. "That's not really true."

"What do you mean?" I asked. "Uncle Stanley didn't gamble a lot?"

"No," Dawn said. "You weren't named after Dad's uncle. You were named after your father."

"That doesn't make sense, Dawn," I said. "Father's name isn't Stanley. It's Dick and his middle name is Paul."

"Don," Dawn said.

She didn't speak for a few seconds and when she finally did, she spoke real soft and it was almost like she was whispering.

"The man you call dad is not your father."

"I don't understand," I said. "That doesn't make sense. Why is he not my father?"

After I said it out loud, I thought that maybe I did understand. I thought that maybe my mother had had an affair with a man named Stanley and the man I called "father" all those years wasn't my father.

But I was really wrong because then Dawn said, "He's not your father, Don. Your father's name is Stanley Sullivan. And the woman you've been calling 'mother' isn't your mother."

Now that really confused me. I could kind of understand how my father could not be my father, but I didn't know how my mother couldn't be my mother. And then I thought maybe I was adopted.

But I was really wrong that time too because Dawn said, "I'm your mother."

In one year, I found out that judging chickens was one of the most important things in Horse Island, that my real name wasn't Don, that I might have a twin brother named Stanley, that I didn't have a twin brother named Stanley, that my mother was doing stuff with Mr. Bufford that she shouldn't be doing, that my sister who I thought was dead was really alive, and that my parents were getting a divorce. I didn't think anything would ever surprise me again. But I was wrong, because when Dawn told me that she was my mother, I was so surprised, I couldn't speak. I think I opened my eyes a little wider, and my mouth too, but then one of the mosquitoes that had gotten into the house flew in it and I started coughing. Dawn shook me a little and asked, "Are you okay?"

"Yeah," I told her. "A bug flew in my mouth."

"You didn't know, did you?" she said. "That I was your mom, I mean."

"I don't understand," I told her. "What do you mean?"

I understood what she meant because it explained a lot. It explained why my parents didn't want me to see my birth certificate and why they were always keeping secrets from me. I guess when I said I didn't understand, I meant I didn't understand why she'd left me.

So then I asked her, "Why did you leave me? Did I cry too much? Or were you mad I didn't look like you?"

"No, Don," she said.

Then she grabbed me and hugged me and started crying.

"I'm so sorry," she said. "I didn't want to leave you, but I didn't know what else to do. I couldn't stand living with them anymore because they made my life hell. If they weren't fighting, she was making me dance and he was ignoring me. When I got pregnant with you, I was fifteen, and stupid, and didn't have any money. I knew I couldn't tell them about you because they'd make my life miserable. So I went to Grandma's in Texarkana to have you. At first I wasn't sure what I was going to do, but then the nurse said she'd give you a good home."

"What nurse?" I asked.

"Grandma was blind and dying so she had a nurse who lived with her," Dawn told me. "She said she was going to keep you and take care of you. I don't know why she gave you to Mom and Dad. I guess she got scared. Please don't hate me. I've thought about you so many times."

I kind of understood why she left me because she was really young and didn't have any money and was scared that my mother and father would get mad at her. But I didn't understand why she didn't come and get me after she grew up and got a job. So I asked, "Why didn't you come and get me or visit me when you grew up and got a job?"

"I didn't know where you were," she said. "I figured Grandma was dead and I didn't know how to find the nurse. Please don't hate me, Stanley."

I kind of understood that and I didn't hate her for leaving me and I told her that. But then I started thinking about how she'd called me Stanley and I thought about how she'd told me that I was named after my father and I wondered where he was.

So I asked her, "Where is my father?"

Dawn stuck her tongue out of her mouth a little and moved it around her lips and then said, "I don't know. I never told him about you. I didn't love him. I was young and stupid."

"But when women get pregnant," I said, "they get big stomachs. Didn't everyone see that you had a big stomach?"

"I didn't have a big stomach," Dawn said. "I guess it's because I was so young and because I was dancing all the time and I never put on that much weight. You were a small baby. You were so cute. It was so hard to leave you and the biggest mistake I ever made. But, listen, I want to make it up to you. I want you to come with me and I'll take care of you. We'll leave this place right now and I promise I'll be a good mom."

I couldn't believe that Dawn wanted me to go and live with her. I thought that maybe she and I could move to California and be a real family like the Brady Bunch. Only without the five other kids, father, and the maid. That sounded a lot cooler than living with my mother or father, because a bunch of people on TV lived in California but none lived in Horse Island or Lafayette. I kind of figured that I'd miss my mother and father, but I didn't want to have to choose between them and if I chose Dawn, I wouldn't have to.

Besides that, though, Dawn seemed really nice, and like she'd be a good mom and ask me how my day at school went and take me to the circus and remember my birthday. So I decided that I would leave with Dawn, but before I said yes, I asked, "Can I bring my favorite chicken, KC?"

She laughed and then said, "If you think a chicken named KC wants to come with you, then yes. Bring him."

"KC is a her," I told Dawn, and she said, "Oh. Well, you can bring her."

I didn't think my mother or father would let me keep KC and so I decided that I would go with Dawn. So I pulled my suitcase down from the top shelf of my closet and put it on the floor and started packing. I packed my blue ribbon from the Dairy Festival, some clothes, and my *Standard of Perfection* book. Dawn sat on my bed and watched and asked, "What's your favorite color?"

"Light brown," I said. "The same color as the Brown Leghorn, my favorite breed of chickens."

"Mine's red," Dawn said. "What's your favorite food?"

I told her, "Ice cream," and then she asked, "Flavor?"

I said, "Chocolate," and she said, "That's my favorite flavor too."

She lifted her feet off of the ground a little and then said, "So tell me about this chicken, KC."

I closed my suitcase and then said, "I got her from the Dairy Festival. She was in this glass box and she played "Mary Had a Little Lamb" on the piano whenever you put a quarter in, and after she was finished, some feed fell out. She's okay now, because I took care of her, but when I found her, she had a bunch of missing feathers, and I could tell she was sad because she was stuck in that box all alone. Her name was Henrietta when I found her, but I changed it to KC because, when I brought her home and put her in the yard with all the other chickens, she stood in front of them and let them know that she was new, and she was small, but she wasn't going to let them boss her around, because you know chickens have a pecking order and try to see who's the strongest, and even though she wasn't the strongest, she made them think she was by flapping her wings, and it was almost like she was dancing. So I called her KC, because he used to dance in front of the Sunshine Band, and sometimes he wore an Indian costume with feathers and he kind of looked like a chicken."

I think it was the longest I had ever spoken without stopping. It was because I loved talking about KC and how she could have died if I'd left her in that box. Dawn looked at me like she didn't understand and then her eyes filled up with water. She put her hands on her face and then passed them through her hair, and her bangs stuck up kind of like a rooster's comb.

I thought she looked really pretty, then. Even though she had my mother's eyes, I could tell she was different from her. I don't think my mother could have kicked that drunk man in the privates the way Dawn did. It was kind of like Dawn was a rooster and didn't need anybody to protect her, but my mother was a young hen and couldn't take care of herself. Then I started thinking about how if I left with Dawn or went with my father, that my mother would be alone. She was kind of like KC in a way, and trapped in a glass box, and if she had feathers, they would be all gone or dirty and they'd probably stay that way until someone took her out of that box. I thought about how much she'd cried earlier and how she thought she was a bad person because Dawn left her and my father was going to leave her.

And that made me think about how Dawn had left me. Even though I wasn't mad at her because she left, I kind of wished that she hadn't. Because I felt like it was my fault that she had to run away and couldn't finish high school or go to college or do any other stuff that she might have wanted to do and instead had to dance for a living. I didn't like feeling that way and I didn't want my mother to feel that way because I left.

So I told Dawn, "I don't know if I can go."

She got up from the bed and said, "What? Why? Do you hate me? Do you hate me because I left you?"

I told her, "No. I don't hate you," and she said, "Please don't hate me. Please don't."

She started crying again, and then fell to her knees and hugged me, and I said, "I don't hate you. I love you. Even though I just met you, I love you."

It started to rain really hard and Dawn and I both looked out my window for a couple of seconds like we didn't recognize the sound of the drops hitting the ground. Then Dawn cried harder, and then I started crying.

"I don't know what to do," I told Dawn. "Mother and Father are getting a divorce and Father wants me to go with him and Mother thinks I'm staying with her and I thought it was going to be hard to choose between them and then you showed up and now it's even harder because I really want to go with you, but you're a rooster and Mother's a weak hen and she needs someone to take care of her and I don't want her to think she's a bad person."

Dawn let me go and looked me in the eyes and said, "What? They're getting a divorce?"

"Yeah," I said. "I just found out yesterday."

"Well," Dawn said. "Good! Those two should never have been together in the first place. They ruined my life and I'm sure they were about to ruin yours."

I knew that things weren't always like I wanted

them to be, but I never thought that my life was ruined. And then I just didn't want to think about anything or have to choose anything. I wanted to sing a KC and the Sunshine Band song and just forget about everything that was going on. Then I started thinking about that day I won that KC and the Sunshine Band greatest hits album and how I'd won it. It was because the Magic Number was 33 and my mother had bought thirty-three dollars worth of groceries. And then I started thinking about how Mr. Bufford had decided that thirty-three was going to be the Magic Number. He had put a chicken on a board with numbers on it and whichever number the chicken used the bathroom on was the Magic Number. And that's when I got an idea.

"I want you to come with me to the chicken yard," I told Dawn. "I want to do something and then I'll know who I'm going to live with."

"What are you going to do?" Dawn asked.

"I'll show you when we get to the chicken yard," I told her.

I changed into some jeans and a long-sleeved shirt. Then I grabbed a flashlight, a black marker, and an umbrella and told Dawn to follow me to the chicken yard.

Once we were underneath the coop, I lit some special candles to keep the bugs away and to give us some light. Then I grabbed a sheet of plywood that I was going to use to make a nest for the chickens and put it in the middle of the coop. I took the black marker and drew a circle on the plywood and separated it into three sections. In one section, I wrote an "F" for father. In another section, I wrote an "M" for mother. And I was going to write a "D" for Dawn in the last section but then I looked at her and I changed my mind. In the last section, I wrote, "GM" for Grandmother. And then I put a "G" before the "F" for Grandfather. And I left the "M" for Dawn.

"What are you doing?" she asked me.

"You'll see in a second," I told her. "It's kind of hard to explain."

I pulled a metal cage out of the shed in the chicken yard and dropped it on top of the circle on the sheet of plywood. Then I looked for KC. Most of the chickens were underneath the roof of the coop because of the rain, so it was hard to find her at first because she was white like a bunch of the others. But I could always tell her apart from the other ones because she stood taller than them.

When I found her, I bent down and called her, "Hey, KC. Come here, girl."

She didn't run right to me, but she looked at me. So I bent down and slowly walked toward her until I could pick her up. She flapped her wings a little but calmed down after a couple of seconds. Once she had, I put her in the metal cage and closed the door.

"KC is going to decide who I'm going to live with," I told Dawn.

"How is she going to do that?" Dawn asked me.

"By using the bathroom," I told her. "I'm going to live with the person whose piece she goes on."

"Stanley," she said. "You can't let a chicken decide where you're going to live."

"Why not?" I asked her.

"This is an important decision," she told me. "You have to decide this. A chicken can't do that for you. It's crazy."

KC clucked really loudly and ran around the little cage. I could tell she didn't like it and it was painful for me to watch her in there. I bent down to let her out, but then I thought of something and stood back up.

"Dawn," I said. "It is crazy, but you know what, it's crazy that you left me because you were too scared of Mother and Father. And it's crazy that they told me that you had died and that you were my sister. And it's even crazier that you ran away because you were tired of dancing but you're still dancing. And it's crazy that my best friends in the world are these chickens and now I have to leave them no matter who I go and live with. But I think the thing that's the craziest is that everything I know is going to change and there's nothing I can do to stop it. So if everything around me is crazy, then why can't I do crazy things to make choices?"

When I finished talking, KC went to the bathroom.

THIRTY-FIVE

Dawn was the first one to look at where KC had gone to the bathroom. Her eyes closed in slightly, like she was thinking, and then she said, "GM."

"Grandmother," I said.

I looked down at the board and saw where KC had gone.

Dawn put her hands on top of her head and then pulled her fingers back through her hair. She looked down at the ground and then took a deep breath. Then she squinted her eyes again and asked, "Wait. You've been calling her 'Mother' all night. Why do you call her 'Mother' instead of 'Mom'?"

I told her, "Because she told me to call her 'Mother' and Father, 'Father.' "

Dawn threw one of her hands up in the air and said, "Oh, for Christ's sakes. That sounds like something she'd do. Why would you want to stay with a woman like that?"

Dawn grabbed me by the shoulders and said, "Come with me, Stanley. Please. Let me take you away from that awful woman."

I shook my head and said, "I have to stay with her. But maybe you can stay here with us."

Dawn breathed deeply and pulled her T-shirt away from her skin with one hand and started fanning herself with the other. She looked kind of sick, so I asked, "Are you okay? Do you want a glass of water or something?"

She stopped fanning herself and stared at me and asked, "Are you sure you don't hate me?"

I nodded my head up and down and said, "Yes, I'm sure."

Dawn grabbed my hands and pulled me toward her and asked, "Are you sure you want to stay here with her?"

I looked at her and thought about it again. I had the chance to go with Dawn, who hugged me, and kissed me, and told me how much she loved me, and kicked people who tried to hurt me, or I could stay with my grandmother. Then I got the idea that maybe Dawn and my grandmother could make up and she could stay with us and maybe if she did, my parents wouldn't get a divorce and I wouldn't have to leave my chickens or my friends at school.

So I squeezed Dawn's hand and said, "Yeah, I'm sure. But I want you to stay here with us so we can be like a family."

Dawn shook her head and said, "Stanley, I can't stay here. I don't get along with that woman, and although I don't want to leave you, I can't stand to be around her."

Dawn took a pen and some paper out of her purse and started writing and said, "Here's my number and address in Baton Rouge. I'm going to be there for a while, so if you change your mind, call me, and I'll come and get you. If I move, I'll let you know. Please don't let Mom or Dad know that you saw me or where I am."

She handed me the paper, and I hugged her and told her that I would miss her and that I'd visit her the first chance I could. Dawn walked out of the coop and then to her car. I let KC out of the cage and blew out the candles. Then I went back into the house.

I walked over to the window in the living room and looked at Dawn in her car. She had turned the light on so I could see her. She was smoking a cigarette and looking at herself in the rearview mirror. She turned off the light and started the car and I started singing "Please Don't Go" by KC and the Sunshine Band in my head.

Babe, I love you so
I want you to know
That I'm going to miss your love
The minute you walk out that door

I couldn't believe that Dawn was leaving me again. I almost ran outside and screamed out to her to stay with us, or wait, and that I'd get my suitcase and leave with her.

Please don't go
Don't go
Don't go away
Please don't go
Don't go
I'm begging you to stay

Dawn backed out of the driveway and when she did, her lights flashed into the living room. I heard my grandmother moving around in the beanbag chair, so I turned to see if she'd woken up. She stretched her legs out but stayed lying down. I saw an empty wine bottle next to her and I figured that's why she was sleeping in the beanbag instead of her bed. I turned back toward the window and saw Dawn's car on the road.

If you leave
At least in my lifetime
I've had one dream come true
I was blessed
To be loved
By someone as wonderful as you

I waved, even though I knew she couldn't see me. I knew I was going to miss her, and that sometimes I'd probably wish that I'd gone with her.

Please don't go
Don't go
Don't go away
Please don't go
Don't go
I'm begging you to stay
Hey, hey, hey

When I couldn't see Dawn's car anymore, I backed away from the window and felt something under my foot. It was the music box and I wasn't sure why it was on the ground, but I figured that it was one of the things I'd heard my grandmother throwing. I was going to put it back on the bookcase before my grandmother woke up and saw me holding it, but then I got an idea.

I wound it up as tight as I could, and then put it on the coffee table. Then I knelt down in front of it, opened the lid, and watched the ballerina dance. And after a few seconds, I looked at my grandmother and then back at the tiny dancer and whispered, "Fly."

Acknowledgments

I'd like to thank my agents, Dan Lazar and Simon Lipskar from Writers House, for taking a chance on a new writer; my editor, Jill Davis, for helping me to shape my wild and sometimes downright crazy ideas into a readable format; my publicist, Deb Shapiro, who was an endless source of information concerning the promotion of the book; my British editor, Sarah Odedina, and my German editor, Dorit Engelhardt, for making me known around the world; and everyone at Bloomsbury who contributed to publishing my first novel.

And thanks should be given to Frederic, Mary, Phillipe, Harold, Kurt, Mikey, John Reid, Jeff, Francisco, Heather, and Seb for opening up their sofas and spare rooms to a starving artist; my classmates and teacher, Leslie Dormen, at the Writers Studio, who encouraged me to develop the two-page story entitled *Dance* into a longer piece; the students and instructor, Joseph Caldwell, at the 92nd Street Y, for holding my hand while writing the novel; Troy, for copyediting the manuscript before I sent it to my agent; and Jack, Jay, Peter, and the other Jack, who convinced me that behind my massive forehead there was a novel waiting to be written.

I need to thank my former boss, Lisa, for being so supportive (and also for those beautiful Paul Smith cuff links); and my work colleagues Kurt, Christine, and Leah for reading the first drafts and providing feedback.

But most of all, I'd like to thank my family for providing support and material over the years. I won't name them all here because there are more than thirty of them, but each one of their names is in the book.

Special thanks go to my sister-in-law, Rhonda, who believed in all of my ideas no matter how outrageous they may have seemed at the time and encouraged me every day of my life to be who I am; my sisters, Sandy and Kay, and my brother, Joey, who were my first readers; and Joey and Rhonda's daughter, Taylor. When she was ten years old, she wrote this letter:

Dear Uncle Jacques,

How are you doing? It was fun when you came down. I hope you can come back soon. Are you still writing your book? Don't give up, okay.

Love Taylor

Every time I felt as if I were chasing a pipe dream or out of my mind for attempting to write a novel, I looked at her letter and it kept me going. So I'd like to end by thanking all of the children and adults who have inspired, encouraged, and supported a person's dreams.